Beyond the Grave

Leo McNeir

Enigma Publishing

Copyright

Dedication

For my friends and colleagues

in the

St.Albans Chapter

of the

Crime Writers' Association

Index

About this book

There's a killer on the loose in the quiet country town of Stony Stratford, and the victim is a harmless man who works on behalf of local charities. Why he should be singled out for brutal murder is a complete mystery. Or was it just a random killing? The police mount a determined investigation but no clues emerge about the perpetrator of this vicious crime.

Almost by chance, Marnie Walker becomes involved in helping a homeless woman. It is simply not safe for a female beggar to be sleeping rough in the middle of a murder manhunt. At the same time, when Marnie's personal plans are being thwarted, two further mysteries come her way. A voice from the past embroils her in an intrigue from beyond the grave that threatens to disrupt her own life and the lives of those she holds dear. And unrelated remains from another grave add a further element of confusion to the turmoil in Marnie's life. Unrelated? Who can say?

As the police murder investigation draws a blank, and Marnie's world becomes ever more chaotic, out of the blue comes a resolution that she would never have wished for.

Beyond the Grave

Prologue 1
Time: June, late 1990s

It was a pleasant evening, the day he was murdered. The early summer weather had been mild for much of the previous week or two, with only the occasional shower. He had met some friends for a drink in their favourite pub and had left well before the others; he wanted a relatively early night. They had all had one drink too many, and he needed to clear his head before turning in. Tomorrow was Wednesday, a working day, and he had a full diary of meetings and appointments waiting for him in the office. The decision taken on the spur of the moment to walk for a few minutes in the park by the river proved to be ill-advised.

Down past the church he walked, enjoying the calm before the pubs turned out. Further on, he crossed the short bridge over the ancient mill leat diverted in centuries past from the Great Ouse – such a grand name for such a modest waterway, he always thought – and strolled along the footpath that was lined on one side by a thick hedge. Tut-tutting to himself, he stepped over some empty beer cans and thought he glimpsed a syringe discarded by the wayside, in the faint light from the houses across the water. It never used to be like this. All sorts of undesirables now roamed the parks and streets of his home town. Standards everywhere seemed to be in decline.

He heard a rustling sound and stopped, thinking that someone was coming up behind him on the footpath, but he saw no one when he looked back. It was nothing more than a light breeze ruffling the hedgerow and the trees that were scattered here and there by the water. He resumed his walk, but decided it was time to turn and make for home. The rustling sound when it came again didn't even arouse his curiosity. At the last moment – which turned out to be his last moment – the rustling became a rushing footfall. Before he could even turn to check it out, the blow crashed into the back of his skull. Shattered by a searing pain, lights flashed chaotically in his head and he collapsed to the ground. One blow was enough. He twitched once or twice, moaned faintly and expired with both eyes open as a dark red stain spread across the path.

There were no witnesses, not even a passing dog-walker to offer a modicum of solace, and no one to come to his aid. Twenty minutes would pass before an inebriated reveller stumbled in horror upon the body. By that time the silent perpetrator had slipped away like a shadow in the night.

Prologue 2

"Coo-ee! It's only me.'

It was an announcement that she had made on entering the house every Tuesday and Friday for the past twelve years. Occasionally there would come a reply from somewhere in the cottage, but not always, so on that morning at nine o'clock sharp it was no surprise when her greeting was met with silence. For a moment or two she hesitated in the hall listening, her head canted on one side. Odd. There was something final about the silence. She had once heard someone say that you could sense if a building was empty. On that Tuesday morning she had that feeling.

Being a practical kind of person, she accepted that there was a simple reason for the lack of a response. The owner of the house – the lady of the house, to her mind – had just popped out to go shopping. No time was to be wasted in getting down to work. She went to her cupboard – it was always referred to as her cupboard – and pulled out the hoover. She always called it the hoover, even though it was another make entirely. For the next half hour she dusted then hoovered downstairs. She had read in a magazine article that that was the correct order, though it didn't really seem to make sense.

She always left the kitchen to last, so she lugged the vacuum cleaner up the stairs and hoovered the landing. Next stop: the main bedroom. She pushed open the door with her bottom and entered backwards, pulling the cleaner behind her. It was only after plugging it into the wall socket that she straightened up and glanced round the room. Her employer always had the bed made by the time she arrived, and that day seemed at first sight to be no exception. Except ...

To her surprise – and, let it be said, shock – she saw that the bed was still occupied. She gasped and raised a hand to her mouth.

'Oh, I'm terribly sorry. I didn't realise you were ...'

Her voice faded away as she saw that the shape in the bed made no movement. It lay utterly still. She had always dreaded that, with such an elderly employer, this might happen one

3

day. Everything in the room looked as orderly as before. The dressing table was tidy. There were no clothes lying about. The bedroom was a model of orderliness, just as her employer would have wished it. On the bedside table there was a book and the water that she always had to hand.

For a few moments, she stood with head bowed and hands clasped together and said a little prayer. Then, having ascertained beyond any doubt that the occupant of the bed had enjoyed her final slumber, she went quietly down the stairs and picked up the phone on the hall table. She dialled the number for the local doctor's surgery and, while waiting for a reply, vowed that she would continue her day's work as usual so that the whole house would be spotless. It was the least she could do. Standards had to be maintained.

It was only much later that she realised that the death of her employer had not caused her to shed a single tear. Such a display would have been frowned on by that austere lady as an unnecessary extravagance.

Chapter 1

It began with two phone calls and one letter, all on the same day. Two of the three were disruptive; all of them had far-reaching consequences.

After receiving the first call Marnie Walker had a lot on her mind. None of it was good. She put the phone down, slumped forward on her desk, head in hands. That call had come from the district registrar. Marnie thought it was the worst news she could have that day. As it turned out, she was wrong.

Marnie Walker was in her mid-thirties. She was above average height for a woman and slim, with the kind of figure that looks good in jeans. Her hair was dark, wavy and shoulder-length, and her eyes were brown. She had an attractive face, with a good complexion and clean intelligent features.

That Wednesday morning she was alone in the office. Her assistant and close friend, Anne Price, had gone to the village shop for a few provisions; her lover, Ralph Lombard, was on his way to Oxford. Ralph was also her fiancé, but she couldn't bring herself to think of him like that. *Fiancé* – a title from a bygone age, she thought.

Ralph was almost a decade older than Marnie, but had kept himself in good shape, both physically and intellectually. Just over six feet tall, with strong features, dark hair and piercing grey eyes, his manner was confident but not over-bearing. His passions included economics, boating and, of course, Marnie.

Marnie left the office barn and set off through the spinney towards the canal, desperate for fresh air to clear her head, It was a mild day in early June, and the trees were now in full leaf. She stepped out of the spinney fifty yards later, stopped, closed her eyes and breathed in deeply. The fresh clean smell of the water and the countryside was soothing to a degree, but her thoughts were still punctuated with question marks. She breathed out audibly and contemplated the scene before her.

Ralph's narrowboat, *Thyrsis*, was moored on the mainline of the canal to her right. On the left, her own boat, *Sally Ann*, also a forty-five footer, nestled in a private docking area cut into the main line of the waterway at right-angles.

Marnie walked past *Sally Ann* and headed towards the accommodation bridge spanning the canal about forty yards away. It was a brick structure dating back to the late eighteenth century, and had an elegant simplicity of design. It had been built to allow cattle and sheep to cross over the waterway. Marnie walked to the centre of the bridge and leaned against the parapet, looking down towards the boats. A good place to find peace and calm. Within moments that atmosphere evaporated as the mobile in Marnie's back pocket began vibrating. The ID window revealed that the caller was her sister.

'Was that a sigh, Marnie?'

'Possibly, Beth, or something like that.'

'What's up?'

'Where do I begin?'

Beth changed the subject. She often did that. 'Have you heard the news?'

'The Martians have landed?'

'Apart from that.'

'Enlighten me.'

'There's been a murder up in your neck of the woods.'

Marnie stiffened. 'What are you talking about?'

'It was on the news just now. I think it happened last night.'

'Up here?'

'Somewhere near Stony Stratford, they said on the radio. That's just a few miles from Knightly St John, isn't it?'

'That's terrible!'

'Yeah, in fact it's really quite tragic. Seems the victim was a man who worked for a *charity*. Why would *anyone* kill someone like that, someone who just wanted to help people?'

'Well, someone obviously did.'

'Yeah, poor guy. I think they said he was about our age, middle to late thirties.'

'Was that it? You just rang to brighten my day?'

'No. I was wondering how the wedding plans were coming along.'

Another sigh. 'They're not. We've had a glitch, as of this morning. Staffing problems at the registry office, something to do with cutbacks. We're postponed till the end of the summer.'

'But what about your honeymoon plans ... Venice on the Orient-Express? All that's postponed, too?'

'Inevitably,' Marnie said.

'A shame you can't do something else in the meantime.'

After disconnecting, Marnie gazed down at the canal. Perhaps Beth had a point. She and Ralph had cleared time in their diaries for a week or two without meetings. With their original plans in shreds, it dawned on her that the solution was staring her in the face. Literally.

****

Marnie walked back through the spinney to the cluster of buildings that was Glebe Farm. Her mind was now troubled by thoughts of the poor man, the charity worker, whose life had cruelly been cut short.

Reaching the cobbled courtyard, she turned right into the office barn. It had been the first building renovated when she took over the property a few years earlier. She'd turned a near-derelict small stone barn into an attractive and efficient work space, with modern blond-wood furniture and up-to-date computers and equipment. The walls were emulsioned in apricot white, and the floor was covered in natural hessian carpet. Cork-boards displayed drawings and photographs of past and pending projects. At the rear Marnie had installed a kitchen area and beyond it a shower room.

On that side of the office, Marnie had provided a desk for Anne Price, who had worked as her assistant from the beginning. To Marnie, Anne was like another sister. She was nineteen and taking a foundation course at the local art school. Almost as tall as Marnie, she had pale blonde hair cut very short, almost sculpted to her head. The generous would say she had a slender, boyish figure; others might say she was skinny.

The generous would say she was fair-skinned; others might say her complexion bordered on anaemic.

Anne had now returned from shopping and looked up as Marnie entered.

'Everything okay?'

'I needed to get out to clear my head.'

'Have you heard the latest news?'

'About the Martians?'

'Martians?' Anne sat back in her chair end eyed Marnie appraisingly. 'You've been talking to Beth, haven't you?'

'What makes you think that?'

'You're always a bit ... *loopy* when she's been on the phone.'

'A fair cop, guv. She rang while I was mulling things over. So what news?'

'There's been a murder in Stony Stratford.'

'I know and, in case you're wondering, I have an alibi.'

Anne said, 'There you go again. Loopy's the word. And I'm betting Beth didn't exactly help with whatever you were thinking about.'

'Funnily enough, she did ... sort of. You see, we've lost our booking at the registry office. I got a call while you were out. It seems they've got staffing problems. We can't tie the knot till late summer.'

'But what about your honeymoon ... the Orient-Express, Venice?'

'That goes back too.' Marnie reached for the phone. 'I'd better break the news to Ralph.'

Anne looked up at the clock. 'His seminar will be starting soon.'

'I'll leave a message on voicemail.'

Anne went back to sorting the post. When Marnie hung up, Anne was staring at an envelope, her expression puzzled.

'Something the matter?'

Anne said, 'It's franked with the name Burnett Haydock and Lang.' She pronounced each name slowly and distinctly.

'Architects?' Marnie suggested.

Anne squinted closely at the franking. 'Looks like ... *solicitors*.'

She took it over to Marnie and turned back to her desk. At that moment the phone began ringing. Marnie picked up the receiver. It was Ralph.

'Can't speak for long, but I just got your message about the registrar. It's all very inconvenient, right at the last minute. What's going on?'

'There's nothing anyone can do about it. We're stuffed.'

'Good job we hadn't planned a big event,' said Ralph. 'Though of course we've cut out everything in our diaries for the next two weeks.'

'Listen, Ralph, I've had an idea. Why don't we take a short break, anyway?'

There was a pause on the line. 'You're thinking maybe a canal trip?'

'Why not? We haven't had any sort of holiday for well over a year.'

'Okay. Look, gotta go. I've got twenty economists waiting to get their teeth into the Celtic tiger.'

'Mind it doesn't bite back.'

'That's rather the point of the seminar. See you later.'

Marnie slotted the phone into its holder.

'That's something else you do.' It was Anne, now back at her desk.

'What's that?'

'When you speak to Ralph, you're always smiling afterwards.'

Still smiling, Marnie picked up the envelope and slit it open. Within moments the smile had vanished and turned to bewilderment.

****

It was late afternoon when Ralph Lombard turned through the field gateway onto the rough track leading down to Glebe Farm. He'd replaced his venerable Volvo with a Jaguar a year earlier. Low-slung and capable of high performance, for Ralph its greatest virtue was four-wheel drive. It made light work of the field track in all weathers.

Ralph – full title, Professor Ralph Lombard, visiting Professor and Senior Research Fellow in Economics at All Saints' College, Oxford – enjoyed the freedom given him by his role. It combined a modest amount of postgraduate supervision, while devoting the remainder of his time to research, writing and giving guest lectures around the world. It amused many of his university colleagues that his study was located in rural Northamptonshire on a narrowboat.

On that particular day he was happy to return home to Marnie, his partner, lover, officially *fiancée*. On the other hand, he was vexed that their wedding plans had been thwarted, though the prospect of a short holiday on the canal softened the blow.

He parked the Jaguar in its usual space in one of the small stone barns and walked round to the farmhouse. They had converted and modernised it to create a spacious and comfortable home. As he dropped his briefcase in the hall, he was greeted by a medley of enticing smells emanating from the kitchen: prominent among them were cucumber and onions with a background of *quiche lorraine*. The door to the kitchen was ajar. Ralph pushed it open and stepped in.

'I think I've died and gone to heaven,' he said.

If he expected a cheerful response, he was disappointed. Marnie was laying the table while Anne was reading a letter beside the Aga.

'Don't do it just yet,' Marnie said. 'We need your opinion on this letter we've received from ... who is it again, Anne?'

Anne checked the letter heading. 'Burnett Haydock and Lang, solicitors.'

Marnie added, 'The envelope was stamped: PERSONAL, PRIVATE AND CONFIDENTIAL.'

Ralph crossed the room, pausing on the way to kiss Marnie. He took the letter and gave Anne's arm a friendly squeeze.

'Can you read it out loud, Ralph?' Marnie said. 'I've been trying to read between the lines. It's all very mysterious.'

Ralph sat at the table and accepted a glass of wine from Anne. He took a sip before reading.

Dear Mrs Walker,

We have been instructed to act on behalf of a client in regard to a legal matter in which you have been named as an interested party. I therefore write to invite you to a meeting in our offices in London. On that occasion I shall be able to give you more information concerning the nature of the matter and the action required to fulfil our instructions.

I should be grateful if you would kindly get in touch to arrange a meeting at your convenience.

Yours sincerely,

Seymour Lang
Partner

Ralph took another sip of wine and re-read the letter silently to himself.

'Have you spoken to Roger about this?' he asked.

Roger Broadbent had been Marnie's solicitor for several years.

'Not yet. I thought I'd get your opinion before doing anything.'

'Well, it seems quite straightforward,' said Ralph. 'Why not just give this Lang a call?'

'What about Roger?'

Ralph shrugged. 'Can't hurt to run it past him first, I suppose.'

****

Marnie had known Roger Broadbent for years as a fellow boater and a friend, as well as a wise counsel. She contained her impatience until nine-thirty the next morning, the time she knew Roger normally arrived in his office. He had handled her divorce, the sale of her flat in Hampstead, north London, and the purchase of Glebe Farm when she moved from her well-paid job in an architects' practice to set up in business on her own. He had also acted as adviser when she had been caught up in more than one murder investigation.

Marnie regarded Roger as a safe pair of hands. His number was on her speed-dial.

'Mr Broadbent's office, good morning.'

'Judith, hi, it's Marnie Walker. Is Roger available?'

'You must be psychic, Marnie. He's just walked in. I'll put you through.'

There was a click on the line followed by a familiar voice.

'Marnie!' Roger's voice was tinged with suspicion. 'Please tell me you're not involved in the murder in Stony Stratford.'

'Murder? Oh, *that*. No, no.'

Roger's tone lightened. 'Praise the Lord!'

Marnie explained about the letter and read it to him. There was a pause after she finished.

'Mm ...' Roger murmured eventually.

'Do you know this firm at all, Roger?'

'No, but that's not surprising. There are thousands of solicitors in London.'

'What do you make of the letter?'

'Slightly odd. On the face of it, it's a simple invitation to meet. What's different is, this Lang doesn't give any clue as to what it concerns.'

'What would you expect?'

'At the very least an inkling of the subject.'

'Such as?'

'If it involved an inheritance he might have said, *where you will learn something to your advantage*. If he has a client intending to *sue* you, he might give you some sort of warning.'

'Well, Roger, I'm certainly not in line to inherit anything, and nobody's threatened me with legal action. So where does that leave us?'

Another pause, another murmur. 'Mm ... It's all very vague.'

'*Vague* is the word. I wonder why he's being so mysterious.'

'One way to find out.'

'Roger, do you think you should come with me to the meeting?'

'Probably no need at this stage. If anything that comes up bothers you, just say nothing and leave the meeting. Then keep me posted and we'll take it from there.'

Marnie was bursting to contact Seymour Lang, but first she rang Ralph in Oxford. She connected with him straight away and outlined her conversation with Roger.

'We can surmise all we like.' Ralph said. 'But the only way to move forward is to phone Lang.'

Marnie agreed, but she was out of luck. Seymour Lang was in court that morning, followed by a lunch engagement and back-to-back meetings with clients all afternoon. Marnie was invited to leave a message.

'He sent a letter asking to arrange a meeting. Actually, if you're his secretary perhaps we could just compare diaries?'

'I'm afraid Mr Lang manages his own diary, but I can pass on a message. What name shall I say?'

'It's Marnie Walker.'

'Oh.'

'Is that a problem?'

'No, it's just ... er ... if you'd like to give me your number, I'm sure he'll be in touch as soon as possible.'

Marnie guessed she was being fobbed off, but a call came in just as Anne was suggesting lunch.

'Walker and Co, good afternoon ... Yes, she is. Who's calling, please? ... I'll put you through.'

Anne pressed a button and announced Seymour Lang of Burnett Haydock and Lang. Her accent was pure lah-di-dah. Marnie was grinning when she picked up the phone.

'Thanks for getting back to me, Mr Lang.'

'Not at all, Mrs Walker. Good to talk.'

Marnie pulled a face across the office to Anne who almost choked, straining to suppress a guffaw.

'You asked for a meeting, Mr Lang. Can you give me some idea of its purpose?'

'Well that's just it, you see. I'm not exactly sure.'

'I'm sorry, I don't understand. Presumably you know what we're going to talk about. Otherwise we'll be having a rather quiet meeting.'

A laid-back chuckle. 'Oh, very droll, yes indeed.'

'Mr Lang, I'm being serious. How can we have a meeting if you don't know what it concerns and I'm completely in the dark? What's the context?'

'Context?'

'I mean, is someone threatening to sue me, or what?'

'Well ...'

A few seconds drifted past.

'Let me be frank with you, Mr Lang. If you want me to travel to London for a meeting, you'll have to give me a clue about what we're discussing.'

'Yes ... of course ... I take your point. I can tell you that it concerns ... a delicate matter.'

'Obviously.' Marnie was losing patience.

'Its precise nature has not been revealed to me or either of my former partners.'

'I'm intrigued, but I still don't follow.'

'I can perhaps tell you that our client is a person of your acquaintance ... or perhaps I should say *was* such a person.'

Marnie's stomach turned over. 'Are you talking about ... my late former husband?'

'Oh no, not at all.'

'You really can't keep me dangling like this, Mr Lang. If you want me to come to see you, you'll have to give me a name.'

More time passed. Eventually Lang said, 'My instructions were ... oh well. It's ... Miss Iris Winterburn.'

Marnie felt a wave of grief wash over her. 'She's dead?' she said quietly.

Across the room Anne sat up in her chair. She leapt to her feet and hurried across the office. She mouthed, 'Who's dead?'

Marnie said, 'Sorry, Mr Lang. I missed that. Are you saying that Iris Winterburn has died?'

Anne covered her mouth with both hands and flopped onto the visitor's chair.

'I'm afraid so,' said Lang.

14

'That's quite a shock. Now can you tell me what it's all about?'

'That's just it, Mrs Walker. As I said, I don't actually know.'

'Look, Mr Lang, I'm sure you're not being deliberately obscure, and I'm not usually slow on the uptake but –'

'Mrs Walker, I've told you all I can. My instructions were simply to hand you a letter in person, nothing more. When we meet I'm sure everything will become clear.'

And that was how they left things. Lang offered a meeting in his office on the following Thursday morning. Marnie accepted, and Anne entered it in the diary.

Chapter 2

On Friday morning, preparations for the journey to London were in full swing. Marnie and Ralph decided to stick with their original plan of a trip on *Sally Ann*. They would set off early on Saturday morning, leaving Anne in charge of the office. Anne was in her element, producing to-do lists. She added a supplementary list of shopping, the provisions needed for the journey south to London on the Grand Union Canal.

Marnie and Anne sat in the office reviewing progress on all their projects. Anne had created an up-to-date chart, a situation report, which she called a 'sitrep' – she liked using jargon – and the folders for each project lay in a neat pile beside them on Marnie's desk, waiting for action. At least, that was the theory. In fact, Marnie spent more time making last-minute phone calls. In between, there were cheques and letters to sign, orders for materials to confirm and invoices to approve for posting. As always, Marnie was amazed at how much work was generated by such a small practice and at how much she relied on Anne; another safe pair of hands.

Meanwhile, Ralph was on the boat, working through his own list. While he checked the level of diesel in the fuel tank, and cleaned the fuel pump and drop filter, the water tank was filling from a hose pipe. *Sally Ann* was built for long-distance cruising, and the water tank in the bows held around three-quarters of a tonne. Next, Ralph packed the stern gland with grease and checked the main gas bottle and the spare.

Marnie had once told him she thought of the boats as big animals that needed to be looked after. Anne's boyfriend, Donovan, had pointed out that in some respects a narrowboat was like a submarine. If its systems failed, you were in serious trouble; hence the checking and double-checking before a long journey.

When Marnie pressed the speed-dial button and connected with her sister, Beth, Anne decided it was time to go shopping. She was making hand-signals to Marnie when she heard tyres crunching on gravel. Outside, she found Angela Hemingway climbing out of her car. Tall and thin, wearing a clerical grey dress complete with dog collar, Angela was the local vicar. She had become a good friend, despite the fact that Marnie, Ralph and Anne were devout agnostics. She smiled when she saw Anne.

Anne smiled back. 'If you've come to save our souls, you're too late. We've already flogged them on eBay.'

Angela looked puzzled. 'On what?'

'It's a new website where you can … Oh, never mind.'

'Hope you haven't sold – or rather *flogged* – them to a Mr Lucifer.' She smiled sweetly. 'Could be tricky.'

'You've come to see Marnie?'

'Yes. I've got a busy week ahead so I just wanted to wish them a happy honeymoon. I envy them the Orient-Express and Venice, even if they are just getting married in a registry office.'

Anne glanced back through the window. 'Marnie seems to be chained to the phone at the moment.'

Angela checked her watch. 'I'll pop back later. I've got a lot on today.'

'I'll let Marnie know. Actually, Angela, I should tell you there's been a change of plan: the wedding and honeymoon have been postponed till September. Staffing problems at the registry, apparently.'

'So what are they going to do?'

'I'll tell you as we – Blimey! What's happened to your car?'

Angela's car was a maroon Ford Escort, elderly but lovingly cared for. That day, it looked as if vandals had filled it with junk.

'I'm taking some things to the hospice charity shop in Stony Stratford.'

'You're confident you'll make it back up the field track?'

'I live in hope.' She smiled sweetly. 'It goes with the job.'

'Why don't I follow you in my car and help you unload that stuff? I can get my shopping in Stony.'

'If you can do that, Anne, I'll apply to get you beatified.'

Anne stared back, deadpan. 'Don't bother. Looks like I'm gonna be martyred. Come on, let's go.'

17

****

Stony Stratford is a small town located on the old Roman road, Watling Street, from London to the north-west of England. It boasts two famous coaching inns. According to tradition, news brought up from London by stage-coach would be told in the Cock Hotel and later repeated with much exaggeration – after copious consumption of alcohol – in the Bull Hotel, further along the High Street; the origin of the 'Cock and Bull story'.

The town has been by-passed for many years by the modern A5 dual-carriageway, part of the impressive Milton Keynes road network. This is fortunate, as the old main road through the town's centre is narrow and often cluttered with parked cars. On that Friday morning a farmers' market was underway in the market square, which further reduced the number of parking spaces available.

Angela and Anne parked in tandem on double yellow lines opposite the charity shop and trudged backwards and forwards across the road, dodging traffic, transferring the second-hand items to the sanctuary of the shop. Angela was praying – literally – that no traffic warden would appear with a parking ticket.

They had finished off-loading when Angela's prayers were answered. A large van pulled away from the kerb a short distance ahead of them, leaving two spaces free. They rushed to claim the vacated slots.

'What next?' Anne asked.

Angela glanced quickly at her watch. 'Anne, have you time for a quick cuppa? My treat, to thank you for your help.'

Anne reflected for a millisecond before accepting. They agreed on a plan: Angela would order coffees while Anne hit the supermarket.

Within minutes Anne arrived at the café, a shopping bag in each hand. Outside, a youngish woman wearing a hoodie was sitting cross-legged on the floor. Beside her was a rucksack on top of which lay a rolled-up blanket. Between her feet lay a grubby baseball cap containing a few copper coins. Anne stepped around the woman and entered the café.

'I hope your coffee's still warm,' Angela said. She had laid the saucer on top of the cup to keep the heat in.

Anne took a sip. 'It's fine.' She glanced towards the front window. 'Did you see that woman out there on the pavement, begging?'

Angela shook her head. 'She wasn't there when I came in.'

Anne sighed. 'I hate to see people begging. Life can be so unfair.'

'That's why I think Randall's hostel is so good,' said Angela. 'Of course, being down in Brackley, it's not much use to anyone begging up here.'

Randall – formal title, the Reverend Dr Randall Hughes – was the rural dean of Brackley in the southernmost tip of Northamptonshire. He was also Angela's boyfriend. Before his promotion he'd been the vicar of Knightly St John and a controversial figure in the village. Two years earlier he'd opened a residential centre for homeless people and itinerants. The locals thought of them as 'tramps', a term Randall heartily disliked. Anne had dubbed it a 'drop-in centre for drop-outs', a name of which Randall fully approved.

Anne said, 'I told you about the postponement of the wedding and honeymoon.'

'Yes, a real pain in the ...' She thought carefully. '... neck. They must be really upset.'

'And there's more news. Marnie's had a letter from a solicitor in London. D'you remember an old lady who visited us a couple of years ago ... Miss Iris Winterburn? She'd worked on canalboats in the war. She was one of the famous girls, about my age, who later became known as the *Idle Women*.'

'I do,' said Angela. 'Very striking looks and lots of ... character.'

'I'd call it *attitude*,' said Anne. 'That's her. Well, she's died and this solicitor wants Marnie to go to his office in London because –'

'Marnie's mentioned in her will?'

'That's just it. He couldn't say. It's all a bit of a mystery. All we know is he's going to give Marnie a letter.'

'What about?'

Anne shrugged. 'Even he doesn't know what's in it.'

'That's very odd. So are they driving down today?'

'No. They're travelling down on *Sally Ann*. They're seeing the solicitor, a very plum-in-the-mouth bloke, next Thursday morning.'

'*Sally Ann*?' Angela sounded incredulous. 'Can they get to London in that time?'

'No probs. They can do it in four or five days, no sweat. They'll leave on the morning tide ... well, first light, anyway.'

'I hope the weather stays fair for them, Anne. Have you noticed there's been a shower of rain while we've been in here?'

Anne looked over towards the window. There were streaks of rain on the glass, and she could just see the top of the hoodie of the woman on the pavement.

'Are we ready to go now?' she said.

'Yes.'

Instead of gathering up her shopping bags, Anne said, 'Hang on a minute. Won't be long.'

Angela settled back, assuming that Anne was heading for the loo. But she veered off towards the counter. A minute later she made for the door carrying a take-away mug and a paper bag. Thinking she had misunderstood Anne's intentions, Angela was pushing back her chair to stand when Anne returned and picked up the shopping.

'Ready?' she said and made for the exit.

Angela hustled after Anne, catching up with her outside. From behind them they heard a quiet voice.

'Thank you.'

Anne hesitated, half turned, smiled and continued on her way. As Angela looked back, the woman on the pavement raised a mug. In her other hand she was holding a croissant. Angela sped after Anne and almost collided with her when they reached Anne's Mini.

'You gave that woman those things?'

Anne nodded. 'I thought she might not have had much breakfast.'

'That was very kind of you, Anne.'

Anne shrugged, 'I was worried she might think I was patronising her.'

'Surely not. That was an act of real charity.'

'I ought to get back,' Anne said. 'Marnie will be wondering where I am.'

Angela gave Anne a brief hug and they parted.

****

Anne walked into the office to find Marnie looking pleased with herself.

'Hi, Anne. Did you manage to get all the things we needed?'

'Yeah. I've put them on the boat.'

'Great.' Marnie added, 'Aren't you going to ask me how I got on?'

'Would it have anything to do with your rather smug expression?'

'My rather ...? Well, yes, actually, it might. The fact is, I've completed all the tasks on my list.' She added, '*And* ... I've been in touch with the gardeners who are coming in the next few days. They weren't even *on* the list.'

Anne sighed. 'And there I was, thinking you might be wondering what had become of me.'

'Quite the opposite in fact.'

'And I thought I was indispensable. So tell me about these gardeners. Do I have to produce a list for them?'

'Not really. They're just going to be digging up the garden now that it's been ... what's the appropriate word?'

'Deforested?' Anne suggested.

'That'll do, yes. In fact, they're going to be *double*-digging the garden to get it ready for planting.'

'What on earth's that?' Anne asked.

Marnie paused. 'Not sure how it works, but they seemed to know what they were talking about. Apparently it improves the soil by aerating it, or something.'

'So my job will be strategic management and overall coordination of landscaping projects on the principles of management by objectives and action-centred leadership.'

'Exactly,' said Marnie. 'You'll be the tea-girl.'

Anne dropped an undignified curtsy and transformed herself into Eliza Doolittle. 'I knows me plice. Oi'm a good gel, Oi am.'

Chapter 3

Good fortune accompanied Marnie and Ralph as they travelled south to London on *Sally Ann*. The locks were largely in their favour, and the weather was fair. The boat chugged happily along through varied pastoral landscapes, the engine never missing a beat, long days leaving the crew pleasantly weary, ready for a pub supper and an early night.

In the evening of the second day's cruising, Marnie phoned Anne to check that all was well at Glebe Farm. She had a surprise.

'Guess who's here, Marnie.'

'Amaze me.'

'Donovan. He came up on *Exodos*, got here this afternoon.' The name painted on the boat was in fact *XO2*, but pronounced as *Exodos*.

'He came on the boat?'

'Yep. He's come up for a few days, moored just opposite *Thyrsis*. He's going to write up his uni project.'

'I *am* amazed. He must have passed us. Can't think how we missed him.'

'Ships that pass in the night,' Anne suggested.

Marnie said, 'That really is a stealth narrowboat.'

'He says he spotted *Sally Ann* yesterday evening tied up at Leighton Buzzard, thinks you were probably having a pub supper. I told him about your mission to the solicitor. He's very intrigued.'

'So am I. Does he have any thoughts about it?'

'He thought it would probably concern some sort of legacy, but he can't understand why they're going about it like this.' She lowered her voice. 'You know he was involved in his parents' will when he was ten years old. He has vague memories of the process.'

'We've come to the same conclusion, Ralph and I, and we're equally baffled by all this mystery.'

'Oh well ...' Anne yawned. 'You'll find out all about it on Thursday.'

'Was that a yawn, Anne? Are you finding the responsibility of running Walker and Co too demanding?'

'Late night. Donovan didn't get here till gone eleven and we sat up talking for a while.'

'Give him our love. How are the gardeners getting on with the double digging?'

'They're *amazing*. You wouldn't believe how much they can do in a day. It's tiring, just watching them.'

****

The rest of the week cruised gently on, as did *Sally Ann*, southwards through the Home Counties – Buckinghamshire, Bedfordshire, Hertfordshire – up and over the Chiltern Hills, across the Tring Summit and down the other side, reeling off the miles to London. Then through the north-western suburbs before turning left-full-rudder at Bull's Bridge into the Paddington Arm, with no more locks to face all the way to their destination, the basin of Little Venice.

On the last leg of the journey Marnie and Ralph stopped to replenish their stores at the Sainsbury's supermarket opposite the cemetery of Kensal Green. It was the last resting place of poets, artists, architects, engineers, the Great, the Good and the Worthy, and even one, Betsy Balcombe, who as a young girl had befriended Napoleon Bonaparte during his exile on St Helena.

While Ralph wheeled the trolley along the aisles, Marnie stood on the bank and phoned the British Waterways office in Little Venice. She spoke to Rob Frazer, the manager, who had reserved a temporary mooring for them.

That evening, at journey's end, Marnie and Ralph entertained two old friends to dinner in the saloon on *Sally Ann*: Jane Rutherford, who taught the traditional castles-and-roses painting of the canals, and Mrs Jolly, an elderly lady who lived opposite the moorings and was regarded with affection as an honorary member of the Little Venice boating community. To celebrate the occasion – a return, however brief, to Marnie's original home port – Ralph had decided that a bottle of champagne was required. There were no dissenters.

Back home at Knightly St John, the week passed equally smoothly at Glebe Farm. Anne kept on top of the paperwork in the office, which was largely routine, and Donovan helped out until he returned to London by train to hand in his project. Anne fulfilled her duties as tea-girl to the gardeners and was impressed with their progress.

On Thursday morning of that idyllic week everything was about to change.

Chapter 4

At breakfast the next morning on *Sally Ann* there was a divergence of view between Marnie and Ralph. The question was how to reach the offices of Burnett Haydock and Lang which were situated in High Holborn near the city centre. Ralph mentioned that it would be an easy journey by tube to Holborn, followed by a short walk. Marnie had assumed they would go by taxi.

They decided on a compromise or, what Ralph called, *letting fate take a hand*. They left the moorings in good time, locking the gates behind them and setting off in the direction of Warwick Avenue tube station. They had barely walked twenty-five yards when a taxi came by. Fate had intervened.

They arrived at their destination with minutes to spare and announced themselves at the reception desk. Almost immediately they were ushered into an office, the door to which bore the nameplate:

Seymour F. Lang
Partner

Neither the office nor its occupant were what Marnie had expected. Instead of a gloomy room lined with dark mahogany bookcases ceiling-to-floor filled with learned tomes and statutes untouched for generations, they entered a spacious and inviting workplace. Bookcases there were, but painted white with the occasional houseplant and ceramic vase between the books. The overall effect was tasteful, relaxed, almost domestic. In the centre of the office stood a large desk, but this was no Victorian behemoth. It was an ultra-modern structure with shiny steel legs and an oval glass worktop, entirely uncluttered save for a widescreen Mac computer and keyboard.

Behind the desk sat a young man – younger than Marnie expected – who got to his feet as the visitors entered the room. Not much more than forty, he had a mop of bushy dark hair and wore gold-rimmed glasses with a faint blue tint. In a well-cut navy pin-stripe suit, he exuded energy as he stepped around the desk and thrust out a hand. Watching him as he shook hands with Ralph, Marnie noticed that he was barely taller than herself and moved with the staccato articulation of a marionette. For all his languid way of speaking, he reminded Marnie of a musician or a poet as he turned towards her. His grip as they shook was firm and dry.

'Seymour Lang. Good of you to come.' That drawl again. 'I hope it wasn't inconvenient. Please take a seat.'

For the first time Marnie noticed an envelope lying on the desk. Lang continued.

'Would you care for coffee ... tea?'

They opted for coffee and heard the door click shut behind them.

'I'm very intrigued, Mr Lang,' Marnie said. 'It was quite a shock to learn that Iris had died.'

Lang nodded. 'Yes ... yes, I'm sure. Tell me, Mrs Walker, are you related?'

'Not at all. In fact we only met a few times. That's one of the reasons why we're intrigued. It's not as if we were ever really close.'

'Yet you use her first name when you speak of her. That's rather unusual, considering the difference in your ages, if you're not a relative.'

Marnie thought fleetingly of her friend Mrs Jolly, of whom she was very fond, and who was always 'Mrs Jolly'.

'I agree. Actually, I was rather surprised when she asked me to call her Iris. It was the last time I saw her.'

'Surprised because she was so much older than you?'

'Partly that and partly because she was a slightly forbidding character in many ways. Did you know her well, Mr Lang?'

Lang shook his head. 'I never met her. Her affairs were looked after by my former partner, Toby Haydock. He's been retired more than two years. I think when she first became a client she dealt with the then senior partner, Tristan Burnett. Tristan died several years ago. My only contact with Miss Winterburn is this letter ...' He picked it up from the desk. '... and one or two other items that we may or may not come to.'

'This is all very mysterious,' said Ralph.'Oh yes,' said Lang. 'In fact, it's as much a mystery to me as it is to you.'

Marnie was about to speak when she heard the door open. Lang shifted his gaze to a point beyond his visitors.

'Thank you, Janet.' He indicated the desk where the woman from reception set down a tray. 'Please, help yourselves.'

Marnie observed that the cups were of fine china, the milk jug and sugar bowl were silver.

'Mr Lang,' she said, 'there's something I need to ask you. You haven't told us how Iris died. Was it a long illness?'

Lang cleared his throat and looked down at the desk. He said quietly, 'My client passed away peacefully in her sleep. Her GP signed the death certificate. As cause of death he wrote 'heart failure'. There was no post mortem, of course. Miss Winterburn had been suffering from angina for some years and was almost ninety.'

'Natural causes,' Ralph said. 'A gentle end to a long life.'

Lang looked up. 'Indeed.'

Marnie said, 'I wonder, Mr Lang, if now might be a good time to look at the letter, or am I supposed to take it away with me?'

Lang stirred his coffee. 'The instructions in the file are explicit about that, Mrs Walker. Frankly, I think it's up to you, but the procedure set out by my late client envisages your reading the letter now and giving me a decision. I'm in no position to judge how reasonable that requirement might be.' He shrugged. 'You could need some time to think about whatever is in the letter before reaching that decision. Who knows?'

Ralph said, 'Perhaps if Marnie could read the letter here and now she'd be in a better position to know how to proceed.'

Lang sipped his coffee and set down the cup. 'Quite so.' He raised an eyebrow in Marnie's direction, then reached across the desk and passed her the envelope. 'Mrs Walker?'

Marnie stared at the envelope for a few moments. It was cream vellum, and her name was written on it in black ink. The writing looked a little shaky, the hand of an elderly person.

Marnie felt momentarily sad at the thought that that rather austere, strong character was after all frail and mortal. She opened the envelope with her thumb and pulled out the letter. It was hand-written on good quality paper that matched the envelope. The writing was a little unsteady but perfectly legible.

'If you'll bear with me I'd like to read it to myself,' she said.

'By all means,' said Lang, reaching for his coffee cup.

Marnie read in silence.

April Cottage
Little Haddon
Herts

Dear Marnie,

You are reading this letter because I have died. I owe you an explanation and probably an apology, but that rather depends on what you decide to do after you have read what I have in mind.

I have no immediate family and no close friends to whom I could entrust the role of being my executor. Never having married, I leave behind no heirs; my siblings have predeceased me and, like me, they died without issue.

You are probably wondering why I am not asking my solicitor or the bank to act as executor to the small resources which might be called my 'estate'. The fact is, there is a complication that requires what I can only describe as a special touch. On the basis of our few meetings, my dear, I have reached the conclusion that I can trust you. There is also a link between us of which you are at present entirely unaware, though I did once allude loosely to it some time ago.

At this stage all I ask of you is that you inform the solicitor of your decision, whether you accept the role of executrix or not. Please feel under no obligation. If you do not wish for any reason to perform this duty, that is perfectly acceptable; Mr Lang knows what follow-up action to take, and you will not be troubled further. It will of course make no difference to me, as I am writing to you – sorry to be melodramatic – from beyond the grave.

However, it is only fair to warn you that acceptance will involve a considerable obligation on your part and I will ask that you sign a strict confidentiality agreement.

I must add one last thing. I have named you as a beneficiary in my will. Whatever you decide to do one way or the other will not make any difference to the provisions in that document.
It was a pleasure knowing you and I wish you every success and happiness in your life.
Very sincerely, and with much affection and gratitude,
Iris

Marnie read the letter a second time before passing it to Ralph. She drank her coffee lost in thought while he read. After a few minutes he took a mouthful of coffee and read the letter again. He looked up at Lang.

'Are you aware of the contents of this letter, Mr Lang?' he asked.

'No. I'm aware only that I am to await a decision from Mrs Walker, depending on which I have instructions as to how I should proceed.'

Ralph handed the letter back to Marnie. 'Do you need time to think about this, darling?'

Marnie stared at Ralph without speaking for several seconds then said, 'It's certainly very intriguing. I don't quite know what to –'

Before she could complete the sentence a faint humming sound emanated from her shoulder-bag on the floor.

'I'm sorry. That's my mobile. It's in silent mode, but that means I have a message. It can wait.'

Lang made a languid gesture. 'Please check it, Mrs Walker. There's no hurry.' He smiled. 'My instructions are that in no circumstance am I to rush you into anything.'

Marnie reached down and pulled out the phone. To Ralph she said, 'It's from Anne.'

Ralph said, 'She must need a decision on something.'

'I don't like to interrupt a meeting,' Marnie said quietly.

'No harm in just checking it,' said Lang.

Marnie pressed a button and read from the screen. 'Oh.' She held the mobile up for Ralph to see.

> Something has happened.
> Please speak soon.
> I need advice.
> Anne

'Something has cropped up in the office,' Marnie said to Lang. 'My colleague wouldn't send a message if it wasn't urgent.'

'It's not a problem, Mrs Walker, I mean as far as Miss Winterburn's letter is concerned. Please let me have your decision when you can.'

Marnie turned towards Ralph. 'Iris is trusting me to do something for her, something obviously important to her.' To Lang, 'I want to help, but I'd like to discuss it with Ralph first. Could we see you after a short interval for some lunch, perhaps?'

'I shan't be taking a break today. I'll be here if you'd like to come back in an hour or two. Would that suit you?'

****

There was a pub about a hundred yards down the road offering the usual fare: 'good food, cask ales, fine wines'. Marnie and Ralph decided to give it a whirl and they set off at a brisk pace. It was just after twelve noon, and the lunchtime rush had barely begun. They ordered sandwiches and spritzers and found a corner table. Marnie's head was spinning as a result of the letter 'from beyond the grave'.

'Well,' she began, 'that was a real surprise ... Iris Winterburn, wanting me as executrix.'

31

'I didn't realise you knew her so well.'

'I didn't, Ralph. As I told Seymour Lang, I met her on just a few occasions. But I liked her. She was a strong character. I'm sorry she's died.'

'She's made you a beneficiary in her will as well as her executrix, so she must have had a high regard for you.'

'I suppose. Even so, it's quite a mystery. What did you make of it, Ralph?'

'All sorts of things. It's obviously not just a straightforward legacy, though it seems that will come later. Shall we go through it and share thoughts?'

Marnie smiled at Ralph. 'Is that what you do with your students?'

'How else can we work out what's involved?'

Marnie laid the letter on the table between them, and they read it once again in silence. When they finished, Ralph raised an eyebrow.

'How odd ... intriguing.'

'You go first, Ralph. What are you thinking?'

'I'm wondering why she mentions the need for an apology, presumably if you decide you're willing to go ahead as executrix.'

'There must be more to it than just the normal probate, I suppose.'

'Must be,' Ralph agreed. 'What next?'

'I'm wondering about this *complication* and the need for a *special touch*. Why does she say she trusts me? I wonder what that's about.'

'It must be to do with this *obligation* she refers to later. And what about this link between you?'

Marnie pondered. 'I told you, I only met her a few times, Ralph. The first was when I sort of rescued her when she had an injured ankle and I found her sheltering from a storm. That can't be it.'

Ralph said, 'I met her just once, that time when she came to Glebe Farm and we all went for a tootle on *Sally Ann*. Anything there come to mind?'

Marnie closed her eyes and thought back. 'Vaguely. She told me she'd stayed at Glebe Farm for a short time in the war. Her boat's engine had broken down apparently and she had to wait for spare parts. I can't remember her *alluding loosely* to anything at the time, certainly nothing that would require a *confidentiality agreement*. It's all very –' Suddenly Marnie exclaimed and raised a hand to her mouth.

'You've remembered something?' Ralph said.

Marnie hauled her bag from the floor. 'Anne's message! I forgot all about it. I must call her. I'd better do it outside.'

The phone rang several times before Anne picked it up. She sounded breathless.

'Sorry, Marnie, I was outside with the gardeners.'

'What's happened?'

'It's Ray and Sammy, digging in the garden. They've found a skeleton.'

Marnie was stunned. 'Bloody hell! You've seen it?'

'Yes, well, partly. They've only uncovered some of it. Then they came to the office to tell me about it.'

'You're sure it's human?'

'Looks like a human skull. Marnie, what do I do? I've just given the men some tea and told them to stop work.'

Marnie's mind was racing. She opened the door to the pub and signalled to Ralph. A waitress was just serving their order. Ralph explained hurriedly that they'd be straight back and picked his way quickly across the dining area.

'What is it?'

'You're not going to believe this.' Marnie explained what had happened. 'Anne's asking what to do. I'm trying to think straight here, but my heads all a-jumble over the will thing.'

Ralph nodded. 'I'm sure the police have to be informed. That's the first thing to do.'

'Oh God,' Marnie murmured. 'What a thing to land on Anne while we're away. We've got to get back.'

Ralph held Marnie by the arms. 'Let's think things through clearly and methodically. Yes?' Marnie nodded. Ralph continued. 'I think we should inform the police ourselves, not leave it to Anne. Then we get back home as quickly as we can.'

'Yes, yes, of course. You're right.'

'Do you have the local police number on your phone?'

Marnie grimaced. 'It's practically a hot line.'

'Then ring them now. Ask for CID.'

Marnie pressed buttons on her mobile. 'I expect I'll get my old friend Chief Inspector Bartlett.' She pulled a face. 'He'll be thrilled to hear from me.'

While Marnie waited to be connected, Ralph rang Anne. He told her to do nothing but wait either for the police to arrive or for a further call from him or Marnie. They disconnected simultaneously and looked at each other quizzically.

'You first, Marnie,' said Ralph. 'But I think we ought to get back in there and have some lunch.'

'Ralph, I don't really feel –'

'I know. Neither do I, but we have to keep our strength up. Come on.'

Ralph led Marnie back to the table and encouraged her to make an attempt on the sandwich. He took a gulp of spritzer and asked her to go ahead.

'Well, I didn't get Bartlett – praise the Lord! – but I spoke to Sergeant Binns. You remember he was involved when that mugger was about?' Ralph nodded and took a bite of his sandwich. 'He's taking a team of crime scene people to Glebe Farm to see what's what.'

'He's treating the find as a crime, then.'

'He said he had no choice. Standard procedure with human remains. I told him we were in London on business, but we'd return as soon as we could. He said we should do that. Tell me about your call to Anne.'

'I just said we were notifying the police and she should sit tight with the gardeners. As soon as we've finished here I'll –'

'Ralph, I think she needs to know right now. We don't want the police suddenly descending on her. I'll send her a message.' Marnie smiled. 'At least she'll be comforted that it will be Sgt Binns coming.'

'Oh?'

Marnie was still smiling as she sent the message. 'She once said that if he was from the Metropolitan Police he'd be called Binns of the Yard.'

Ralph chuckled and shook his head. 'Typical! That girl …' Another bite from the sandwich.

'There,' said Marnie, 'it's sent. I expect she's already writing lists of things to do.'

Ralph swallowed. 'And so should we. I'll get onto Rob Frazer at the BW office and see if we can leave *Sally Ann* in Little Venice for a while.'

'And I'll talk to Seymour Lang,' Marnie said.

'Do you know what you want to do about the will and whatever else is involved?'

Marnie looked perplexed. 'Iris trusted me to do something that was important for her. It was her last wish.'

'True.'

She sighed. 'I've really got enough on my plate with work and everything else. And now we'll have the police crawling all over us at home.'

'Only you can decide about Iris Winterburn, Marnie. Whatever you do, you know I'll support you in every way I can.'

Leaving the pub, they set off in opposite directions, but were of one mind.

Chapter 5

The journey back to Knightly St John was appreciably quicker than the journey south on *Sally Ann*. Rob Frazer agreed to an extended stay on the mooring in Little Venice, so Marnie and Ralph returned to the boat to collect their bags then caught a train from Euston. Once settled in their seats, Marnie phoned Anne.

'The garden's swarming with people dressed like astronauts,' Anne said. 'They're excavating the skeleton. Sergeant Binns is here. He hasn't told me anything about what's going on.'

'They never do. Listen, we'll get a taxi from the station and _'

'Marnie, I have to tell you something. Donovan's coming back. In fact, he's driving up right now. I can probably get him to meet you at MK Central. What d'you think?'

They agreed on a plan. By the time the train began rolling, it was arranged that Donovan would drive straight to the station in Milton Keynes, and they would travel to Glebe Farm together.

Donovan had been a regular visitor to Glebe Farm for the past two years. Not quite as tall as Ralph, he was lightly built with blue eyes and blonde hair, not quite as pale as Anne's. He had on occasion been taken for her brother, in view of their similar colouring, but their relationship had been anything but fraternal from almost the first time they met. He habitually wore black, or sometimes dark grey, a taste in colours which extended to his car and his narrowboat.

His car was a VW Beetle from the 1970s, inherited from his parents, his mother German, his father Anglo-Irish. They'd died in a coach crash while on holiday in South Africa. Donovan, who was then ten years old, had been sitting on the other side of the coach; he was shaken but otherwise uninjured. He inherited the VW and other things, including the family's house in west London.

The ride home from the station was a twenty minute journey. With three adults and their luggage, the little car was cramped. Ralph, who had long legs, had to sit in the front. While he rode shotgun, Marnie sat in the rear with two weekend bags piled on the seat beside her.

At the entrance to the field track they were stopped by a police constable. He waved them on when they gave their names. Donovan drove carefully down the rough slope, avoiding bumps and tussocks, as the roof of Glebe Farm came into view through treetops. He pulled over at the end of the trail where police cars and vans obstructed access to the site.

Lugging their bags, the three of them threaded their way through the parked vehicles. The space beside the farmhouse leading into the rear garden was cordoned off with blue and white tape. Beyond it they could see scene-of-crime officers – SOCOs – in their all-enveloping white tunics, with hoods and masks, moving purposefully about. Anne was standing in the doorway to the office barn watching proceedings. Her face lit up when she saw Marnie, Ralph and Donovan. She rushed out and hugged them all in turn, with a kiss for her boyfriend.

'*So* glad you're back,' she said and gestured towards the garden with her head. 'The invasion of the Martians began just after your first phone call.'

'Have they told you anything?' Donovan asked.

Marnie said, 'No chance of that.'

'Here comes Sergeant Binns,' Ralph said. 'He'll probably prove your point.'

The detective was a little older than Marnie and an inch or two taller. He was solidly built and looked tough, but his manner was quiet and unthreatening. He was wearing light blue overalls, similar to those worn by the 'Martian' SOCOs.

'How's it going?' Marnie asked, not expecting an answer but ever hopeful.

'Early days.' True to form.

'But it's definitely a human skeleton?' said Ralph.

'It looks that way.'

'Any clues as to how long it's been in the ground?'

Binns should his head. 'Not till our expert has had a good look.'

Ralph said, 'You're waiting for the pathologist?'

'I wanted a forensic anthropologist, but division's sending a forensic archaeologist.'

'You're expecting the remains to be ... antique?' Ralph suggested.

Binns turned to Marnie. 'You've been here a few years now ... is that right?'

'Yes, but my priority's been renovating the buildings. Judging by the state of it, no one has been in that garden for quite a time.'

Anne added helpfully, 'We usually call it the jungle.'

Binns made no comment. There was an awkward silence. Eventually Marnie spoke.

'I was rather expecting to see DCI Bartlett or DS Marriner.'

'Lucky dip, or unlucky dip, as the case may be. I was available when your call came in, and that was that. Actually, this may be my last case in Northamptonshire.'

'Promotion?' said Ralph.

A modest smile from Binns. 'I've passed the Osprey exam for promotion to inspector.'

'Congratulations.'

'Thanks.'

'So you'll be moving away?' Marnie said.

'Yes. I've heard from the Metropolitan Police and decided to–'

'Sarge!'

A call came from one of the SOCOs inside the taped-off area. Binns excused himself and hurried away. They were in a huddle for a few minutes while Marnie, Ralph, Anne and Donovan looked on.

'I wonder what's going on,' said Marnie.

'Something's got them excited' said Ralph. 'I don't suppose we'll ever find out what it is.'

But he was wrong.

Marnie was suggesting that they dump their weekend bags in the house when Donovan gestured.

'He's coming back.'

The four turned expectantly towards Binns. When he reached them he held out one gloved hand palm upwards. The four of them craned forward. He was holding a small piece of metal, aluminium or tin, roughly the size of a two pence coin. It was oval with three perforations in the form of slits across the middle. There were three more perforations in the form of small round holes. The object had been wiped just clean enough to reveal markings, though they weren't decipherable.

'What is it?' Marnie asked.

'We don't know yet,' said Binns. 'Perhaps our archaeologist will be able to tell us.'

Ralph said, 'Is there anything on the other side?'

Binns shook his head. 'No, it's blank.'

At that moment Donovan leaned in closer. 'Can I have a look at that?'

Binns extended his hand. Donovan murmured something inaudible.

'What was that?' Binns said. 'Do you know what this is?'

'*Erkennungsmarke*,' Donovan muttered softly. 'How odd. I've seen one before, but certainly not here. An old neighbour of ours in Germany had one in his box of medals.'

'It doesn't look like any medal I've ever seen.' Binns sounded doubtful.

'It's not a medal,' said Donovan. 'I think you'll find it's a dog-tag.'

'A *German* soldier's dog-tag?' Doubtful had turned into highly sceptical.

By now Donovan's nose was almost touching the object as he strained to decipher the markings.

'I don't see how that's possible,' Binns continued. 'Are you seriously suggesting it's a dog-tag from World War Two, found in a grave in this village?'

Donovan shrugged. 'Presumably. I can't make out what's inscribed on it.'

'What do you think it might be?' Ralph asked.

'The one I've seen had the person's service number, the unit mark and his blood group.'

'But what makes you so sure it's a dog-tag?' Binns was still unconvinced.

Donovan pointed. 'You see those slits across the middle? The idea was that if this man was killed in action, they could easily split the tag in two. One half would go to the HQ of his unit to register him as a fatality and then notify his family. The other half would stay on his body as identity.'

In a flash, Donovan picked up the tag, licked his finger and rubbed it firmly across the metal surface. Faint markings were revealed.

'Hey, that's evidence!' Binns said.

'Surely not of any crime,' said Ralph. 'It must be very old.'

Donovan laid it back on Binns' glove. 'Hold it there,' he said.

Binns was taken by surprise as Donovan pulled out a small digital camera and photographed the tag. Too late, Binns snatched it away.

'What are you doing?' he said.

Donovan slipped the camera back into his pocket. 'It just intrigues me, that's all.'

'Are you really sure it's a dog-tag?' said Binns. 'I mean the Germans never had any soldiers on English soil.'

'Almost certain,' Donovan replied. 'But I'm as baffled as you are about how this man came to be here. Is there anything else in the grave ... buttons, buckles, insignia ... anything like that?'

Binns said, 'They're still excavating.'

'Will you stop now and wait for your archaeologist?' Ralph asked.

'The SOCOs are just as thorough,' said Binns.

'Where was this found?' Marnie asked. 'I mean, in relation to the skeleton.'

Binns said, 'Roughly between the head and the rib cage, according to my colleague.'

Marnie fingered her throat. 'So he was wearing it round his neck.' She exchanged a glance with Donovan.

Binns stared down at the object. 'I suppose we can't know anything more about this person, whoever he was, until our forensic guys have reported.'

Donovan said, 'We know one thing for certain about him.'

'What's that?'

'He died in a foreign land and his family never found out what became of him. That dog-tag is still intact.'

'We have another mystery too,' Ralph said. 'The question is, how did he come to be in Knightly St John?'

Everyone looked baffled. No one had an answer.

Chapter 6

That evening after supper Marnie and Ralph decided to relax in the living room in the farmhouse while Anne and Donovan retired to her attic room in the office barn. During the meal they had gone over the events of the day and reached only tentative conclusions. The mystery of the skeleton and its German military dog-tag defeated them all. When Ralph entered the room carrying two cups of coffee he found Marnie writing a list.

Without looking up, she said, 'There's just so much to do.'

'We'll share it out,' Ralph said. 'Would you like a small cognac with your coffee?'

Marnie smiled. 'Yes, just a double.'

'What's top of your list?' Ralph asked.

'I suppose I ought to let Roger know about our meeting with Lang ... see what he makes of it all.'

'You could ring him at home this evening. He wouldn't mind. You can't tackle the rest until office hours tomorrow.'

While Ralph went in search of the brandy bottle and glasses, Marnie rang a familiar number. Roger Broadbent was fine with a call at home.

'Of course I don't mind, Marnie. In fact I've been wondering all day about your mysterious communication from those solicitors. So is it all now cleared up?'

'Not really. I've told this guy, Seymour Lang, that I'm willing to go ahead as executrix for Iris. I've arranged to go back to London to see him on Monday. That's when I'll find out what this extra task will be.'

'I've been thinking about that, Marnie. Something has occurred to me. Has there been any hint that the will might possibly be contested? That's the only added complication that I can think of.'

'No, nothing like that so far, but I've been wondering about that myself. I suppose I'll just have to be patient for another few days. Okay to keep in touch with you on this?'

'By all means ring me whenever you want. And if there's anything that bothers you about this extra task, stall for time and let me know. There is just something I ought to mention.'

'What's that?'

'I've got to take *Rumpole* for its annual safety inspection in a couple of weeks. Assuming there are no problems, Marjorie and I are planning a short trip on the boat ... just a few days away.'

'Okay. Hope it all goes well. I don't think anything urgent is likely to crop up.'

'Even if we're away I can interrogate the answerphone remotely, so I'm not completely out of touch.'

'Thanks, Roger. There's something else I want to tell you. The people working in the garden have uncovered a skeleton.'

A pause. 'Human?'

'Not only that. There was a German military dog-tag buried with it.'

'In your garden? Are you sure about that?'

'Donovan's here. He identified it. Apparently he's seen one before.'

'That's incredible. The German army didn't have any boots on the ground in mainland Britain in the war.' Roger paused. 'Actually ...'

'What?'

'Perhaps your skeleton didn't date back to the war. Perhaps the tag was a war trophy ... a memento ... a *memento mori*, in this case.'

'I hadn't thought of that,' Marnie said.

'Plenty of items were brought back by servicemen as keepsakes. My father had an Iron Cross that he found near Cologne in that last push before they surrendered.'

'I'll mention it to the police. Did I tell you they were here?'

'Inevitable when human remains are discovered, Marnie. I'd be glad to know how that progresses. Everything in your life seems to be a puzzle at the moment.'

Marnie agreed to keep Roger informed, and they disconnected.

Ralph said, 'I've had an idea. If there really was a German soldier here in the war, you can bet your life someone would know about it ... everyone, probably. The word would get round the village in no time.'

'That's for sure,' said Marnie. 'I wonder who'd be the best person to ask.'

'I was thinking of George Stubbs.'

'He was just a child at the time.'

'But George knows everything about the village, and everyone. If he didn't know then, he'd find out about it later.'

George Stubbs was born and brought up in Knightly St John. His family had been key members of the local business fraternity for generations. They were butchers, well-off and with political connections. George and his wife lived in a fine stone farmhouse near the centre of the village and were closely involved in every aspect of community life.

Marnie stood and picked up the phone. She knew George wouldn't mind being phoned late in the evening. He was in his sixties and had a soft spot for her, which he made rather obvious.

'Are you kidding, my dear?' Marnie winced. 'A Kraut soldier in our village during the war? He wouldn't have lasted five minutes.'

'That's just it, George. We've found a dog-tag in the garden down here.'

'A what?'

'You know, a military dog-tag ... identity tag.'

'And you're sure it's German?'

'Positive.'

A pause. 'A war trophy, surely. People brought back all manner of stuff after the war. It's a wonder nobody nicked a Tiger tank as a memento.'

'So you've never heard of any military presence here? What about a POW who might've got permission to work on a farm? I believe it did happen.'

'No POW camps round here, Marnie. And I can't imagine anyone wanting a bloody Nazi on their land. Oops ... sorry about that.'

44

'Thanks, George. Sorry to disturb your evening.'

'Any time, my dear.' Another wince. 'Tell you what, I'll have a think and ask around, just in case. But I'm pretty sure I'll draw a blank.'

****

Over in Anne's attic room another phone call was made. Donovan judged that it was rather late in the evening in Germany to ring the elderly neighbour whose dog-tag he'd seen in the past, but he was anxious to check his facts about dog-tags before the day was out. A friend of his uncle Helmut had been conscripted into the *Wehrmacht* as a boy soldier in the last months of the war. Recently retired, the friend was still fit and active and more than willing to talk about his experiences at that time. Their conversation was in German.

'Sorry to ring out of the blue like this, Herr Beckmann' said Donovan.

'Not a problem, my boy. What can I do for you?'

'You remember your dog-tag – your *Erkennungsmarke*?'

'Of course. I still have it in a drawer somewhere. What about it?'

Donovan described the tag found with the skeleton. Herr Beckmann agreed with Donovan's assessment in principle; his recollection of details was accurate. But on one key point Herr Beckmann was adamant.

'No. This was no German soldier. The *Wehrmacht* never landed in Britain, apart from those islands in the Channel, of course.'

'So I understood,' said Donovan. 'Can you think of any explanation for a dog-tag like that turning up in the middle of England?'

There was a lengthy silence. 'No idea. But then, remember, I was only a conscripted soldier straight out of the Hitler Youth. What could I know about such things?'

'Could he have been a spy, perhaps?' Donovan suggested.

'Wearing an army dog-tag? Seems unlikely. But there is one thing – assuming you're not mistaken. Is there any sign of a harness on him?'

'You're thinking of a paratrooper, Herr Beckmann?'

Another silence. 'No, not really. The army wouldn't have sent one man to conquer England. Even on a bad day, Hitler wouldn't have been so stupid … probably.'

Donovan was smiling when they ended the call and he outlined the conversation to Anne.

'It just doesn't add up,' she said. 'I don't suppose there's any chance this tag thingy might be something different?'

'Well, I must admit, I'm starting to have my doubts. But I have seen one before and it was just like the one Binns showed us today. Herr Beckmann seemed to think I'd got it right.'

'So how do you explain how it turns up in the garden of Glebe Farm?'

'I can't, Anne. I'm completely flummoxed.'

They fell silent, each lost in their own thoughts, both wrestling with the problem, until Anne started laughing.

'What's the joke?' said Donovan.

'I just thought of Sergeant Binns.'

'What about him?'

'You heard him say he's been promoted.'

'That's funny?'

'Don't you get it?'

'It must be the way you tell them.'

'Donovan, he said he'd be going to join the Met in London.'

'Yes, I heard him say that.'

'That's it. He really will be … Binns of the Yard!'

Anne laughed like a fishwife. Donovan hung his head.

Chapter 7

It was Friday morning and Anne was impressed. There was no other word for it. Straight after breakfast Marnie homed in on her desk like a heat-seeking missile and cranked up the computer. Within minutes she was typing a document, consulting a notepad beside her on the desk. Anne's curiosity was aroused. She sidled across the office and gazed over Marnie's shoulder.

'That table,' she said. 'Is that a list?'

'Yep. I'm on fire.'

Anne leaned forward to read the first items. 'Contact Orient-Express …' she read out loud. 'Finalise visit to Seymour Lang, Monday morning …'

Still typing, Marnie muttered, 'I want to get all these things sorted out this morning.'

'Wow,' said Anne, impressed. She set off towards her desk but stopped halfway across the room and turned to look back at Marnie. 'I've just worked out what the last item on your list will be.'

Marnie stopped typing and looked up. 'Tell me. I'm intrigued.'

'It'll be: *order form P45 for Anne.*'

Marnie looked bewildered. 'P45? Isn't that … oh, I get it.'

'Yes. You must be making me redundant. I always thought Principal List-maker was my job title at Walker and Co.'

Marnie stared back deadpan. 'You always gave me to understand it was *Indispensable* Principal List-maker, but these things I really have to do for myself before Ralph and I go to London on Sunday.'

'In that case,' said Anne, 'I'll pop into the supermarket in Stony Stratford and stock up with provisions for your trip. How long will you be gone?'

'A few days and we'll travel back on *Sally Ann.* Do you want me to do you a shopping list?'

Anne smirked. 'As Indispensable Principal List-maker I have a generic list already drawn up on my computer.'

'Silly of me to ask,' said Marnie and returned to her typing.

Donovan volunteered to go to Stony Stratford with Anne as her 'beast of burden'. With the supermarket car park teeming with Friday morning shoppers, Anne gave up trying to park, reversed the Mini out of the melee and drove round the block. Near the church a large BMW estate car was trying optimistically to squeeze into a tiny slot. The driver gave up just as the Mini was approaching, and roared off in frustration. Anne manoeuvred the little car into the space with ease and they made their way back to the supermarket.

All along the high street were notices on lamp posts, telegraph poles and in shop windows. The police were asking for anyone with information concerning the murder of the 'charity worker' to contact them. A phone number and e-mail address featured prominently under a photo of the victim. The crime had shaken the whole community.

A short while later they emerged from the supermarket with everything ticked off Anne's list and a trolley-full of provisions. Rather than lug all the bags back to the car, Anne opted to fetch it while Donovan waited by the entrance. Some time elapsed before he caught sight of the Mini returning. As Anne pulled up beside him, she looked troubled.

'Everything okay?' he said. 'You were gone for ages.'

'Let's load the shopping and I'll explain later.'

They filled the tiny boot and the rear seats, and set off.

'So what was the problem?' Donovan asked.

'I'll show you.'

They retraced their route through the town. Anne slowed as they passed the church on their right and a row of shops on their left.

'There.' She pointed in the direction of the charity shop.

'That notice in the window about the murder?' Donovan said. 'What of it?'

'No. That person sitting on the pavement, begging.'

'You stopped to give her something ... chatted to her?'

'Yes, I did. But that's not the whole picture. I had to coax it out of her.' Anne turned a corner and accelerated up the main street. 'It seems she's been homeless for some weeks, sleeping rough in the park down by the river.'

'Why's she homeless?' Donovan asked.

'I couldn't make it out. She wasn't very coherent. There was something about looking after her mother who'd died. She had to get out of their home for some reason.'

'Couldn't pay the rent?' Donovan suggested.

Anne shook her head. 'I dunno. But it's really upsetting.'

'You're wanting to do something about it? Is that what you're thinking?'

'What *can* I do? Contact the Social Services department ... the Housing department? Is there such a thing these days? I just don't know. What do you reckon?'

'I reckon we talk it over with Marnie and Ralph, see what they think.'

****

Ralph was in the office having coffee with Marnie when Anne and Donovan returned. Anne outlined her conversation with the woman begging outside the charity shop.

'You think she's the same person you saw before?' Marnie said.

'Pretty sure, yes.'

'And that's all she said, no other details?'

'Nothing that I could make out.'

'She's really got to you, hasn't she, Anne?' Ralph said.

Anne sighed. 'I keep thinking back to the time I ran away from home. I could've ended up sleeping on the street.'

Donovan looked startled. 'You ran away from home?'

Anne nodded. 'My dad had just been laid off again from the factory. I thought I'd be one less mouth to feed.'

'What happened to you?'

'Marnie happened. I met her and she persuaded me to go back and face up to things. That's how we met. She was wonderful. She saved me.'

Ralph said, 'Marnie has a way of saving lost souls.' He didn't elaborate.

'Can we get back to your begging lady before my halo gets tarnished?' said Marnie. 'What d'you want to do about her?'

Anne looked forlorn. 'Can't we do something to help her? I hate just leaving her there on the street. I can't help thinking about that murder in Stony Stratford. Who knows what might happen to her?'

Donovan said, 'Sounds as if you want Marnie to happen to her.'

'Not just Marnie. Couldn't we all do something?'

'Well ...' Marnie began tentatively, '... there's Randall's hostel in Brackley. That might be a place to start.'

'We don't know she'd be willing to go there,' Anne said. 'In fact, we don't even know if she's still begging in Stony.'

Marnie reached for her car keys. 'Anyone coming?'

****

They met a steady stream of traffic flowing out of Stony Stratford as the Freelander rolled into town. The road was arrow-straight, a vestige of the ancient Roman highway, Watling Street. Reaching the town centre, Marnie made a sharp right turn at the church. From the back seat, sitting beside Donovan, Anne was craning her neck, desperate for a sight of the beggar-woman.

Ralph pointed. 'That must be her.'

Anne was relieved to see the woman still sitting on a blanket on the pavement with a rucksack at her side.

'I'll pull over,' said Marnie. 'You can get out and I'll find somewhere to park.'

Anne was already opening her door. 'I'd better go first by myself. Don't want to scare her off.'

As soon as Anne was out of the car, Marnie took off. First stop was to park in the market square beyond the church. The three of them climbed out, walked through the churchyard and halted by the church's west entrance. They peered round the corner and saw Anne kneeling beside the woman. They seemed to be in conversation, the woman casting occasional glances in Anne's direction but otherwise not making eye contact.

'I'm going over,' said Marnie.

50

She strolled casually across the road while Ralph and Donovan looked on. When she was about ten feet away she stopped. The woman had her hood lowered, and Marnie guessed her age at forty or so. Her hair was an unwashed dark blonde, tied back with a red elastic band in an unruly ponytail. She looked drawn and weary. Anne glanced around and spoke quietly.

'This is my friend. Her name's Marnie.'

The woman looked up, suspicious. 'Are you from social services?'

She had an educated voice. Marnie was surprised.

'No,' Marnie said. 'I'm an interior designer, and Anne works with me. We'd like to help you if we can.'

'That's more than I ever got from social services. So how d'you think you can help me?'

'I'm not quite sure right now, to be honest. But is there something you need that we might be able to provide?'

A sad smile. 'You mean apart from a roof over my head?'

'Look ... Sorry, I don't know your name.'

A moment's hesitation. 'Sylvia ... Sylvia Harris.'

'My name's Marnie ... Marnie Walker. And you know my friend is Anne.'

'Anne Price,' Anne added. 'That's Anne with an 'e'.'

Sylvia smiled faintly. 'Anne with an 'e'.'

'We're serious about helping,' Marnie continued.

'And you're really not from social services.'

Marnie shook her head. 'Really not.'

Anne said, 'We hate to see you out on the street like this.'

Marnie reached forward and lightly touched the sleeve of Sylvia's hoodie. 'Anne said you've been sleeping in the park.'

'Yeah.' It was little more than a whisper.

'For long?'

'A few weeks.'

'That must be tough.'

'It's not easy to keep yourself clean when you're living rough.'

'We can do something about that,' Marnie said.

'What d'you mean?'

'You can use our shower room. We've got plenty of towels, shampoo ... stuff like that.'

'And what happens afterwards?' Sylvia asked.

Marnie checked her watch. 'It's coming up to lunchtime. We can work something out while we eat.'

Sylvia stared at Marnie appraisingly. 'We *eat*?'

'It'll just be something light,' Anne said. 'We've got soup and rolls ... fruit for dessert ... maybe yogurt.'

'I wouldn't want you to have any surprises,' said Marnie. 'There are four of us at Glebe Farm.'

'Glebe Farm? You said you were a designer, nothing about a farm.'

'I've renovated an old farm. It was almost derelict. We live and work there.'

'Four of you?'

'At the moment, yes. There's Ralph, he's my partner ... well, my fiancé ... and Anne's boyfriend Donovan is up for the weekend from London. They're here, waiting for us by the car.'

'What d'you think?' Anne asked. 'Please come. We'll do what we can. I'm sure we'll think of something.'

More hesitation. Then Sylvia nodded decisively. 'Thank you.' She began struggling to her feet.

'I'll carry your bag,' said Anne, reaching forward.

'No.' The abrupt reaction surprised Marnie and Anne. Sylvia grabbed the rucksack and clutched it to her chest. 'It's okay. I can manage.'

Marnie suspected that the bag contained everything that Sylvia possessed in the world. 'Then let's go,' she said.

For the first time Sylvia smiled openly. 'What was that you said about a shower?'

****

Anne opted to stay in the office while Sylvia used the shower room. The phone rang as Anne was booting up the computer. It was George Stubbs.

'Hello, Mr Stubbs. It's Anne here.'

'Hello, sweetie.' Anne mimed vomiting into the receiver. 'And it's George to you.'

52

'What can I do for you, er ... George? I'm afraid Marnie's not in the office at the moment.'

'A message then, please. Would you just tell her that there was definitely no German soldier in the village in the war. I promised to check. No POWs, no volunteer farm workers. The dog-tag must've been a war prize.'

Anne offered to pass on the message and rang off. She wrote a note for Marnie and put it on her desk.

The next fifteen minutes she spent on the computer, checking her 'generic list' of provisions required for a week's journey on the boat. She was so engrossed in ticking off the items from her shopping list against the manifest for *Sally Ann*, that she was unaware of Sylvia standing behind her.

'That looks complicated.' Anne jumped at the sudden sound. 'Oh, Anne, sorry. I didn't mean to startle you.'

'No probs. Did you find everything you needed?' She pressed keys to save her work.

Sylvia let out a long contented sigh. 'I certainly did. It was *wonderful*. I've put the bath towel in the Ali Baba basket you left by the shower.'

'Fine. Er ... Marnie put it there, thinking you, er ... might want us to put your clothes in the washing machine.'

'Nice thought, but maybe not a good idea? It's not really practical to hump damp things around.'

Anne shut down the computer and stood up, amazed. It was as if she was seeing Sylvia for the first time. This was a new woman. Her hair was damp, hanging down to her shoulders, but clean and fragrant. Her skin glowed. Looking wholesome and not unattractive, but more thin than slim, she had changed into a clean pair of jeans and a navy sweatshirt. There was a light in her eyes that had been absent before.

'It's like this, Sylvia. Marnie figured you might like to stay here tonight. We've got to talk about plans. We can do that while we're eating. Anything that gets washed can go in the tumble-dryer overnight and be fresh and dried for tomorrow ... if that's okay by you.'

Sylvia looked stunned. 'You're *serious*?'

Anne feared she'd overstepped the mark. 'We're sort of making it up as we go along, Sylvia, but we wouldn't do anything without your agreement.'

'What happens next?'

'A spot of lunch.'

'Soup and a roll sounds great. You can't imagine.'

'Slight change of plan,' Anne said quietly.

'Oh?' Wary.

'Marnie thought you might like something a bit more substantial.'

'Such as?'

'Let's go and see.'

****

Conversation stopped when Sylvia was ushered into the farmhouse kitchen by Anne. Sylvia guessed that they'd been talking about her, but Marnie's first words dispelled that idea.

'Wow, Sylvia, you look great!'

Sylvia smiled. 'I think you mean I look clean and perhaps tidy.'

'No, I mean it. You're a new woman.'

Sylvia quickly changed the subject. 'Something smells good.' She looked wistfully across at the dark blue Aga cooker with its gleaming heavily-chromed lids. 'We used to have one of those.'

'You did?' said Marnie.

Sylvia nodded. 'It was cream. My grandparents had it installed. That was years ago. I think my dad was just a toddler. It had a little tap on the front. You could get hot water from it any time you wanted.'

'I know the sort,' Marnie said. 'I've seen them in magazines.' It occurred to her that this was probably a painful memory. 'Come and have some lunch.'

The refectory table had been laid with blue and white gingham napkins, two chunky white candles and wine glasses. As Sylvia took her seat, Donovan lit the candles while Ralph rummaged in the fridge and extracted a bottle of rosé wine.

'Soup and a roll, you said,' Sylvia observed. 'This looks like you're ready for a dinner party.'

'It's only simple fare,' Marnie said. 'We had a quiche in the freezer – salmon and asparagus – and some frozen peas. I simmered them with a sprig or two of mint while the new potatoes were cooking. Nothing elaborate.'

'And we had some wine in the fridge,' said Ralph. 'I think it should be nicely chilled.'

'Is any of this not to your liking, Sylvia?' Marnie asked. 'It's all a bit last minute and off the cuff.'

'And totally wonderful,' Sylvia said. 'You're too kind.'

'Nonsense.' Marnie turned to the Aga and opened the door to the bottom oven. Wearing oven gloves, she placed two serving bowls on cork mats in the middle of the table. Anne removed the lids while Marnie retrieved the quiche from the top oven.

Anne was picking up two serving spoons when Sylvia suddenly gasped, put her head in her hands and began to sob. Marnie set the quiche down and was round the table in a flash. She knelt beside Sylvia and put an arm round her shoulders.

'Sylvia, please don't upset yourself. I promise you we'll do all we can to help.'

Marnie felt Sylvia's thin shoulders tremble and heard her laboured breathing. Her words came out as a series of breathy, half-swallowed utterances.

'I'm sorry, Marnie. It's all just ...'

'I know. Listen ... we'd like you to stay here tonight, and for tomorrow we have a suggestion. It may not be perfect but it could be a start. We can talk about it while we eat if you like.'

Sylvia nodded. 'I don't want your lovely food to be spoilt. I'm afraid I'm rather overcome by all this. I know I'll never be able to repay you for your –'

'No need.' Marnie gave her shoulder one last squeeze. She stood up. 'Here. Let me give you a slice of quiche. Ralph thought a rosé would hit the spot. What do you think?'

Sylvia smiled through her tears. ' Perfect. It's all just perfect.'

****

Over lunch Marnie outlined a tentative plan: Sylvia would spend one night at Glebe Farm then go to Brackley while they worked out the next step. She suggested that Sylvia should sleep on it and come to a conclusion in the morning.

That afternoon Marnie and Ralph packed their bags for the return trip to London. Anne put Sylvia's clothes in the washing machine and suggested a walk by the canal. The plan was agreed and, while the clothes swished around in the drum of the machine, Anne and Donovan gave Sylvia a tour of the Glebe Farm complex.

'This place is amazing,' said Sylvia. They were walking through the spinney towards the canal. 'And it all belongs to Marnie?'

'It didn't look like this when she bought it a few years ago,' Anne said. 'In fact for the first two and a half years we were sleeping on *Sally Ann* while the builders did up the cottages.'

'Not the main house?'

'No. Marnie needed the income from letting, so the cottages got priority.'

'I can imagine she was really stretched for a while, with all that going on, plus having to set up her own business in a new place.'

'Oh yes,' said Anne. 'Her friends in London said she was taking a very *courageous* decision.'

Sylvia nodded. 'And we all know what that means.'

'Yes,' Donovan chipped in. 'They all thought she was completely mad.'

Sylvia laughed. 'It was a great help that you were involved from the beginning, Anne.'

'You're right there,' Donovan said. 'Anne keeps the firm running smoothly.'

As they left the spinney Sylvia stopped in her tracks.

'This place is full of surprises. It's all so lovely ... a real secret hideaway. So whose boat is that?'

'*Thyrsis* belongs to Ralph,' Anne explained. 'He uses it mainly as a study now. He and Marnie used to sleep on it for a while.'

'A floating study ... That's original.'

'He calls it his floating Oxford college.'

Sylvia turned to Anne. 'So you have your attic room in the ... what d'you call it? ... the office barn?'

'That's right.'

'And Marnie and Ralph are in the farmhouse.'

'Yes.'

Sylvia looked thoughtful. 'They have a guest room in the farmhouse?'

'They haven't got round to sorting one out just yet.'

'And the cottages are all occupied?'

Anne said, 'You're wondering where you'll be sleeping tonight.'

'Well, I was thinking ...'

'About Donovan,' Anne completed the sentence.

'Sort of ...'

Anne pointed towards the opposite bank of the canal. 'You see that boat over there?'

'The sinister-looking one with the strange name?'

'That's my boat,' said Donovan.

'Oh, sorry.' Sylvia looked embarrassed. 'I didn't mean –'

'That's okay. I'm not offended, Sylvia. It does look rather unusual compared with most other boats. In fact, Anne calls it a U-boat or even a stealth narrowboat.'

Donovan's boat was painted matte dark grey all over, with a black hull. Its interior was similarly monochrome. *Sinister* was a good description, but Donovan had developed it into a comfortable. functioning travelling machine, and he kept it in tip-top condition.

'So how do you say its name?' Sylvia asked.

'It's pronounced *Exodos*. I'll tell you the story some time, but basically it means *way out* in Greek. Donovan chose it when he dropped out of a university course.'

'I think I get it.'

'Coming back to your question,' Anne said. 'If you'd like to sleep in my attic room, that's fine by us. We have a camp bed. It's quite comfortable, and I can let you have some pyjamas.'

'But what about Donovan?'

'*Exodos*,' he said, gesturing across the canal. 'As Anne would say ... no probs.'

****

And so that night's sleeping arrangements were sorted: Marnie and Ralph in the farmhouse; Donovan on *X O 2*; Anne in her attic room, plus Sylvia on the camp bed.

Anne and Sylvia installed themselves comfortably in the attic room. It was lit by three table lamps over each of which Anne had draped a coloured chiffon scarf. The light had a jewel-like quality: gold and emerald and ruby. Sylvia was happy enough on the camp bed. Beside her stood the rucksack, now almost emptied.

'Are you okay over there?' Anne asked.

'Are you kidding? I've been sleeping under a hedge. Well, I say sleeping. It was really dozing between waking up wondering if that strange sound was some sort of animal prowling around or some loony pervert coming to rape me ... or worse.'

'Blimey!'

'This camp bed is like the Ritz, believe me. And fresh, clean pyjamas ... *bliss*.'

'You can keep them if you like, Sylvia. They're new. I've never worn them, and they're about your size.'

'Oh, Anne, I couldn't, I really –'

'I mean it. There's a limit to how many pairs of pyjamas anyone needs. I've got plenty. And when Donovan's here I ... well, never mind. Okay if I turn out the lights?'

'Sure.'

Sylvia yawned. 'You and Marnie have made a wonderful home for yourselves here,' she said in the darkness.

'I know I'm very lucky,' Anne said. 'It must have been horrible, sleeping rough like that for all those weeks. I hope Marnie's plan works out, if it suits you.'

'I've got a few questions to talk about tomorrow, Anne. I don't really know Brackley.'

'Have you always lived around here?' Anne said. 'Oh sorry. You probably won't want to talk about it.'

'We lived on the other side of Stony Stratford. My grandparents had the house built between the wars. The place was surrounded by fields back then. They wanted somewhere semi-rural to bring up a family. Now I'm the only one left and, of course, the house is gone.'

'What ... you mean actually demolished ... like built over by a housing estate?'

'No. It's still there. It's just not ours any more.'

Anne had no desire to rake over unhappy memories for Sylvia. She was on the brink of drifting off to sleep when Sylvia spoke again, her voice firm and wide awake.

'After my dad died, there was just mum and me. I had no brothers or sisters and I was unmarried, living at home. I worked in the library in Milton Keynes; it was a good job and I enjoyed it ... pretty good salary, too. Then mum gradually became crippled with arthritis and found it hard to get about. In the end she was bed-ridden. There was nothing for it; I had to give up my job to look after her.'

'Awful for you both,' Anne said quietly.

'Dad had left us with some money ... his life savings ... and we got half his pension from work. That kept us going for a few years. Then mum got dementia and started to go really downhill. After a couple of years the money ran out. I tried to get support from the council. By then the spending cuts were hitting the social services budget. I tried to go back to work ... just part-time to make ends meet, you know. But it was the same old problem ... the cuts again ... no chance of a job at the library.'

'What did you do?' Anne asked.

'We ended up on benefits. Things were really tight. What made it worse was newspaper articles talking about 'benefits scroungers', 'the work-shy'. You know the sort of thing. In the end I tried for jobs stacking shelves in supermarkets, anything. But it was no good. They kept saying I was 'over-qualified for the job'. Mum got worse and had to go into a care home. It cost a fortune.'

'What did you do?'

'Borrowed, of course, against the house. What else?'

'So you ran up debts so she'd be looked after?'

'Yeah. That's when it happened, and I went to pieces.'

'What happened?'

'I was out trying to get a job one day. I came home – no job – and got a message to phone the care home. Mum had died suddenly while I was out. I never even got to say goodbye.'

'Oh, Sylvia ...'

'Everything went wrong after that. I'd lost my mum, I was in debt ... couldn't cope with anything. It was a nightmare. I don't like to think about it.'

'I'm really sorry, Sylvia.'

'That's how I was when you found me.'

Anne was lost for words. Now wide awake, her eyes open, she lay staring up into the dark void of the attic roof, fearful that anything she said might only make Sylvia's painful memories worse. After a long interval Sylvia spoke quietly.

She sighed. 'I think I'm dropping off. It's so comfortable here.'

'Good night, Sylvia. We'll do our best for you.'

'Night, Anne. Sweet dreams.'

Chapter 8

On Saturday morning Anne left Sylvia folding her newly-cleaned and dried clothes into the rucksack and hurried over to the farmhouse. In the kitchen she found Marnie, Ralph and Donovan laying the table for breakfast. She outlined Sylvia's story, and reactions were predictable; all three were horrified.

Marnie said, 'What a life she's had. No wonder she went to pieces, losing her mother, her home ... everything.'

'Sylvia's had a horrible life since her mum died,' Anne said. 'It must've been terrifying sleeping out in the park like that, listening to every sound.' With an intake of breath she covered her mouth with one hand. 'I've just thought. She said she was worried that someone might rape her ... or worse. Oh my God ... There was that poor man murdered in that very park.'

The conversation was interrupted by the ringing of the doorbell.

'I'll go,' said Marnie. 'It'll be Sylvia.'

****

They sat round the refectory table after breakfast. Marnie outlined the plan again, this time in more detail. At the end of the exposition, Sylvia sat quietly looking down at her hands.

'This place is in Brackley, you said?'

'It's a converted Georgian townhouse – quite grand – close to the centre in a quiet side street.'

'And it's run by a vicar, right?'

'Yes,' said Marnie. 'Randall's actually a former vicar of this village, Knightly St John. His full title is Dr Randall Hughes and he's about your age, I'd guess. He's now the rural dean for the Brackley area.'

'But basically it's a hostel for homeless people.'

'A well-appointed one, yes. I thought you'd find it comfortable. You'd be safe there and you'd have breathing space, an opportunity to work out what comes next.'

Sylvia mulled things over. 'Brackley's a small town, isn't it?'

'Quite a bit larger than Stony Stratford,' Ralph said.

'I was wondering about job prospects down there. Stony's not far from MK, which is really big.'

Marnie found this an encouraging sign. Sylvia was not dismissing the idea out of hand; she was thinking it through.

Ralph again. 'It's within striking distance of Oxford and Banbury, and Bicester's not far away.'

'What about costs?' Sylvia asked. 'That hostel sounds like a smart place. It can't come cheap.'

'There are no charges,' said Marnie. 'They accept donations, but it's not a requirement. The house is supported by a fairly well-endowed trust set up by Randall. I think there are two members of staff in the office. They could deal with benefits if that would be helpful.'

'Sounds almost too good to be true,' said Sylvia. 'Is there a catch? I mean, do I have to go to church twice on Sundays, or anything like that?'

Marnie shook her head. 'Not at all.'

'So what's the next step?'

'Well, if you're up for it, I'll give Randall a call and see if he has a room.'

'You mean it's not definite, Marnie? You haven't got it arranged already?'

'Not without your say-so. You might want to think it over, or you might have a better plan.'

Sylvia smiled. 'What do you think?'

****

The distance from Knightly St John to Brackley was about twenty miles, an easy cross-country run of about half an hour. Marnie offered Sylvia the front passenger seat in the Freelander, but she preferred sitting in the back with the rucksack beside her on the seat. Anne was keen to go with them, so she rode shotgun up front.

For the first ten minutes there was no conversation in the car, and Sylvia was content to watch the countryside roll by.

Feelings of excitement and apprehension washed over her as they headed south and west. The excitement arose from the realisation that people were doing their best to help her at a time of desperate need. The apprehension came from the prospect of a step into the unknown, one more uncertainty in her life. What next? Eventually a number of questions took shape in her mind.

'Marnie? This Randall Hughes, the vicar ... rural dean. He's basically a priest ... Church of England?'

'Yes,' Marnie said over her shoulder. 'He's rather a forthright character, a bit of a traditionalist in some things ... quite good-looking too.'

'Will he ask me about religion?'

'No.'

'Only I've never been a church-goer, not even Sunday school.'

'Sylvia, the house isn't that kind of place. Don't worry about it. Randall makes no bones about his own faith, but he really doesn't shove it down your throat. None of us is a church-goer, but we're friends with Randall and with Angela Hemingway. She's the current vicar in our village, and I should tell you that she and Randall are an item.'

Sylvia fell silent while she pondered the idea of vicars having boyfriends and girlfriends. In the rear-view mirror Marnie noticed that Sylvia was smiling.

'Marnie? Can I ask you something else?'

'Sure. Go ahead.'

'The sleeping arrangements in the hostel ... I was wondering if it has dormitories or what?'

'Sorry, Sylvia. I meant to tell you. When I spoke to Randall on the phone he said he was going to reserve a single room for you. I think it's on the first floor. They also have some double rooms, but they're mainly just for men. If you're worried about privacy, don't be.'

'Marnie, believe me, anything is better than sleeping rough. A hedge gives no privacy at all.'

Anne turned in her seat. 'I know the room Randall has in mind. I'm pretty sure it's just opposite a bathroom. You'll be almost self-contained at one end of the building.'

Sylvia relaxed for the rest of the journey. As Marnie drove into the town Sylvia became more alert, taking notice of the surroundings that would become her new home, at least for a while. The main street widened nearer to the centre and, ahead of them, Sylvia was pleased at the sight of the town hall, a fine building some three hundred years old, that dominated the view. They turned into a street of eighteenth century houses and pulled up outside an impressive double-fronted building made of stone. Beside the door was a sign with a name carved in slate in elegant lettering:

Magdalene House

The front door opened as Sylvia got out of the car. Randall Hughes stood smiling on the doorstep. He was tall and willowy with curly dark hair, a long intelligent face and piercing brown eyes. For a moment Sylvia had the impression that she'd travelled back in time to another age; Randall was wearing a full-length black cassock with buttons down the front from top to bottom. His shoes were shiny black wingtip brogues. He cut an imposing figure.

Marnie walked round the pavement and received a kiss on the cheek and a hug from Randall. She turned to Sylvia.

'Randall, I'd like you to meet Sylvia, Sylvia Harris, your new guest.'

Randall thrust out a hand. His long fingers enveloped Sylvia's smaller hand in a grip that was firm but not overpowering.

'Sylvia, welcome. It's a pleasure to have you join us.'

'I'm glad to be here. Thank you.'

Anne pointed. 'Is that a new sign, Randall?'

'It is ... a new sign and a new name. Lovely to see you, darling.'

Anne stepped forward; another kiss, another hug. Sylvia looked on, surprised at this show of affection. Her impressions of how vicars behaved were dissolving rapidly. Randall released Anne and turned towards the sign.

'I had it carved by a woman in Burford. She's first class, don't you think?'

'Why that name, Randall?' Marnie asked.

'I did wonder about using 'Brackley House', but then I thought of Mary Magdalene. She was a generous person who gave freely of herself. I can think of no better name. I used the biblical spelling so as to avoid any confusion with Magdalen College School here in town.'

'So Magdalene with an 'e',' said Anne with an 'e'. 'I approve.'

'Good. Let's go inside. Is that your rucksack, Sylvia? Allow me.'

'No, it's fine, thanks. I can manage.'

Sylvia braced herself when she crossed the threshold, expecting the interior to feel like an institution, with the faded smell of stewed cabbage hovering in the air. But she had a pleasant surprise. The hall was bright and spacious with a winding staircase at one side, its mahogany handrail shining. Ahead of her stood the reception desk, an actual Victorian desk of polished oak. On the wall above it was a large sign:

WELCOME

Behind the desk sat a young woman. She stood as they crossed the hall and smiled.

'Hi, I'm Jo. You must be Sylvia.'

Another hand-shake.

'I expect there's some paperwork that needs doing,' Sylvia said.

'Oh, there's always paperwork,' Jo said cheerfully, 'but no need to bother just now. It'll keep for later. You can settle in first. Here's the key: room eight on the first floor. It looks out over the garden. Hope you like it.'

Randall stepped forward. 'Let me show you the way, Sylvia. Are you sure I can't carry that bag for you?'

'It's fine.'

'We'll wait for you here,' said Marnie. 'Randall will want to show you round once you've dumped your things.'

Randall and Sylvia climbed the stairs together. As they disappeared from view, Marnie heard Randall asking about food allergies and dislikes.

****

'I think she'll be happy there,' Marnie said. They were driving home after leaving Sylvia to settle in. 'At least it'll give her somewhere pleasant to stay while she sorts out the rest of her life. And Randall made a good impression. I thought she rather took to him, and he seemed to like her.'

'She certainly scrubs up well,' Anne said. 'And you're right; she brightened up as soon as she met Randall.'

'And saw Magdalene House,' Marnie added.

Anne said, 'Have you thought about what comes next?'

'I'm too preoccupied with this legal business down in London, not to mention the wedding-honeymoon malarkey.' Marnie sighed. 'And to think, I moved to Northamptonshire with the misguided notion that life would be simpler. Huh!'

Anne laughed. 'So it's back to London tomorrow?'

'Yeah, in time for the meeting on Monday.'

'Are you staying on *Sally Ann* or in the flat?'

'Might be a good idea to give the flat an airing. We can drop your extra provisions off on the boat. They'll come in handy for the journey home.'

'I'll order you a yak to carry them,' said Anne. 'You'll need it.'

'Not a bad idea,' Marnie reached over and hit the radio button. 'Can you find the local channel, Anne? Be good to catch up on what's going on.'

Anne deftly located a local radio station just in time to catch the noonday news summary. It was the usual heady mixture: a lane closure on the M1 following a tyre blow-out on a lorry, staff shortages in the county ambulance service and a drugs bust in Corby. The presenter was on the point of announcing the end of the bulletin when a news flash came in:

One last-minute item to report. Thames Valley Police are widening their hunt for the murder of charity worker, Phil Braywell. Mr Braywell died as a result of injuries sustained while walking home from his local pub in Stony Stratford three days ago. They are asking anyone with any information to contact them or the Northamptonshire Constabulary. All calls will be strictly confidential. And now it's over to the weather centre for –

At a signal from Marnie, Anne switched off.

'Phew!' she said. 'I'm really glad we got her away from that place.'

'Mm ...' Marnie sounded unconvinced.

'You don't think so, Marnie?'

Marnie glanced at her friend. 'Can you really imagine someone lurking at night in Stony Stratford in the hope of waylaying some passer-by?'

'Well, somebody did,' Anne said.

'I suppose so. It's a good job we got Sylvia to safety. But where we go from here ... who knows?'

Anne was racking her brains for a solution as she watched the countryside speeding by, but inspiration failed her.

Chapter 9

Marnie and Ralph drove down to London early on Sunday morning leaving Anne in charge of Glebe Farm with Donovan keeping her company.

Traffic was light all the way to London and through to Little Venice. The weather was mild though overcast; good conditions for travelling. They parked illegally on yellow lines long enough to transfer provisions to *Sally Ann*, then continued on their way to Docklands.

Marnie had misgivings whenever she used the flat. It was located in the Butlers Wharf complex, one of the most desirable upmarket residential developments in Docklands. The flat was on the fifth floor of the riverfront side of the building, directly opposite Saint Katherine Docks, with views down the Thames towards the skyscrapers of Canary Wharf. It was spacious, well-appointed, quiet and exclusive. Marnie's misgivings derived from the fact that it had been bequeathed to her by Simon, her late husband, or rather ex-husband. It was worth a considerable sum.

Marnie parked the Freelander in her reserved space in the underground car park. They made their way to the lobby on the ground floor and used the entry card and keypad to summon the lift.

Once inside the flat, Ralph walked across the open-plan living area and gazed down at the river.

'That is a *wonderful* view,' he said with feeling.

Marnie joined him at the window and slipped her arm around his waist.

'You say that every time we come here, Ralph.'

'And I mean it every time. It never ceases to please me.'

Marnie thought how sad it was that Simon hadn't lived to enjoy it more. She kept the thought to herself.

****

The phone rang just before ten o'clock that evening. Anne apologised for ringing at that hour, but she had just finished a call from Randall Hughes and wanted to bring Marnie and Ralph up to date.

'Is Sylvia finding it difficult to settle in?' Marnie asked.

'Quite the opposite, in fact. Randall said he'd arranged to have a chat with her after lunch yesterday. He was impressed with how positive she was about being there.'

'Quite a change from rough sleeping,' Marnie said.

'Exactly, but there was more to it. It seems she asked if they could have another talk when she'd dealt with the paperwork for her stay. She'd seen an announcement on the notice board: nominations were invited for a 'guest delegate' to join the management committee.'

'I didn't know there was such a thing,' said Marnie.

'Well, Sylvia remarked on it casually to the woman in the office, the one we met in reception. She told Sylvia none of the *guests* ever applied. That's what Sylvia wanted to talk to Randall about. Anyway, long story short, he persuaded her to join, and she said she would. He rang to ask if I knew how long Sylvia might be staying there.'

'Good question, Anne, and interesting that Sylvia obviously didn't come up with an answer.'

'I'd imagine she's waiting to find out what you have in mind for her.'

Marnie sighed. 'I haven't thought that far ahead. We haven't discussed it with Sylvia because we didn't know how it would work. We seem to be going round in circles.'

'Okay, so Randall said would you give him a call when you can.'

'It's up to Sylvia to decide what she wants to do.'

'I think maybe Randall has the idea that you've sort of parked her there as part of some master plan.'

'Then he has more faith in me than I deserve. I'll phone him tomorrow, once we've seen the solicitor about the will. I can't get my head around anything else till I know where that's going.'

'Oh, there was something else, Marnie. I had to pop into Stony Stratford this morning. I needed whipping cream, and the village shop didn't have any.'

'Would this possibly have anything to do with Donovan?'

'You guessed. Donovan says Sunday isn't right without coffee and cake. He says *Kaffee und Kuchen* is a ritual with his German family. Anyway, we went to the supermarket in Stony and found three police cars in the high street. The cops were doing house-to-house inquiries about the murder.'

'On a Sunday?'

'Probably thought they'd find more people at home. There were lots of uniforms about.'

'They must think there's still danger from the killer. I'm so glad we've got Sylvia away. She'll be safe at Randall's place.'

Chapter 10

Monday morning, ten o'clock sharp. Marnie and Ralph mounted the stairs to the first floor offices of Burnett Haydock and Lang. Suddenly to Marnie nothing felt right. She didn't want to be there, didn't want Iris Winterburn to be dead, and certainly didn't want to be attending the reading of her will. Marnie had a weight in the pit of her stomach and was overcome with misgivings. Everything felt wrong. She stopped and steadied herself on the banister.

From behind her on the stairs Ralph said, 'Are you all right, Marnie?'

'I'm not sure.'

'What is it? Are you in pain?'

Ralph stepped up and took hold of her arms.

'It's silly,' she said. 'Embarrassing.'

'Tell me. But first let's get up to the landing. I don't want you to fall.'

They climbed the last few steps and halted outside the door to the solicitors' offices. Ralph hugged Marnie and held her close. She eased herself gently away.

'I'm not feeling ill. It's just ... this whole situation ... I've got a bad feeling about it.'

'In what way?'

'That's just it; it's crazy.'

'Try me.'

'It was like a premonition that things are going to turn out badly.'

'A premonition?'

'I told you it was embarrassing, but it just came over me.'

'You can tell Lang you've changed your mind. You don't have to go ahead if you don't want to.'

Marnie took a deep breath. 'I don't run away from things, Ralph. It's not what I do. Even so, I'm wondering what I might've let myself in for.'

'D'you think you're upset because Iris died ... perhaps that you never had the chance to say goodbye?'

'I don't know what it is. Maybe it's a combination of all the things happening to us just now ... postponing the wedding ... the Orient-Express ... this horrible murder back home ... trying to sort out Sylvia. It's all so unsettling. And on top of all that we've got this business with Iris, her will and whatever else has to be done, this mysterious *obligation*.'

'One thing's for sure,' Ralph said. 'You can opt out of being executrix, and you can do that right now. One less thing to worry about.'

From below they heard the door onto the street open and close, footsteps on the staircase. Marnie breathed out audibly and shook her head.

'Oh, come on. Let's just do it,' she said. 'It's time.'

****

When they were seated in the office, each with a cup of tea served in bone china, and a plate of digestive biscuits before them, Seymour Lang opened the envelope. He took out the last will and testament of Iris Winterburn, late of April Cottage, Little Haddon in the county of Hertfordshire. Lang adjusted his glasses, moving them up to the bridge of his nose, and cleared his throat as he unfolded the document.

'It's the custom that where possible the solicitor reads the will in the presence of the beneficiaries,' he explained.

Marnie and Ralph were the only other people in the office.

'Isn't anyone else coming?' Marnie asked.

'No,' Lang said. 'The will is quite brief. Would you like me to read it out?'

Marnie and Ralph had both attended will readings before and knew there would be a degree of verbiage in the form of preambles before arriving at the main terms. Marnie had no wish to plough through the 'hereinafters' and 'afore-mentioneds'.

She said, 'Could you perhaps just give us the main points, Mr Lang?'

'Of course.' He quickly skimmed through the paragraphs, then looked up. 'Mrs Walker, there is just one beneficiary, namely yourself. Miss Winterburn has left you her house – the cottage in Hertfordshire – and its entire contents. In addition she has bequeathed you some shares and savings. The share certificates are kept in a box in her bureau; the bank account and building society statements may be found in a drawer in the same bureau. I think you will find your role as executrix quite straightforward.' He handed Marnie another envelope. 'This letter is from me. It authorises you to act as executrix for Miss Winterburn and gives you the right of access to all her documents, accounts and so on. You'll need it when you go to the bank.'

Marnie looked blank. 'Is that it?'

'As far as the will is concerned, yes it is.'

'There are no other beneficiaries?'

'None.'

'Is it possible the will might be contested?' Marnie asked.

Lang shook his head. 'To the best of my knowledge, there's no one who could contest it.'

'I thought there was some sort of extra obligation that I had to fulfil.'

Lang sat back in his chair and steepled his fingers. 'Ah, yes ... that.'

'Is that not mentioned?'

'Not in the will as such, no. That is an altogether separate matter.'

'Can you tell me what it involves now?'

'I'm afraid I can't. I thought I'd made it clear at our first meeting that the additional matter had not been revealed to me or my predecessors.' He picked up a single sheet of paper and passed it across the desk to Marnie. 'You'll remember, though, there was the question of a confidentiality agreement. I've drawn up a very brief document. If you're happy to go ahead, I'll need your signature on this paper. Professor Lombard, perhaps you'd be good enough to witness Mrs Walker's signature?'

'Is that in order?'

'As you're not at present in any way related, yes.'

'One thing first,' said Ralph. 'The contents of the will aren't dependent on Marnie signing that agreement and going ahead with the extra task?'

Lang shook his head. 'Not at all. There's no obligation undertaken up to this point, other than acceptance of the role of executrix. However, by signing that agreement, Mrs Walker is accepting what you call the extra task.'

'And how does she find out what that involves?' Ralph asked.

'It's yet another envelope, I'm afraid.' Lang smiled as he picked up another document from the desk. 'Its contents are not to be revealed to any third party.'

'Even to you?' Marnie said, taking the envelope.

Lang nodded. 'Even to me.'

'Or me?' Ralph said.

'Being realistic, professor, I think it would be difficult, if not impossible, to impose that condition, given the closeness of your relationship.'

Marnie had now read the short confidentiality agreement three times. She looked up.

'So this is the moment of truth,' she said. 'This is where I get to find out what Iris had in store for me. If I sign this I'm committed. Is that right?'

'Yes, and when you learn what the specific task is, I must remind you that you cannot ask my legal advice on any aspect of it. Our only other contact will take place when you receive my invoice for professional services which it will fall to you as executrix to settle from Miss Winterburn's assets.'

'This agreement seems very simply worded, Mr Lang. Do you think I should discuss it with my own solicitor?'

'It can't do any harm.' Another smile. 'But then I would say that, wouldn't I? We solicitors stick together.'

'When do you want the document back?' Marnie asked.

'At your convenience, Mrs Walker. No pressure.'

****

Out on the street, Marnie checked her watch and dug out her mobile.

'I'm going to ring Roger straight away. I want to get this thing sorted once and for all.'

She was in luck. Roger was between meetings with clients.

'So you now know what you have to do for Miss Winterburn?' he said.

'No, there's one more hurdle. I have to sign the confidentiality agreement I told you about. I'd be glad if you could run your eye over it, please Roger.'

'Is it just asking you to accept the confidentiality terms?'

'Yes. It's quite short and to the point, but once I've signed it I'm under an obligation to pursue the matter that Iris wants me to resolve. Mr Lang has made that clear.'

'Then that's the main thing, Marnie. Does it give any details of this task?'

'None, not a word.'

'Can you read me the relevant sentences?'

'There's one that requires me to maintain confidentiality.' Marnie read it out. 'There's not much more than that.'

'This is all very mysterious, Marnie. I've never come across anything like it. You've told Lang that you'll do it ... whatever *it* turns out to be?'

'Yes.'

'Then it sounds as if your Mr Lang is involving you in a kind of verbal contract at this stage.'

'Is that legal? Didn't someone once say a verbal contract isn't worth the paper it's written on?'

Roger chuckled. 'That was attributed to Sam Goldwyn, the film producer. In fact, it's not strictly speaking true. Verbal contracts date back to the time when your word was your bond.'

'And they're still acceptable?' Marnie said.

'In some cases, yes, quite acceptable, especially when the word was given in the presence of a witness.'

'Such as now?'

'I would say so. Mr Lang would say you've entered into a verbal contract dependent on your accepting the requirement for confidentiality.'

'I don't get it,' said Marnie. 'I can't see why he didn't just draw up an agreement for Iris setting out what I have to do.'

'Oh, I think that's quite clear, Marnie. Iris Winterburn had something in her past that she wanted kept secret.'

'Even from her own solicitor?'

'Precisely. That task is so secret it's for you alone to know.'

'And Ralph?'

'That's you're decision, Marnie.'

****

For the second time that morning Marnie and Ralph climbed the stairs to the first floor. Seymour Lang's secretary didn't seem surprised to see them again. She buzzed through to his office and announced their return. Before entering, Marnie asked the secretary if she could produce a photocopy of the confidentiality agreement. The secretary smiled up at her.

'No need. Mr Lang already has one on his desk.'

Marnie signed both copies there and then in the office of the solicitor. He handed her a final envelope, asking her not to open it in his presence. They shook hands, and he wished Marnie well.

'I don't suppose we'll meet again, Mrs Walker. There is just one thing I'd like to add to what has been said so far. My former partner, Toby Haydock, left me a note concerning Miss Winterburn. It's always struck me as rather curious.'

'In what way?'

'He stressed the wish of our client that you should – and I quote – clean the house carefully.'

'*Clean* the house?' Marnie looked incredulous, then bewildered. 'That can't be the special task.'

'I would have thought not,' Lang agreed.

'Carefully?' Marnie repeated. 'Odd choice of wording.'

'Those were apparently her exact words,' said Lang.

Marnie glanced at Ralph who looked equally blank.

'What does that mean?' Marnie asked.

'That, Mrs Walker, is for you to find out, and only you.' He held out his hand. 'Goodbye and good luck.'

****

Outside on the pavement, Marnie and Ralph stared at each other. Marnie looked at her watch. Ralph looked at his watch. It was past coffee time, but still too early for lunch. Marnie gazed down at the envelope in her hand.

'Well, Marnie,' Ralph said. 'Are you bursting with impatience to know what the letter involves or shall we just stand here for a while and breathe in particulates?'

'I'm wondering if I've done the right thing, Ralph. Too late now to change my mind. I suppose we could go back to that pub and see if they do brunch, or we can go back to the flat.'

'Shall we toss a coin?'

'What *is* the matter with me? I've been feeling strange all morning.'

'Then, let me decide,' said Ralph. 'Brunch at the pub. Are you on?'

'Let's go for it.'

Good news: the pub offered an all-day breakfast. They ordered scrambled eggs and coffee and settled at the table they had occupied on their previous visit. As soon as they had placed their orders, Marnie slid open the envelope and unfolded the single sheet. Marnie felt a twinge of sadness at seeing the now familiar handwriting. It made Iris Winterburn seem immediate and close. And although Marnie knew she would never see her again, she suspected that Iris would be playing a part in her life for some time to come. She read the letter in silence while the waitress poured coffee.

> April Cottage
> Little Haddon
> Herts

My dear Marnie,

You are reading this letter because you have not only agreed to be my executrix but you have also undertaken to carry out a special task for me. I will come straight to the point.

I have bequeathed you my house – in fact it is a quite modest cottage in a small village – not only because I would like you to have it but because it is the keeper of a secret that I have carried for almost all my adult life. I'm not going to explain here what the secret involves. I am instead going to invite you to discover it for yourself once you have made acquaintance with the cottage. Essentially, I would like you to clean everything very carefully. Then, if fate plays its part, you may come to resolve the conundrum. If not, then perhaps it was never meant to be resolved and it will simply pass into history, like me.

I apologise for being so mysterious, but even after all these years I find it difficult – even impossible – to put into words what has been an emotional burden on me. I can think of no one better able to resolve this problem than you. I know I leave it in safe hands and that you will do the right thing.

Bless you, Marnie.

Iris

Marnie read the letter a second time and looked across at Ralph.

'Mystery revealed?' Ralph asked. 'Or, judging by your expression, perhaps not.'

Marnie's brow furrowed and without speaking she re-read the letter one more time.

'Unclear?' said Ralph.

'No. It's quite clear and explicit.'

'Then why are you frowning?'

Marnie passed the letter to Ralph. 'Because it doesn't give me a single clue about what she actually wants me to do. See what you make of it.'

Ralph turned his attention to the letter as the scrambled eggs arrived. Marnie thanked the waitress but Ralph appeared not even to have noticed her or the plate set down before him. He concentrated intensely. Marnie could almost feel an energy field between his brain and the page.

'Ralph? Your eggs will get cold.' Marnie began eating hers. 'Ralph?'

'Mm ...'

'Earth to Ralph, Earth to Ralph, do you read me? Come in, please. Over.'

'Mm?'

Marnie reached over and laid a hand on his sleeve. 'Your food has arrived.'

'Oh.' He gazed at the plate as if he had never seen one before. 'Yes, good. Thanks.' He took a fork-full.

'What d'you think?'

'Quite tasty.'

Marnie chuckled. 'The letter!'

'Well ...'

Marnie said, 'Clear and explicit and doesn't give a clue about what Iris wants.'

After a second fork-full of scrambled eggs Ralph said, 'The clue's there, all right. It's just rather obscure. *Clean the house very carefully*, she says. That wording again.'

'Not very helpful, Ralph. I mean the letter, not you.'

'Not sure I'm very helpful either.'

'Any idea where this village is ... Little Haddon?'

'Up near St Albans, I think. We could look in on the way home. Wouldn't be a major diversion.'

****

Ralph was proved right. They collected the car from Docklands, crossed London and took the M1 motorway for a short distance before turning off in the direction of the cathedral city of St Albans. Little Haddon was located in gently rolling, partly wooded countryside between St Albans and Wheathampstead. An elderly lady walking a Labrador in the high street was able to give directions to April Cottage. Marnie was putting the car into gear when the lady leaned forward and spoke softly.

'I'm afraid you won't find anyone at home.' She glanced up the empty street as if anxious not to be overheard and added, 'The person who lived there has unfortunately passed away.'

'Yes,' Marnie said. 'We did know that. Thank you.'

'Are you from the coroner's office?'

'No,' said Marnie. 'Can I ask why you thought we might be?'

Another glance up the street. 'It's just that it wouldn't surprise me. Miss Winterburn has always been a person who kept to herself and seemed rather ... how can I put it? ... rather *mysterious.*'

'In what way?'

'Oh dear, I've probably spoken out of turn. I've just realised you're probably relatives. I do hope I haven't caused offence.'

'Not at all,' said Ralph.

The lady stepped back and pointed straight ahead. 'As I said, take the first turning on the left. You'll find April Cottage a little way up the hill. You can't miss it. There's a large cedar tree at the side of the house. Goodbye.'

With that, she patted the head of her dog and set off down the street.

Marnie drove away from the kerb. '*Coroner?*' she said. 'What was that about?'

'Didn't Lang say she died peacefully in her sleep?' Ralph said. He pointed. 'Here's our turning.'

The road climbed steadily past rows of thatched cottages. April Cottage came into view on the right, with a magnificent cedar dwarfing the house and dominating the skyline. The cottage itself was of brick under a steep-pitched roof of dark red tiles. It was double-fronted with a small covered porch. Marnie parked on the gravel drive at the side of the cottage beneath the boughs of the cedar and switched off the engine. She turned to Ralph.

'Yes. It was heart failure, Lang said, and she'd been suffering from angina for some time. Not much call for a coroner, surely.'

'Marnie, have you noticed that Lang didn't mention her funeral? I suppose she has had one.'

'Good point. I've no idea. I'll check with him. But first, I'm curious to see the house.'

Marnie unlocked the front door and pushed it open. There was a faint musty, unoccupied smell in the house. She was surprised not to find a scattering of letters, leaflets and junk mail littering the doormat. Instead she saw a neat pile of correspondence on the hall table.

'Someone's been keeping the place tidy,' Marnie said.

The layout of April Cottage was simple and conventional. On the ground floor was a sitting room on the left of the entrance hall and a dining room on the right. The furniture looked comfortable and traditional. It reminded Marnie of her grandmother's house, remembered from childhood. A passage led through to a kitchen that occupied most of the rear of the building, adjacent to a utility room and pantry. A staircase led up to a landing from which radiated three bedrooms and a bathroom. The bedroom looking out over the garden appeared to be used as a study and sewing room. Opposite the door stood a bureau. Marnie thought it might have been Victorian or possibly a 1930s reproduction.

A slightly larger bedroom was fitted out with two single beds, and probably served as a guest room. On the opposite side of the landing, next to the bathroom, was the largest bedroom. It contained a medium-size bed with a quilt in gold-coloured satin.

'This must have been Iris's room ...' Marnie said quietly. '... the room where she died.'

'Someone's made the bed,' Ralph observed. 'You were right about someone looking after the place. I wonder who it was.'

'You know, Ralph, I keep thinking of that strange instruction in her letter, about cleaning the house *carefully*.'

Marnie stepped across to the bed and examined it closely.

Ralph said, 'It looks to me as if someone has cleaned it pretty thoroughly already. I expect Iris had a cleaner who's been in since her death. Probably wanted to leave the cottage to the standard that Iris expected. That person probably made the bed, too. Don't you think?'

Marnie was turning back the bed cover. 'Probably. The bed's been remade with fresh linen. It's odd ...'

'I can imagine that a cleaner would want to make one last effort for their employer ... perhaps a way of saying goodbye.'

'Mm ...' Marnie nodded thoughtfully. 'You said the house looked as if it had been cleaned thoroughly.'

'Don't you think so, Marnie?'

'I was thinking of something else. Iris didn't suggest cleaning the place *thoroughly*. She said clean it *carefully*. Was that a different message, or am I reading too much into it?'

'Hard to tell,' said Ralph.

'She was a very precise sort of person, Ralph, not one to choose her words loosely. But what could she have meant by *carefully?*'

'Whatever she meant, we can't do anything about it today, can we?'

'No, not today. We've got enough to sort out, but I want to get this business cleared up soon. I think it'll mean returning in a day or two.'

Ralph said, 'While we're here we could get the documents from the bureau ... the bank statements and so on.'

'Why not?' said Marnie. 'It'll be a start, at least.'

They crossed the landing to the study. Marnie pulled down the lid of the bureau. In a gap between the lowest row of cubby holes stood a metal box. It was not locked. Inside, she found a small batch of share certificates. In the drawers were neat folders of bank and building society statements. Tucking these under her arm, she gave the box to Ralph to carry as they made their way out of the house and back to the car.

'So, you have some homework to do,' Ralph said, fastening his seat belt.

Marnie inserted the key in the ignition. 'Yep. And I haven't a clue what I'm supposed to do with these things.'

'You'll learn, Marnie. Didn't Iris describe you as a safe pair of hands?'

'So no pressure there, then.' Marnie grimaced and started the engine.

Chapter 11

On Tuesday morning Marnie lived up to Iris Winterburn's assessment of her. The previous evening Anne and Donovan had gone into town to eat out and see a film at the Milton Keynes multiplex, so there had been little time for conversation. In the office Marnie had given Anne the papers from the solicitor to file, and Anne began reading them.

'Oh,' she exclaimed. 'Aren't these supposed to be top secret or something? Didn't you sign a confidentiality thingy?'

'They are and I did,' said Marnie.

'Does that mean if I read them you may have to kill me, like in spy films?'

'I expect so. More likely that I'll get carted off to the Tower of London and thrown into a dungeon.'

Anne looked thoughtful. 'Well, before you get beheaded –'

'Yes, I know. I have to phone Randall about Sylvia.'

'You remembered.'

'Even without one of your lists.'

'Seriously, Marnie, would you rather I didn't look at these papers … just filed them away?'

'As far as I'm concerned, what's confidential stays with us in this office.'

'What about me?'

They turned to find Donovan emerging barefoot from the direction of the bathroom. He was wearing a towel round his waste, his hair still damp from the shower.

'Same applies to you, Donovan,' Marnie said. 'I'll need all the help I can get with this Iris business, so we all need to be in the picture.'

Donovan nodded. 'Fair enough. We just treat it like your normal client confidentiality.'

'Don't you have to get back to university?'

'This term's set aside for writing a dissertation. I have to give that priority before I tackle the photo of the dog-tag. I can do the writing from anywhere … assuming that's okay with you, of course.'

'Stay as long as you want, Donovan ...' Marnie reached for the phone, '... even with clothes on.'

Donovan laughed and withdrew while Marnie pressed buttons for Randall at the rectory. She was in luck; he answered straight away.

'So ... Sylvia Harris,' Marnie said. 'She wants to join your management committee and you're wondering how long she'll be staying.'

'It's like this, Marnie. We meet once a month. If I give her the papers for the next meeting and she's left before it even happens, we'll have wasted her time completely.'

'You've talked it over with her?'

'Yes, when she expressed interest. The trouble is, she thinks you may have some sort of plan for her future.'

'Excuse me while I laugh out loud.' Marnie's voice dripped with irony.

'You don't have a plan?'

'I just wanted to get her off the street. Frankly, Randall, I've got so much happening right now, I don't know if I'm coming or going. D'you think you could have another chat with her, find out if she has any idea what she might do?'

'Will do. She's certainly settled in here very well ... doesn't show any sign of wanting to leave.'

'Then if you're happy to have her, and she's happy to stay for a while, let's leave it like that for now.'

And that was how they left it.

****

Ralph made an announcement at coffee time that afternoon. The Master of All Saints' College had phoned to ask Ralph to meet him for lunch in Oxford the next day. He wanted to discuss a proposal from a benefactor. It was a controversial project to build a new centre for management studies. The benefactor, an immensely wealthy Arab prince, had studied at the college for his PhD some years past. So far, so good. However, his name had been linked with a number of scandals involving actresses (*call girls*, according to the tabloid press) and Russian oligarchs (*mafia bosses*, according to the tabloid press).

'That should be a fun meeting,' said Marnie. 'Perhaps he'll bring along some of his little friends to entertain you and then make you an offer you can't refuse.'

Ralph groaned. 'It's just a quiet lunch for the two of us, the Master and me, no prince, no little friends, no mafioso-oligarchs.'

'How sad for you. Even so, you'll have to go. The Master will probably need moral support.'

'As opposed to *immoral* support,' Ralph said. 'Though I'm thinking of crying off on the grounds that we planned to go to Iris's house tomorrow.'

Marnie chewed her bottom lip. 'So we did. Perhaps we could –'

'No, Marnie. You've got to deal with the will and Iris's other matter, whatever it is. They're your priority right now, while we've got this interlude.'

'I don't even know exactly what the so-called *other matter* is.'

'Precisely. The sooner you get it sorted, the better.'

'Why don't you take Anne if you need help?' Donovan said. 'You two are usually partners in crime.'

Marnie looked doubtful. 'Who'd mind the shop?'

Donovan said, 'If it's just manning the phone and taking messages, I can do that. There's not a lot happening right now. Your clients all think you're away on honeymoon.'

Marnie looked thoughtful. 'I suppose ...'

'Right,' said Anne. 'I think that's settled.'

'Works for me,' said Ralph. 'Oh, there is just one other thing. We seem to be low on provisions. I'm not sure we have much for supper. I can take care of the liquid side, but as for the rest ...'

'I feel a list coming on,' Anne piped up.

'There's a surprise,' said Marnie.

****

Anne found a parking space in Stony Stratford high street. Climbing out of the Mini, she became aware of an increased police presence in the town. Two patrol cars were parked further up the road, and uniforms were everywhere. They were mounting an all-out effort to track down the *Stony Stratford killer*.

As they walked along to the supermarket Donovan said, 'No wonder you were keen to get Sylvia away from here.'

'Absolutely,' said Anne. 'She was in *real* danger. It's a relief to know she's safely tucked away in Randall's place.'

When they'd finished shopping, Anne popped into the newsagents and bought the local paper. As they carried their bags back to the car, they were confronted by a young constable. He looked about the same age as Anne, and his helmet seemed about three sizes too big for him. With a serious expression he held up a leaflet.

'We're conducting inquiries about the recent murder of this man. Do you recognise him?'

They studied the photo. The victim had a friendly, open face. He looked mild-mannered, harmless, smiling, ignorant of his fate. Anne shuddered to think that he was brutally murdered, an innocent man who devoted his working life to charity. She looked at the constable.

'I'm sorry. I've never seen him.'

'Nor I,' Donovan added.

The policeman said, 'Could you have seen any strange characters in the area lately?'

Donovan said, 'Does a murderer look any different from anyone else?'

'We understand there was a beggar hereabouts at the time of the murder,' said the officer.

'I saw a beggar,' Anne said, 'a woman, sitting on the pavement outside the café.'

'Can you give me a description?'

'You're treating a beggar woman as a murder suspect?'

'It's routine to follow up all leads.' Anne looked dubious. 'We have to be thorough, miss.'

'Of course you do. Well, the woman looked about forty or so. I gave her something and she thanked me. I'd never seen her before.'

'She asked you for money?'

'She didn't ask for anything. I gave her a coffee and a croissant. I guessed she was homeless and hungry. She looked desperate.'

Anne glanced down towards the café about forty yards away. The policeman followed her gaze.

'We've had reports that she's left the area,' he said.

'Moved on,' said Donovan.

'Well, thanks for your help.'

Anne and Donovan walked back to the car. They waited until they were inside before speaking.

Anne said, 'I can see why Marnie always says she never quite gives the right impression to the police.'

'You didn't actually tell a lie,' said Donovan.

'No. But there was no way I was going to complicate things by telling him everything I know. I'm just glad Sylvia's safe.'

'They seem to think the killer's still a threat. I thought most murders were one-off spur-of-the-moment things.'

Anne shrugged. 'The police seem to think the danger's still there. Look at that paper.'

Donovan stared at the newspaper that Anne had dumped in his lap. The front page was filled with the photo of the victim and the latest news of the investigation.

POLICE STEP UP MURDER HUNT
Stony Stratford killer still at large

****

While Anne and Donovan were unpacking the groceries in the kitchen, Marnie walked in and suggested a glass of wine.

Donovan said, 'I put two bottles of dry Mosel riesling in the fridge this morning. Not Ralph's usual choice, but I think you might like it.'

'Sounds good to me. Oh … a real cork. I'm impressed. Shall I pour three glasses?' There were affirmative murmurs from the pantry. 'Did you get all we needed at the supermarket?'

'And more besides,' said Anne. 'We got questioned by the police in the high street.'

Marnie glanced down at the newspaper on the table. She read the headline. 'Why did they question you?'

Anne said, 'They showed us that photo of the victim and asked if we knew him. He looked a really ordinary, pleasant sort of guy. It's all so sad.'

Marnie set out the glasses of wine on the table. 'I'm glad for once I'm not on the suspects' list.'

'Makes a nice change for you,' said Anne.

Marnie was giving her the heavy eyelids treatment when they heard the front door open. Anne produced a fourth wine glass and reached for the bottle.

Chapter 12

On Wednesday morning it felt like old times, with Marnie at the wheel and Anne riding shotgun beside her, the road atlas on her knees. They were both thinking back to their first journey together when Marnie collected Anne from her home in Leighton Buzzard and they headed north up the A5, destination Knightly St John. Back then everything was an unknown quantity; they had no inkling of what was in store for them. For both it was an adventure, a journey into the unknown.

Back then, they were filled with hope and expectation. Now travelling south to Iris Winterburn's cottage in Little Haddon, they were intrigued, filled with apprehension and uncertainty. Marnie's head was buzzing with questions about the obligation that Iris had imposed on her.

She glanced briefly at Anne. 'Cut across to the M1 then down to junction 9?'

'You got it. At junction 9 take A5183, direction Harpenden. I'll give you directions from there. It's all quite straightforward.'

'Okay.'

'Does this remind you of the journeys we used to take, Marnie?'

'We've come a long way since then, in more ways than one.'

'Marnie, can I ask you something?'

'Sure.'

'It's a bit sombre.'

'That's all right. I expect we've been thinking the same thing.'

'It's about Miss Winterburn,' Anne said.

'You're still wondering about her funeral?'

'Yeah.'

'I haven't a clue. I've been so concerned with this extra task that I forgot to ask Seymour Lang about it.'

'You really don't know?'

'Nope, no idea.'

'Is it possible you might have to organise the funeral as part of your executrix duties?'

'Blimey! I hadn't thought of that. I'll ring him as soon as we get to the cottage.'

The traffic on the motorway was heavy, but they cruised along and made reasonably good time. Once they left the M1 Anne came into her own. She was a good navigator and gave timely succinct directions. Soon, Little Haddon was appearing on the road signs, and Marnie found the way back to April Cottage. She parked on the drive and reached for her bag on the back seat; she dug out her mobile.

'Seymour Lang?' Anne said.

Marnie nodded and pressed buttons. Lang's secretary connected her without delay.

'Mr Lang, there's something I forgot to ask you. It's about Miss Winterburn's funeral arrangements.'

'Remiss of me, Mrs Walker.' That now-familiar drawl. 'It was stipulated in her will that she was to have a green burial in a wicker coffin.'

'Is that something I have to organise?'

'No. It's taken place already. Miss Winterburn wanted a simple interment in a green burial ground not far from the village. It took place about two weeks ago or perhaps a little earlier, and her grave is unmarked.'

'You mean no headstone?'

'I gather it's the custom with that kind of burial that there are no markers.'

'Oh ... so there's no way of paying my respects?'

'Mrs Walker, I think Miss Winterburn only wanted you to carry out what she requested in her letter. That would be the best way of paying your respects.'

'But the letter doesn't specifically tell me what I'm supposed to be doing.'

'I'm afraid I can't help you with that. Naturally, I'll assist you in any way I can, but my ability to do so is strictly circumscribed.'

Marnie disconnected and sat staring out at the cottage. Anne waited while Marnie collected her thoughts.

Eventually Marnie said, 'This is a really bizarre situation. I'm supposed to carry out Iris's wishes even though she doesn't tell me what they are. Her own solicitor is being deliberately kept in the dark. She's been buried already in a wicker coffin in an unmarked grave. There's virtually no one I can contact who can give me the slightest help or guidance.'

Anne murmured, 'Bummer.'

'Exactly,' said Marnie. 'On that positive note, let's go and check out the house … again.'

****

Inside the cottage they made their way in silence from room to room, upstairs and down. Nothing had changed; nothing had been touched since Marnie's first visit. Standing in the kitchen, they peered out into the garden through the half-glazed back door. They were turning away when Anne placed a hand on Marnie's arm.

'What is it?' Marnie asked.

'When did Miss Winterburn die?'

'Not sure of the exact date. Lang said a few weeks ago.'

'That's odd.'

'What is?'

'The garden. I'd have expected the grass to be taller than that. The weather's been good … mild with a little rain. What my dad calls *growing weather*. He does the lawn every week from about March onwards. Iris's lawn looks freshly mown to me.'

Marnie looked out. 'You're right.'

'You know what I think, Marnie? She kept on the person who does the garden.'

'I think you're right, and I'm supposed to clean the house … *carefully*.'

'But she wouldn't expect you to be a cleaner as part of being executrix, would she?'

'Frankly, Anne, I think anything might be possible. This whole business is *totally* weird. I don't know where to start.'

'I do.'

'Go on.'

'We've got to do what she said.' Anne opened a cupboard door in the corner of the kitchen and found the equipment and materials. 'We've got to get cleaning.'

For a moment they looked at each other and then said in unison, '*Carefully.*'

'Whatever that means,' Marnie added.

'I'll make a start on hoovering,' said Anne.

'Okay, though it hardly needs it. I'll go up and have a thorough go at the bureau.'

Anne pulled out the vacuum cleaner. 'Isn't that a bit obvious, Marnie?'

'What d'you mean? That's where she kept all her household papers … bills, receipts and so on.'

'But there's nothing straightforward … *obvious* … in her instructions, is there?'

Marnie shrugged. 'Perhaps we'll gradually work out what she meant. In the meantime I do want to go over the bureau. It seems a logical place to start, even if it is obvious.'

****

Marnie pulled out the chair and sat at the bureau. She imagined that stern, enigmatic old lady sitting in that very chair. Iris's bureau. The sheen of the wood and the quality of workmanship told her it probably was Victorian, a genuine antique. The whine of the vacuum cleaner drifted upstairs as Anne set to work on the ground floor.

Marnie was faced with the array of cubby holes, some empty, some containing folded papers. One by one she withdrew them, examined them and sorted them into piles. There were guarantees, receipts, invoices – all of them marked 'paid' – plus a collection of brochures. Most poignantly, one was for *Woodland Burials – your green haven for eternity.* Marnie laid it aside for further reference. She noticed that not a single bill had been left unpaid, not a single account unsettled. Iris Winterburn had left her affairs in order.

That thought reinforced for Marnie the impression – the certain *knowledge* – that Iris was not one to use words lightly. *Clean carefully.* What on earth could that mean?

Lying alone in one cubby hole was a single sheet of A5 notepaper. It contained just two lines, two names:

Mrs Allen

Duncan

Who might they be? There was a tick beside each name.

Still pondering these questions, Marnie slotted the other papers back into their holes and made to stand up. As she reached for the green burials brochure, something caught her eye at the back of a cubby hole. She reached in and extracted a business card with a hole neatly punched in at one end. Attached to the card by a short length of fine string was a small key. The card was from Gresham's Bank. Under the name Karen Gossard was printed the title: personal banker. At that moment she noticed that the vacuum cleaner was no longer humming. Anne was calling something indistinct up the stairs. Marnie slipped the card and key into a pocket and crossed to the door.

'Sorry, Anne, I missed that. Can you say it again?'

'We have a visitor, Marnie, a gentleman.'

Marnie skipped down the stairs to the hallway. The front door was open, and a burly man in shirtsleeves was standing on the doorstep. He was balding, middle-aged and apprehensive.

'Hello,' Marnie said with a smile. She strode forward, extending her free hand. 'I'm Marnie Walker. What can I do for you?'

'I was wondering ... well, I saw the car and thought perhaps I ought to, er ... see who was here.'

'I'm a friend of Iris Winterburn, the executrix of her will. This is my colleague, Anne Price.'

'Hello ... again,' Anne said cheerfully.

The man nodded. 'So are you a solicitor, then?'

'No, but her solicitor has authorised me to act in the matter of Iris's estate. Sorry, I don't believe I caught your name.'

'I'm … Robert Maxwell.' Again, that apprehensive look. 'I know. It's embarrassing, isn't it? Everyone calls me Bob.'

'Are you a neighbour, Mr Maxwell?'

'Bob.'

Marnie smiled. 'Bob.'

He stood there as if uncertain what to do next. Marnie prompted.

'A neighbour?'

'Yes.' He glanced to his right. 'I live next door.'

'Have you lived here long?' Marnie asked.

'Nine years, come November.'

'Perhaps you can help me. Would you mind? I'd invite you in, but … things are a bit upside down at the moment.' Marnie realised she was treating the house like a crime scene. She looked at the sheet of paper in her hand. 'Do these names mean anything to you, Bob?'

He read the first name out loud. 'Mrs Allen … I think she cleans – er, cleaned – for Miss Winterburn. She lives in a cottage at the other end of the village, just beyond the pub.' His brow creased. 'Shepherds, I think it's called.'

'Thank you. And Duncan?'

'Oh, yes. He's like a handyman and does gardening jobs, too … mows the churchyard and things like that. He was here just the other day.'

'Mowing the lawn?' Marnie said.

'That's right.'

'Do you know where I might find him?'

'He lives just opposite the church. You can't miss his place. It's a mass of flowers … two flowering cherry trees in the front … always has a lovely display.'

'You've been very helpful, Bob. Thank you so much.' Marnie pulled a business card from her back pocket. 'It's good of you to keep an eye on the house. If you need to get in touch with me at any time, this is where you'll find me.'

'Right you are, er …'

'Marnie.'

'Yes. Thank you. I'll do that. Well, I'll let you get on.' He seemed more relaxed as he turned to go. Before leaving, he looked up at the cottage. 'It's funny. I was just thinking yesterday. All these years I've been here, I never knew she was called Iris. She liked to keep to herself, did Miss Winterburn.'

****

Marnie sat at the table in the kitchen and made notes on the paper with the two names. Next to 'Mrs Allen' she wrote 'Shepherds'. Alongside 'Duncan' she added, 'opposite church – flowers'. Anne came in from the hall and laid a hand on Marnie's shoulder.

'Shall I see if there's any tea or coffee?'

'Good idea.'

Anne put the kettle on the stove and lit the gas. 'Something to put on your list,' she said.

'What's that?'

'Cancel utilities. I'll take the vac upstairs while the water's heating up.'

Anne was down again a minute later and found Marnie looking in cupboards.

'Better be coffee,' she said. 'No milk in the fridge. You okay with black?'

Anne pointed in the cupboard. 'Isn't that a tin of evaporated? That's how Donovan does it ... what they do in Germany.'

They sat opposite each other at the table. It was quite a domestic scene, with a plate of Hobnobs to go with the coffee.

'I almost imagine Iris coming through that door any minute,' Marnie said. 'It feels like we're interlopers in her house,'

'Only it's *your* house now, Marnie,' Anne observed.

'I hadn't thought of that. I'm starting to acquire a property empire!'

'All right if I hoover upstairs after we've had coffee?' Anne asked.

'Of course. It's nice of you to do it.'

Anne said, 'Only, I think you're wanting to check everything before it gets disturbed.'

Marnie stared at Anne. 'You're right. I keep telling myself it's just an ordinary cottage … nothing sinister about it.'

'And yet all the time you're wondering about her instructions, aren't you? I know I am. Could we check things together?'

They agreed on a joint inspection. After clearing the table and washing up they climbed the stairs. First stop was the study.

'You've checked the bureau, then,' Anne said.

'Yes. Everything's in order. I've taken a brochure about green burials. I'd like to find out where she's buried. Perhaps we'll find a new grave. I'd like to pay my respects … say goodbye.'

'You've looked in all the drawers?'

'Yes. Nothing much of interest, just spare ball-points, notepads, envelopes … usual kind of thing.' Marnie realised that Anne was staring at her. She smiled. 'No secret compartment in the bureau.'

Anne looked disappointed. 'That would be too easy, I suppose.'

'A bit *too* obvious,' said Marnie.

From the study they crossed to Iris's bedroom. Like the rest of the house it looked neat and tidy. Anne walked over to the bed. On the bedside table stood a jug half-full of water. On top of it was a small piece of material, the size of an old-fashioned lady's handkerchief. It was decorated with a rose pattern, Victorian perhaps, intended to keep dust or flies from reaching the water. It overhung the jug, weighed down with glass beads strung round the edge. Next to the jug was an empty glass and a plastic bottle for still mineral water, a little of which remained. Also on the table was a paperback book. Anne picked it up. Its cover was faded, its pages yellowed with age.

'That's odd,' she said.

'What is?'

'This book … it's German. Did you know she spoke German, Marnie?'

Marnie thought for a moment. 'The first time we met, she used the word *Blitzkrieg.*'

'I think a lot of people of her generation would know that word,' Anne said.

'Yes, but she pronounced it like I imagine it would sound in German. What is the book?'

'It's by a writer I've never heard of: Wolfgang Borchert.' Anne had been learning German and knew how to pronounce the name authentically. 'It's called *Draußen vor der Tür und Ausgewählte Erzählungen.*'

'That funny letter in the first word is an 's'?' said Marnie.

'It's a kind of double 's'. I think the title means *Outside the Door and Selected Stories.* D'you think she could've had a German boyfriend or something like that?'

Marnie made a face. 'Back in those days? I rather doubt it. Germans were interned as enemy aliens. Though, on the other hand ...'

'What?'

'Some German prisoners-of-war were allowed out, I think, to work on farms and such.'

'Like being on parole?' Anne said.

Marnie nodded. 'That sort of thing. But I don't think Iris would have got to know any. Don't forget, she was away working on narrowboats for much of the time.'

'I suppose we'll never know. Shall I hoover in here, Marnie, or do you want me to check the dressing table?'

'I'll do that while you get started. Okay?'

'Fine.'

Anne went out to the landing and plugged in the machine. A moment later she was back in the bedroom and ready to switch on. Marnie passed her on the way out, shaking her head.

'Nothing of note, just underwear, slips, tights ... the usual. Her combs and brushes are top quality, and her mirror's backed with silver. Iris had taste.'

'I'll check the wardrobe when I've done,' Anne said and flicked the switch.

It took Marnie little time to examine the other bedroom to the background noise of the vacuum cleaner. Iris obviously used the wardrobe in the spare bedroom as an overflow for her clothes. Everything was hung and folded away in an orderly fashion. Iris hadn't had the most extensive collection of garments, but everything she had was of good quality. A few of the suits and costumes were wrapped in transparent covers as if recently dry-cleaned. The idea that they could go to a charity shop crossed her mind. Marnie closed the wardrobe door and left the room. On the landing she glanced in at Iris's room and saw Anne kneeling on the other side of the bed.

'Saying your prayers?'

Anne gave her *A Look*. 'Just doing under the bed and then I'll be finished in here.'

'I'll be downstairs when you're ready.'

Marnie had reached the third step when Anne called out.

Marnie stopped and turned her head. 'What is it?'

'You ought to see this.'

Marnie retraced her steps and found Anne standing beside the bed, gazing at the palm of her hand. She held it out as Marnie approached.

'Where did you find this?' Marnie asked.

It was a small white pill with a serial number on the side.

'It was when I got down to do under the bed.'

'Lucky you didn't suck it up,' said Marnie.

Anne shook her head. 'No risk of that. It was lying just behind the leg of the bed near the bedside table, between the bed and the wall. I only spotted it when I was getting up.'

'No doubt why Mrs Allen missed it when she did her last clean.'

'What shall we do with it?' Anne said.

'Not sure. Perhaps we can find out what it is.'

Anne pointed to the dressing table. 'I think there's a pill box over there.'

'Perfect. I'm sure there's someone I can ask –' Marnie was interrupted by the doorbell. 'Seems to be our day for visitors.'

She went downstairs, leaving Anne to move the vacuum cleaner to the second bedroom. This time the visitor was a woman, motherly, aged about sixty, with a round face and a capable expression.

'Hello,' said Marnie. 'What can I do for you? Are you by any chance Mrs Allen?'

The woman looked taken aback. 'I am. How did you know that?'

'Please come in and I'll explain why we're here.'

Mrs Allen stepped into the hall and cocked an ear in the direction of the stairs.

'Shouldn't be any need for hoovering,' she said. 'I did the whole place from top to bottom only last week.'

'And it all looked spotless,' Marnie said, reassuringly. She ushered Mrs Allen into the sitting room and invited her to take a seat on the sofa. Briefly she outlined her role as executrix and explained that Iris had stipulated in the will that they had to clean the cottage *carefully*. Marnie emphasised the last word.

'Carefully?' Mrs Allen repeated. 'What's that supposed to mean?'

'I was hoping you might tell me. It's not an expression Iris would've used?'

Mrs Allen pursed her lips, clearly put out. 'I've been coming here every Tuesday and Friday for twelve years and I never heard her say that. And no word of complaint about my work ever passed her lips.'

'It's not about the standard of your work, Mrs Allen. If Iris hadn't been satisfied with your work I doubt you'd have lasted twelve minutes.'

The trace of a smile crossed Mrs Allen's face. 'You're right there. And she wouldn't have wanted me to call her anything but Miss Winterburn, either.'

'Can I offer you a cup of something?' Marnie said, sensing that the atmosphere was becoming more congenial.

'No thank you, dear. I had one before I came out. Nice of you to offer.'

'You made the bed upstairs, Mrs Allen?'

Mrs Allen lowered her voice. 'I found her. You know, that morning when she was ...' Marnie nodded. 'After the undertakers took her away, I thought it was the right thing to do. She'd always been so particular. I'm sure she would've wanted me to do that.'

'Did you clean the house as well?'

'Oh yes, like I said. And I've been over it again since.'

'Did you notice anything unusual?'

'Not really. I phoned Duncan and told him what had happened –'

'He did the gardening?'

'That's him, Duncan Grisewood. So he came round, and I gave him his envelope and took mine. Then I locked up.'

'Envelope?' Marnie repeated.

'Miss Winterburn told me that if anything happened to her, I'd find two envelopes in the napkins drawer in the kitchen. One for me, one for Duncan. She said there'd be a small thank-you gift for us both.'

'I see. When did she tell you that?'

'Oh, it must have been about Easter time ... March, April, thereabouts.'

'Had she been ill?'

'She never spoke of any illness all the time I knew her, but she was getting on, mind.'

'Did you like working for her, Mrs Allen?'

A hesitation. 'Please don't mind me saying this, dear, but you're asking a lot of questions. Is everything all right?'

'I'm sorry. I'm just curious. I'd known Iris for a few years, though I'd not seen her very often.'

'Well, I did like working for her. She was very fair and generous in her way. Always paid us double at Christmas. And those envelopes ...'

'I really don't want to pry ...'

'She gave us each a hundred pounds ... a goodbye gift, I suppose. Thoughtful. She was like that in an old-fashioned sort of way.'

'So you've been looking after the cottage ever since.'

'Just popping in now and then to make sure it's all nice, you know, the way she would've wanted it to be.'

Neither of them had noticed that the vacuum cleaner was no longer running. Anne was sitting at the top of the stairs, unashamedly eavesdropping on the conversation below.

Marnie said, 'I don't suppose you noticed that Miss Winterburn was reading a German book? There's one on her bedside table.'

'Can't say I noticed, to be honest. Without my glasses on, I can't read things very well. I'll tell you one thing, though. She's got some books in German in the bookcase by the window.'

'I didn't check the bookcase. You're sure of that?'

'Definite. I was dusting the bookshelf one time, and when I moved some books a pressed flower fell out of one of them. It was the first book on the top shelf. Miss Winterburn saw what happened and said it had been a present – the flower. I think she said the book was by a famous German writer.'

After Mrs Allen left, Marnie went up to Iris's bedroom and took out the book in question. She shook it and a pressed flower fell to the floor, together with a slip of notepaper. A single line in German was written on the paper in a firm hand. It was not the handwriting of Iris Winterburn.

****

By the time they locked up the house it was almost one o'clock, so they opted for lunch in the village pub, The Haddon Arms. It was a typical Hertfordshire inn, half-timbered on the outside, low-ceilinged and beamy on the inside. They settled at a corner table with ploughman's lunches and spritzers.

As they clinked glasses, Marnie said, 'I expect you're already writing lists in your head.'

Anne sipped and grinned. 'I was wondering if Duncan Grisewood should be included.'

'Perhaps on a future visit. I think we've spent enough time here this morning.'

'So what's next on the agenda, Marnie?'

'I'm going to contact Woodland Burials. I'd like to visit Iris's grave to say goodbye.'

'I'd like to do that, too,' Anne said. 'Will you wear your *Idle Women* badge when you go there?'

'Perhaps. Will you wear yours?'

'Of course I will.'

Marnie had been given a genuine IW – for Inland Waterways – badge, as worn by the women who worked on narrowboats during World War Two. The badges were made of grey plastic with the heading IW, plus two wavy blue lines to represent waterways and the inscription: NATIONAL SERVICE. It had been a gift from a man in the village the year Marnie and Anne moved in. Then a year or two later Iris Winterburn had given Anne her own badge, a gesture which had touched Anne deeply.

Anne added, ' So, Woodland Burials ... then what?'

'I think I need to sit down and make a list of all the things I have to do as executrix.'

'I can help with that, if you want. Actually ...'

'Don't tell me. I can guess.' Marnie's tone was mock-weary. 'You've already started.'

Anne grinned and took a bite of cheese. She multi-tasked, chewing and nodding at the same time, then swallowed and said, 'Did Miss Winterburn have a mortgage?'

'I haven't found any papers about that, so I think not.'

'And the solicitor said you were the sole beneficiary of the will, so no bequests to deal with.'

'That's right.'

'Then I suppose you need to talk to her bank manager, get any accounts closed and transfer money to your account.'

'She had some investments, too. I'd better ask Roger what I do about that. Also the deeds to the cottage. That will need sorting, and transferring the bills to my name, plus the rates. There's a lot to think about.'

'Roger will advise you. I can send out the letters to companies and the council.'

'Good. But then there's the other stuff, and I don't even know where to begin with that.'

'You mean the mysterious extra task? You haven't worked out what it is?'

Marnie shook her head. 'Have you any idea, Anne?'

'Not the foggiest.'

Marnie chewed her lower lip. 'I think I'll try to find out what that pill is, the one you found under the bed. That's at least something I can do. I'll take it to the pharmacy in Stony Stratford, see if they can identify it. Apart from that, I'm mystified.'

****

There were warnings on the radio of heavy congestion on the M1 motorway, so Marnie opted to cross over to the A5, even though it meant braving the multiple traffic lights of Dunstable. They chugged steadily northbound and made it back to Knightly St John in just over an hour. In the office barn they found Donovan sitting at Anne's desk, working on his laptop. He looked up as Marnie and Anne came in.

'Not too many interruptions, I hope.' Marnie dropped her shoulder-bag on the floor by her desk.

Donovan waved a slip of paper. 'Just three messages ... nothing urgent.'

'And you've got on with your dissertation?'

'Not bad, in fact pretty well advanced.' He smiled as Anne came across, kissed him and took the paper from his hand.

'Could you have a look at something for me?' Marnie said.

'Sure.'

'It's in German. I wonder what you can tell me about it.'

Marnie crossed the room and handed him the notepaper that had fallen from the book in Iris's bedroom. Donovan studied it and quietly read the words out loud.

'*Kennst du das Land, wo die Zitronen blüh'n ...*'

'Do you recognise it?' Marnie asked.

'Everyone in Germany would probably know this. It's very famous. It's a poem by Goethe. I think it was included in one of his early novels, *Wilhelm Meisters Lehrjahre.*'

'What does it mean, that line of poetry?'

'*Do you know the land where the lemons blossom?* It's a love poem, actually. Why are you asking about it?'

Marnie perched on the corner of Anne's desk. 'You're right about that novel. Iris Winterburn had it on her bookcase, and a pressed flower fell out of it. It was marking the page where that poem was included. Any idea why she might've had German books in her house?'

104

Donovan shook his head. 'None at all. Remember, I've never even met her. As a matter of interest, what was the flower?'

'A primrose, I think, though it's very faded and old. Can you tell me anything more about the poem?'

Donovan's brows furrowed. 'Not sure that I know much. I'm pretty sure it was set to music ... Schubert, at a guess, probably one of his *Lieder*. I suppose the flower might've been a sort of love token. Does that make sense?'

'Not really,' Marnie said. 'At least ... I'm not sure. I've only ever known her as an old lady. I can imagine she was quite a looker when she was young.'

'What about the book?' Donovan asked.

'What d'you mean?'

'Was it very old or a recent edition?'

'Come to think of it,' said Marnie, 'it didn't look new. It was a paperback ... in pretty good condition.'

Anne joined in. 'Marnie, I got the impression it hadn't even been read. It looked sort of unused to me.'

'Did you bring it with you?' Donovan asked.

Marnie shook her head. 'No. I put the flower back in its place and the book back on the shelf. It didn't seem right to take it ... too personal.'

Donovan shrugged. 'Sorry, Marnie, I don't think I've been much use.'

'Not to worry. We seem to be up to our necks in conundrums at the moment.'

She walked back to her desk and dug the mobile from her bag on the floor. Bending to retrieve it, she saw the pill box and took that out, too.

'Would you like coffee, Marnie?' Anne was advancing on the kitchen area. 'Or tea?'

'No,' Marnie said. 'What I'd really like is one answer at least to one of our questions. And I'm going to get it. Right now.'

****

The police were no longer thronging Stony Stratford, though their notices were still prominently displayed. Marnie walked into the pharmacy in the market square. She held the door open for two women who were exiting. They were both talking about the murder, the local hot topic. At the counter she asked to speak to the pharmacist in private and was invited to take a seat in a small room beside the waiting area.

After barely a minute the pharmacist entered and took the other chair. She was tall, Asian and wearing a black trouser suit. She oozed confidence and intelligence.

'What can I do for you?'

Marnie reached into her bag and handed over the pill box. 'Can you identify this pill, please?'

The pharmacist took a pair of glasses from her top pocket and scrutinised the pill. 'Was this prescribed for you?'

'No.'

'Then can you tell me how it came into your possession?'

'I found it.'

'Where did you find it?'

'Look, it's like this. I've inherited a cottage from an old friend. When hoovering one of the rooms I discovered this on the floor.'

'Inherited, you say?'

'Yes.'

'Your ... old friend, did he or she die of natural causes?'

'She did, yes. She died in her sleep of heart failure, aged nearly ninety. She'd had angina for some years.'

'That wouldn't explain why she had this tablet.'

'So are you able to tell me what it is?'

'Oh yes. That's quite easy, but I'm wondering why you're curious to know about it.'

'That's just it ... curiosity. I hadn't seen my friend for a couple of years, and I wondered what she might have been taking for her angina.'

The pharmacist stared at Marnie. Her dark eyes had an intensity that Marnie found rather disconcerting. Eventually she said, 'Your friend wasn't taking this medication for angina.

This is a benzodiazepine. You may have heard it referred to as Valium.'

'Isn't that an anti-depressant?'

'Among other uses, yes. Tell me ... I'm sorry to be so blunt, but are you worried that your friend might have committed suicide?'

'No. At least, I wasn't thinking along those lines ... until you mentioned it.'

'Then let me set your mind at rest. A large dose of these pills can induce coma and cause side effects like memory loss. By themselves they're not normally likely to be fatal, but to an elderly person like your friend a large dose could be particularly harmful.'

'I have no reason to think Iris took an overdose,' said Marnie.

'No.' The pharmacist relaxed. 'I quite accept that you were just taking an interest in your late friend. Would you like me to dispose of this tablet?'

'Thank you.' Marnie rose to leave and held out her hand.

As they shook, the pharmacist added, 'I should just say that there are circumstances in which benzodiazepines can be fatal.'

'And what would they be?'

'If taken with a large quantity of alcohol, for example.'

'No question of that, I'm sure,' Marnie said. 'Thank you for your help.'

The pharmacist held Marnie's hand for a little longer than necessary and smiled. 'I hope I've set your mind at rest.'

****

That night Ralph was climbing into bed when Marnie walked in from the bathroom with her jeans over one arm and her free hand held out palm-upwards.

'Something interesting happened when I took my jeans off,' she said.

'So I see,' said Ralph.

Marnie laughed. 'No, idiot. Look.'

'I am looking.'

She gave him the Death Stare. 'At my *hand*.'

'Of course. Where else? Just remind me. What am I looking at?'

Marnie held up a key attached to a business card. 'I found these in Iris's bureau. I must've slipped them into my pocket and then forgot all about them.'

'What are they?'

'Have a look.' Marnie handed the items to Ralph who examined the card closely. He turned it over.

'Have you seen what's on the back, Marnie?'

Marnie sat on the bed and took the card. On the reverse side was an eight-digit number written in blue ball-point ink. Below it in pencil was a note:

(take passport)

Marnie said, 'I think that's Iris's handwriting. I've seen enough of it lately to know it. What d'you think this is?'

'Best guess,' Ralph said. 'I suspect the number relates to an account.'

'You mean like an actual numbered account? I thought they just existed in places like Switzerland or the Caymans.'

'Well, Marnie, I'm no expert but that's what it looks like to me.'

Marnie turned it over. 'The card's in the name of Karen Gossard of Gresham's Bank. It describes her as a *personal banker*.' She looked at it thoughtfully. 'So there's my next stop: Gresham's Bank in the High Street in St Albans.'

'I wonder ...' Ralph mused.

'What are you thinking?'

'Are there still such things as safe deposit boxes? They have numbers.'

Marnie sighed. 'Yet another question. Let's hope Karen Gossard can give me an answer.'

Chapter 13

Breakfast in the farmhouse on Thursday morning looked like a board meeting in progress. As soon as the four of them were settled with coffee, orange juice and croissants, Marnie produced a list which she laid on the table.

'Okay, listen. I've got a plan for today.'

Ralph, Anne and Donovan sat up and paid attention. They each took a sip of coffee. Marnie continued.

'I'm going to try to get an appointment with a bank manager – if there is such a thing these days – to sort out Iris's accounts and investigate a possible safe deposit box – if there are such things these days.'

'Where are you going to find this bank manager?' Donovan asked.

'St Albans, in the High Street ... Gresham's Bank.'

'Today?' said Ralph.

Marnie tore off the end of a croissant. 'If I can get an appointment.'

Ralph grimaced. 'You know I have a follow-up meeting with the Master in college.'

'Yes. But I wouldn't want to keep dragging you around, anyway. You have more important things to do.'

'So I'll be minding the shop while the dynamic duo ride out?' Donovan said.

Marnie blew him a kiss. Anne was mentally already drawing up a list.

****

In the office after breakfast Marnie rang the number on the business card. A recorded message told her it was no longer in use. She grabbed a pencil as the new number was read out. Her second attempt was only marginally more successful. A recorded message offered her several options, and she had to press the button to hear them again before she gave up and held on to be redirected to an 'accounts adviser'. Six rings later a cheerful, chirpy voice responded.

'Gresham's Bank, Cathy speaking, how may I help?'

Braced for another recorded message, Marnie sighed. 'Are you a real person?'

'I was when I last checked. How can I help you?'

'Can I speak to whoever's in charge, please?'

A pause. 'You mean the Group Chief Executive?'

The grandiose title surprised Marnie, and she realised she was off target.

'Can we start again?' she said. 'Am I speaking to the St Albans Branch of Gresham's Bank?'

'You're speaking to the customer services national call centre in Leeds. I can connect you with that branch, but if your enquiry is of a general nature I may be able to help.'

'I think it's the St Albans branch that I need, please.'

'I'll put you through.'

Marnie was trying to identify the jazzed-up version of something that might once have been Mozart when another voice interrupted the flow.

'Good morning Gresham's Bank, St Albans, Barbara speaking. How may I help?'

'Hello. Can you tell me, please, do you have a branch manager?'

'We have a business manager, Mrs Sylvia Lockhart. Would you like to speak to her?'

'Please.'

'One moment.' Marnie was poised for more crypto-Mozart, but after only a few seconds' delay, Barbara came back on the line. 'I'm afraid Mrs Lockhart's line is busy at the moment. Can anyone else help?'

'I really just wanted to arrange a visit.'

'I can make an appointment for you. When would you like to see her?'

Marnie crossed her fingers. 'Any chance of an appointment today?'

'She has a window at two o'clock. Twenty minutes. Is that any good?'

'It's perfect.'

The next call was to Woodland Burials. Marnie was hoping she wouldn't be hanging on for eternity listening to a jazzy version of the Dead March. She was trying to decide if their slogan, 'your green haven for eternity', was comforting or just plain naff when her call was answered promptly by another cheerful if not chirpy voice.

'Woodland Burials, good morning.'

'Good morning. I'm inquiring about a funeral you conducted a few weeks ago for my friend Miss Iris Winterburn.'

'Which burial site was it?'

'That's just what I'm trying to find out. I want to go there to pay my respects and say goodbye.'

'Of course. Can you give me the name again, please?'

'Iris Winterburn. She lived in the village of Little Haddon in Hertfordshire.'

'That's very helpful. You see, we have a burial ground just a mile or two from there. Let me see. Ah yes, here we are. Miss Winterburn. A non-denominational interment, wicker coffin, no wake, no flowers. It was exactly three weeks ago today. Let me give you the location.'

Marnie wrote down the details. 'And I can visit her grave without an appointment?'

'Strictly speaking, yes and no. You can visit at any time during the hours of daylight. Green burials are conducted without traditional markers. You won't find a headstone or a monument. The family might plant a tree as a memorial near the grave, but there won't be a plaque or nameplate.'

'I see,' said Marnie. 'So presumably I won't be able to locate her grave. Is there anything you can suggest?'

'You could take what we call a *memory walk* through the site, and of course you're likely to see a mound over such a recent grave.'

'Do you know if a tree was in fact planted?'

'Let me just check for you … er, no. Our records show there was no planting and there's no mention of any family being involved. Everything was done in accordance with Miss Winterburn's instructions. They were quite explicit.'

111

****

When the 'dynamic duo' rode off, Donovan waved them on their way wishing them a safe and productive journey. He returned to working on his dissertation at Anne's desk in the office barn. Ralph was already long gone on his way to further meetings in Oxford. Silence pervaded Marnie's Freelander for the first mile or two while Anne pored over the road atlas. Eventually she spoke.

'Got it! It's this patch of green north-east of Little Haddon.'

Marnie's voice was transformed to a husky baritone filled with condolence and solemnity. 'Is that our haven for eternal peace?'

Anne pulled a face. 'You're not going to keep that up all day, are you, Marnie? It'll give me the willies.'

'Fair enough. So you think you've found it?'

'Think so. It's heading off in the general direction of Knebworth. It shouldn't be hard to find.'

Anne fingered her *Idle Women* badge from World War Two and was pleased to see that Marnie was wearing hers.

Anne was true to her word and guided them direct to the green burial site. They parked in a lay-by and entered the site by a discreet sign bearing the logo and slogan of Woodland Burials.

'Any idea where we'll find her?' Anne asked.

'Not a clue,' said Marnie. 'I think the idea is, we just walk around remembering her. We might spot a mound where the grave was filled in.'

There was something about Marnie's flat tone and general demeanour that made Anne stare at her. Marnie noticed this and stopped to turn and look at her friend.

'What is it?' she said.

'You don't find it spooky here, do you, Marnie? I mean, it's just like a garden or a park; quite a nice place, really.'

Marnie breathed out audibly. 'Coming here has brought it all home to me. This is a weird business, Anne.'

'You mean you do find it spooky?'

'No. I mean the whole affair ... all this confidentiality agreement and the will and the *cleaning carefully* thing. What's it all about? Iris was an old lady who'd worked on narrowboats in the war. Big deal. I've read about those young women; they had quite an adventure, did important work. In many ways they were inspirational. But I just don't get why she's gone in for all this mystery stuff.'

Anne said, 'I know what you mean. I've been talking about it with Donovan. He wondered if Iris ended up going a bit, you know ... gaga. I don't like to think of her like that – she was so nice to me – but what else could it be?'

They continued their slow walk, deep in thought, scanning the area for signs of a grave mound. Away to their right two men were at work. One was mowing, the other planting a shrub. It was a still morning, thin clouds letting through a weak sun, the air mild. Birds were singing. There was no sound of traffic. Marnie and Anne thought this was a pleasant place to spend eternity. A green haven indeed.

Their walk took them nearer to the men. One was middle-aged, the other somewhat older. As they drew nearer, the men stopped what they were doing and took flasks from a rucksack that was leaning against a tree. They sat on the grass to take refreshment, and Anne thought of the numerous times she had served as tea-girl to workmen back at Glebe Farm. She smiled at them as she and Marnie walked past.

'Morning, my love,' said the younger man.

Anne returned his greeting.

'This is a lovely spot,' Marnie said, adding, 'We've come to visit a grave. An old friend died and was buried here a few weeks ago. Any idea where we might find her plot?'

'A few weeks,' the older man said. 'Now who would that be?'

'Her name was Iris Winterburn.'

The man stared at Marnie. 'You knew Miss Winterburn?'

'We'd met a few times over the years. Do you know where she's buried?'

'I dug her grave myself and I'm still tending her garden at home. She was a good'un was Miss Winterburn.'

'Would you be ... Mr Grisewood?' Marnie asked.

'Duncan Grisewood, yes. And I can surely show you where she's resting.' He got to his feet with no effort. 'If you'd like to come this way.'

Marnie and Anne followed the old gardener to a place where a low mound was visible in the midst of a clump of trees. Mr Grisewood pointed.

'This is her resting place.'

'It's a lovely place.' Anne's voice was little more than a whisper. 'I'm glad she's here. It's beautiful ... peaceful and quiet.'

Marnie put an arm round Anne's shoulders. Mr Grisewood looked at them.

'So you were friends,' he said. 'I don't think I ever saw you at her house.'

'I first met her when I was travelling on my canal boat,' said Marnie. 'Then later she came to visit us at home.'

Mr Grisewood nodded, still staring at the two women. 'Your badges,' he said. 'I've seen them before. Miss Winterburn had a friend who used to come years back. She wore a badge like that. I remarked on it once. Miss Winterburn called it a badge of honour.'

'Miss Winterburn was right,' Marnie said.

Mr Grisewood turned away. 'Well, I'll leave you to pay your respects.'

'Mr Grisewood, before you go, I'd be grateful if you'd continue to take care of the garden at April Cottage. And naturally I'd like to pay for your services.'

'Oh, I don't know about that. I don't want to be –'

'Please, Mr Grisewood. Miss Winterburn has left the cottage to me. I can't look after the garden, and I wouldn't want it to fall below Iris's high standards. Can you do that, please, for me and in her memory?'

'Well, since you put it like that ...'

'Thank you. If you've no objection, I'd like to continue at the same rate as before, for now. I'll send you a cheque each month, starting immediately. I'll leave all the decisions to you for the moment. You must know the garden better than anyone.'

Marnie held out a hand and they shook.

114

'Very will, miss.'

'It's Marnie, if that's all right with you, and may I call you Duncan?'

'Everyone calls me Duncan.'

With that, he left them to their respects and their memories.

****

On the way south to St Albans they called in at April Cottage to check for any post that might need Marnie's attention. Nothing had changed since their last visit. Then it was on to The Haddon Arms for another pub lunch. The landlord recognised them and gave them a friendly welcome.

After placing their order, Marnie went outside to phone Donovan. He reported that the excitement of the morning had been when Dolly brought a mouse into the office. When she released it from her jaws it had set off at a great rate to find a hiding place, while the cat looked on, indifferent. Donovan eventually trapped it under a waste-paper bin and managed to escort it from the premises. He'd rewarded Dolly with a saucer of milk and settled back to work on his project.

In the post there had been a notice from the police asking for any 'persons with information concerning the Stony Stratford murder' to come forward in complete confidentiality. *That word again*, Marnie thought.

'Any phone messages?' she asked.

'Just one or two general enquiries,' said Donovan. 'I'm keeping a list of names. Oh, and Randall phoned. Sylvia seems to be getting on well in the hostel. She's started giving lessons to some of the guests, as they call them: literacy and numeracy. How are things at your end?'

'We found Iris's grave. It's in a beautiful spot. We're stopping off now for a bite to eat and then on to the bank.'

Donovan wished them luck, and Marnie returned to the lounge just as their order arrived at the table. Armed with spritzers and sandwiches, they made themselves comfortable, while Marnie outlined her phone conversation to Anne.

'It's a big relief, not having to worry about Sylvia,' Anne observed. 'I'm glad she's fitting in all right.'

'Yes, but for how long, I wonder.'

'Marnie, are you all right? You've been under a cloud all morning. Was it Miss Winterburn's grave? Did it upset you?'

Marnie put down her glass. 'No, nothing like that. It's what I was saying before, this sense of frustration ... all this messing about. What is it that Iris expected me to do? There's no mystery about her death. She was very old, had a heart condition, died peacefully in her sleep. It's as good a way to go as any. But then there are the strange letters, and everything being secret, even kept from her solicitor. I'm at an absolute loss to know what's going on.'

'And I'm no use, am I?' said Anne. 'Ralph is probably one of the most intelligent people in the country, and he's just as baffled as the rest of us. And I've never known Donovan so totally confused.'

'We're missing something,' Marnie said. 'It's probably staring us in the face.'

Anne nodded. 'Perhaps the bank will help sort things out.'

Marnie looked thoughtful. 'I wouldn't count on it.'

****

Marnie guessed that parking in the centre of St Albans would probably not be easy, but she had a pleasant surprise. She followed a sign to the London Road car park and found a slot about ten minutes walk from Gresham's Bank in the High Street.

The bank presented a Georgian façade, but the inside was modern and functional. Not a large branch, there were just four assistants at the counter, each dealing with a small queue of customers. Marnie chose the shortest queue while Anne held back and studied a rack of leaflets. Only a few minutes elapsed before Marnie announced herself at the counter and was invited to take a seat in a small office near the entrance lobby.

As soon as Marnie and Anne were seated, a youngish woman entered the room and introduced herself as Sylvia Lockhart. Marnie explained her role as executrix and beneficiary and produced the letter from Seymour Lang to confirm this. She also produced her passport for identification.

'I'll need to take a copy of this authorisation, Mrs Walker, as well as your passport, and there are some papers to sign.'

'Inevitably,' said Marnie. 'Would you also take a look at this.'

She passed the business card and its key to Mrs Lockhart who studied it closely.

'Well, well … Karen Gossard. That's a name from the past. I think she left the year I joined … maternity leave. She's got three children now. So what can I do for you?'

'My friend, Iris Winterburn, was a customer of your bank.'

'That's correct. We can transfer funds to any account you wish, Mrs Walker. Then we'll close them all. We'll need to check if there are any outstanding payments to be made, and you'll need to contact third parties in regard to direct debits. If you need any assistance, just let me know.'

'Thanks. This is all new to me. I'm sure I need all the help I can get.'

A reassuring smile from Mrs Lockhart. 'Don't worry. It's all pretty straightforward.'

Marnie pointed at the card. 'There is one other thing. Could you please turn the card over.'

Mrs Lockhart read the markings on the reverse. 'Ah …'

'Yes,' said Marnie. 'I'm not sure what that number refers to. I'm wondering if it – and the key – might relate to a safe deposit box. Any ideas?'

'We don't actually have safe deposit boxes, as such. Not any more. We have a service called *Closed Safe Keeping*. That would be suitable for important documents and items of some monetary value. There's also an Open Safe Keeping Service for things like deeds and life insurance policies.'

'That number refers to one of those?'

'Yes. The first three digits tell me this is for Closed Safe Keeping. Would that seem appropriate, Mrs Walker?'

'I've no idea. But perhaps if you can open whatever it is, we'll find out.'

117

Marnie glanced at Anne who was sitting on the edge of her seat. At last they seemed to be getting somewhere.

'I'm afraid I can't help you there, Mrs Walker. You see, we don't hold that sort of item at this branch. Only branches in major centres offer that service nowadays. The days of cabinets of locked metal deposit boxes in the basement are long since past.'

'I see.' Marnie tried not to betray her disappointment. 'So what do I have to do to locate that … whatever it is?'

'What I can tell you, is that that item is stored in London. If you'll give me a moment I'll check our records and tell you precisely which branch is involved.'

She rose and left the room, taking the authorisation letter from Seymour Lang and Marnie's passport to be photocopied. Marnie turned to Anne.

'Typical! I might've known it wouldn't be so easy.'

'At least we know where to go,' Anne said. 'And London's no problem.'

Mrs Lockhart was absent for no more than five minutes. She returned with another young woman who handed Marnie a sheaf of papers and indicated where to sign. When the young woman had withdrawn, Mrs Lockhart returned the solicitor's letter and passport to Marnie and resumed her seat.

'I'm sorry,' she said. 'We didn't even offer you a cup of tea.'

'That's all right,' said Marnie. 'We weren't expecting to be here for more than a few minutes.'

'Well, I can tell you that the item you need is stored at our City of London branch in Cheapside. It's midway between Bank and Saint Paul's tube stations. You need to ask for Mr Vincent.' She handed Marnie a slip of paper. 'That's his number, if you'd like to phone for an appointment.'

****

They were on their way back to the London Road car park when Marnie suddenly stopped and took hold of Anne by the arm.

'We really do need a plan,' she said.

118

'You're not thinking of going into London now, are you?' said Anne.

'No, not today. I need to clear my head and get things straight in my mind. I could really use a cup of coffee.'

'There's a café over the road.' Anne pointed. 'Any good?'

'I want to have another look round the cottage. I'm *sure* we must be missing something. Perhaps we can get coffee in the village pub.'

****

The area was almost starting to feel like home. Returning to Little Haddon, the names on the road signs were looking familiar. They arrived back in the village in a quarter of an hour and turned into the car park of The Haddon Arms. Behind the bar the landlord was drying glasses.

'You're getting to be regulars. Twice in one day! What can I get you?'

Marnie ordered coffees while Anne drew up two bar stools. They perched while the landlord left to fetch their drinks. There were only three other customers, all at different tables finishing lunch.

'We definitely need a plan,' Marnie said quietly. 'We're here, Ralph's in Oxford, Donovan's back in the office and *Sally Ann*'s in Little Venice. We're all over the place, in more senses than one.'

'Presumably we'll all be back in Knightly St John this evening,' Anne pointed out. 'Except *Sally*, of course.'

The landlord reappeared with two steaming cups and set them down before his guests.

'Moving into the village?' he said.

'Not exactly. I'm acting on behalf of the late owner of April Cottage.'

'Miss Winterburn?'

'You knew her?' said Marnie. She couldn't imagine Iris Winterburn as a regular at the local inn.

The landlord shook his head. 'Not really, but our cleaner used to do for her, if you see what I mean.'

'Mrs Allen?'

119

'That's right, Shirley Allen. She's here for two hours every day. I doubt I'd even recognise Miss Winterburn. So are you a relative, then?'

'No. I'm executrix for her will.'

'You're a solicitor?'

Marnie reached into her bag and produced a business card. 'I'm actually an interior designer.' She handed the card to the landlord.

'Nice to meet you, Miss Walker. I'm Jim Barlow.'

They shook hands, and Marnie introduced Anne.

'It's, er ... Mrs Walker in fact, but Marnie will do fine.'

'Nice to meet you, Marnie. I reckon we could do with some fresh design in this place.' A self-deprecating smile.

'Looks okay to me ... a proper village inn.'

'Don't suppose you've ever done a pub, Marnie.'

'Actually, I've done quite a few in my time. Willards Brewery is a good client of mine.'

Jim stared at her. 'Willards?'

'You must know them ... big firm based in Leicester.'

'You know The Jolly Boatman pub near Bulbourne?' said Jim.

'Very well,' said Marnie. 'Tommy Rodgers ... landlord ... great character.'

Jim looked at Marnie with admiration. 'Respect! That's a really smart pub. And Tommy's my brother-in-law. Put your wallet away, Marnie. Coffee's on the house.'

****

April Cottage looked no different from when they had left it that morning. To Marnie it still felt as if she was a visitor, a guest of Iris Winterburn. She wondered if it would ever seem really to belong to her. This was the one house where Marnie didn't automatically start thinking how she would redecorate it. Like Shirley Allen, the cleaner, and Duncan Grisewood, the gardener, she wanted to preserve the cottage as Iris would have liked it. Stepping inside, she stooped to pick up the post. There were just two circulars and a leaflet advertising a spring barbecue on the village green. She placed them on top of the other mail on the hall table and began her inspection, room by room.

'No change here,' said Anne, coming down the stairs. 'Were you expecting any?'

'Not really. I think I might've been hoping for a bolt of inspiration to strike, but that's not realistic.'

'We have at least made some progress today,' Anne said.

'Better than nothing,' Marnie agreed.

'So what next, Marnie?'

They wandered through to the kitchen and sat at the table.

'Back to the fleshpots of Knightly St John, I suppose.' She rummaged in her shoulder bag. 'I'll give Ralph a ring before we set off.'

Ralph picked up the call almost at once. His meeting with the Master of All Saints' College was over; they had had a pleasant lunch together; he'd borrowed some books from the college library and was ready to set off for home.

'Sounds like your day has been more productive than mine,' Marnie said in a weary tone.

'Tell me about it,' said Ralph.

Marnie gave an account of the visit to the green burial ground and Gresham's Bank in St Albans. 'So all rather inconclusive,' she said.

'I wouldn't say that, Marnie. You're one step away from resolving the question of that key and the business card. You've only got to visit the bank in Cheapside and that mystery will be solved.'

'I expect you're right. I just seem to have this thing hanging over me.'

'And it's understandably getting you down.'

Yes, Ralph, it's getting me down. By now I thought we'd have had our wedding and taken the Orient-Express to Venice. Instead, here we are … Well, no use going over it again. You know the score. I'll be glad to get home.'

There was silence on the line for a few seconds. Marnie could almost hear Ralph's brain working. She waited patiently.

Eventually Ralph said, 'Marnie, I've got a suggestion.'

'Okay.'

'Rather than come back to Glebe Farm, why not stay in London tonight? Tomorrow's Friday, and the bank will be open. Here's my idea. If Anne can bring the Freelander back to Glebe Farm, I'll come direct to London from Oxford and join you this afternoon. We can go to the bank first thing tomorrow morning and sort out whatever they're holding for Iris. Then we can go to Little Venice and set off for home on *Sally Ann*. What d'you think?'

'Hold on a moment.' Marnie explained Ralph's proposals to Anne who straight away agreed. Returning to Ralph she said, 'We have a plan!'

****

The plan worked well, in fact better than Marnie could have expected. After Anne dropped her off at St Albans City station, she had a wait of ten minutes before her train to London St Pancras was due. She used the time to phone Mr Vincent in Cheapside. Success! He was available the next morning and offered her his first appointment at 09.30. The train was on time and she was back in the Docklands apartment in under an hour. With her morale boosted, she booked a table for dinner at a restaurant in Butler's Wharf. It occupied part of the ground floor of the complex, and they could walk there from the flat in two minutes. She was starting to feel more human; life was starting to feel better.

Was it too good to be true? She soon found out.

Her mobile rang. It was Ralph.

'I'm on the train ... due in at Paddington in about twenty minutes. Want some good news?'

'Absolutely!'

'I have a date for our wedding. It's not until September, but it's the best they can do and it's *definite* this time.'

'Did you threaten actual physical violence, Ralph?'

'More or less. Well, I asked nicely and they succumbed. I've also phoned the Orient-Express people and got us booked, plus three extra nights at the Cipriani.'

'Wow! I'm impressed.'

'Oh, going into a tunnel. Gotta go.'

And he went, leaving Marnie smiling for almost the first time that day. Five minutes later the mobile rang again. Marnie picked it up and pressed the green button.

'Is this the light at the end of the tunnel?' she said cheerfully.

'I beg your pardon?'

A different voice. Not Ralph's, but somehow familiar.

'Oh, sorry, I thought it was Ralph. Who's calling?'

'It's Randall, Marnie. If you're expecting a call I can phone you back later.'

She could tell from his tone that all was not well. 'No, Randall, it's fine. What can I do for you?' She felt a stone in the pit of her stomach.

'It's Sylvia,' he said. 'I'm afraid she's been attacked.'

****

The ambience in the restaurant was alive with scintillating vibes. Smartly dressed executives were discussing important deals, while in hushed tones media people were denigrating their rivals' projects. Suave men were entertaining attractive women, some of whom might have been their own wives. Gossip was rife. Occasionally an exaggerated laugh rang out, attracting sideways glances from customers at tables nearby. Wine was flowing freely.

At the table occupied by Marnie and Ralph a serious conversation was in progress.

'Attacked?' Ralph said. 'By whom?'

Marnie suppressed a smile. Ralph noticed. He protested.

'I'm not going to be ungrammatical just because I'm concerned. And yes, I know I sound like a professor. Well, guess what ...'

'Darling,' Marnie said. She reached across the table and laid a hand on his. 'I wouldn't want you to be any other way.'

'I'm glad.' He turned his hand over and gently squeezed her fingers. 'But can we return to my question?'

'The man who attacked Sylvia was just another guest in the hostel. Randall knew him; he'd stayed there before and had never caused any trouble. He wasn't a druggie or a wino. He had no previous form for bad behaviour.'

'Then why attack Sylvia, and what did he do?'

'He went to see Sylvia for help with his arithmetic. You know she's been doing some teaching there ...basic literacy, basic maths and so on.'

'I remember you telling me.'

'Well, according to the man, he went to sit on the armchair in her room and she suddenly got very upset and wanted him to leave.'

'It doesn't add up,' said Ralph. Sorry, no joke intended. I mean, there must have been more to it than that. Did he touch her when he came into the room, perhaps?'

'Sylvia apparently didn't elaborate, but Randall said she was really quite distraught. He didn't like to press her.'

'Did the man say anything else?'

Marnie shook her head. 'He maintains that he just went to sit down, moved her rucksack from the chair and she got – how did he put it? – all aerated.'

'You think he threw the rucksack on the floor?'

Marnie shrugged.

'Where did the attacking part come in?' Ralph asked.

'Well, the man said he was just trying to calm Sylvia down, but as she struggled, they tripped and fell. Sylvia hit her head on the end of the bed and got a nasty cut. Of course that meant a trip to A and E in Banbury hospital.'

'So what's the outcome? Were the police called in?'

'No. Sylvia was adamant; she didn't want to make a fuss. Those were her words.'

''I take it that means she wouldn't be pressing charges.'

'That's right. You can imagine Randall was relieved about that. The last thing he needs in the hostel is any suspicion of violence, especially involving a woman guest. Not everyone in that neck of the woods likes having a hostel for homeless people in their community.'

Ralph nodded. He hooked imaginary quote marks. 'A doss house for tramps and misfits.'

'Exactly,' said Marnie.

'Well, whatever the man says, I think he must have done something inappropriate.'

'I think you're probably right, Ralph. And like a lot of women, Sylvia doesn't want to bring it out into the open.'

They became aware that a waiter was hovering. Ralph looked up at him.

'Let's have a bottle of Chablis,' he said. 'Then we'll be ready to order.'

Chapter 14

Marnie and Ralph set off for their meeting on Friday morning. It was nine o'clock, and London's rush hour was coming to an end. Ralph had worked out a route using the tube, including the underground pedestrian passage between Monument and Bank stations. Marnie and fate had other ideas. As they reached the approach road to Tower Bridge a taxi came by and Marnie waved to the driver. With perfect timing they were deposited on the pavement in Cheapside just as the City of London branch of Gresham's Bank was opening.

Marnie announced herself at the reception desk and they were ushered into the office of Mr Nicholas Vincent, business manager. He was everything Marnie had expected: a sharp youngish man in a sharp suit with a light blue shirt and a yellow silk tie. His handshake was energetic but not overpowering. He gestured to them to take a seat and wasted no time in coming to the point.

'I gather you're here as executrix to a will, Mrs Walker. The paperwork has been faxed to me from the St Albans branch.'

'That's right.' Marnie passed over the business card with the key attached. 'I'd like to have access to the closed-safe-keeping items with the reference number on the back of that card. I gather they're stored here.'

Vincent scanned the documents quickly. 'Ah, yes, of course. I thought the number looked familiar.'

'Familiar?' Marnie repeated.

'This item was accessed not long ago, within the last month or two, certainly.'

'By whom?'

'I can't reveal names, but it was a lady.'

'She took it?'

'No. She examined it here in my office in private, then left it to be returned to the vault.'

'Did she explain why?'

'No, and naturally I didn't ask.'

'That's all you can tell me?'

'It is, Mrs Walker, though now that it belongs to you, you'll be able to examine it yourself.' Vincent pressed a button on his phone. 'Jade, can you pop in, please.'

Seconds later a young woman came in and received instructions from Vincent.

'We shan't keep you waiting long,' he said. 'May I offer you some refreshment?'

'No, really, thanks,' said Marnie. 'We'll need to press on as soon as we've retrieved whatever you're holding.'

Vincent was right. No sooner had this exchange taken place than Jade returned carrying a metal box. She placed it on the desk in front of Marnie, with the business card and key resting on top.

'Will that be all, Mr Vincent?'

'Thank you, Jade.' He turned his gaze back to Marnie and Ralph as his colleague left the office. 'There only remains for you to sign this receipt, if you'd be so kind, and the box is yours.'

'Don't you wish to keep the box?' Marnie asked.

Vincent pointed. 'That was the item being held in our store. It's all yours, and presumably that's its key.'

With the formalities completed, Marnie and Ralph stood. They shook hands and Vincent escorted them out. The whole transaction had lasted little more than ten minutes.

****

Inside the cabin on *Sally Ann* all was quiet. In the centre of the table in the saloon sat the metal box. Beside it lay the shiny key attached to the business card. The box was oblong, its dimensions roughly fourteen inches by eight or, as Marnie would put it, around thirty-five by twenty centimetres. It was solidly built, the kind that was used in times past for petty cash; it had a small hinged handle on the top and a keyhole at the side. With rounded corners, it was an attractive shade of metallic light blue in a stippled orange-peel finish. It must have been quite a few years old, though it looked brand new, having spent almost its entire existence concealed in a bank vault.

Little sound penetrated into the boat's cabin space, only voices heard faintly from the stern deck, and sometimes the hum of traffic on the road that ran alongside the canal in London's Little Venice. The boat was being prepared to cast off and turn on the nose ready for departure. On the towpath Ralph was busy untying mooring ropes while Marnie was phoning Rob Frazer in the British Waterways office to thank him for the use of the mooring.

Marnie ended the call with cordial goodbyes and cranked the engine into life. Beside her, Ralph took the pole from the roof, checked all was clear in both directions and poled the stern firmly away from the bank. When the boat had travelled as far as Ralph could reach, Marnie threw the tiller hard over and pulled the gear lever towards her. The water round the stern began to boil, and *Sally Ann* was moving under her own power, swinging in an arc, her nose button pressed firmly against the bank. Ralph slid the barge pole onto the cabin roof.

The boat swung round till the stern was in mid-channel, where Marnie eased back on the accelerator and pulled the tiller towards her. She pushed the gear lever forward with a momentary pause in neutral and reversed across the water. When the stern button was within a yard of the opposite bank, Marnie eased off and pulled the gear lever smoothly back. She adjusted the tiller to keep *Sally Ann* on a course down the middle of the canal, straight and true. It was a manoeuvre they had performed many times.

They skirted Browning Island in the pool of Little Venice, past the barges that included the famous art gallery and the puppet theatre, and steered towards the narrow entrance of the Paddington Arm of the Grand Union Canal. Ahead of them now lay several hours of steady navigation through London and out beyond its suburbs, with no locks to delay them until tomorrow when they left the great city behind. Ralph turned to Marnie and offered to take the tiller.

'Well?' he said.

'What is it?' Marnie tried but failed to sound casual.

'Marnie, you know you've been aching to open that box ever since we left the bank. Why don't you go below and see to it? I'll steer *Sally*. Go on.'

'Don't you want something to eat first?' she said.

Ralph grinned. 'I'll try not to die of malnutrition in the next half hour.'

Marnie took a deep breath and released her grip on the tiller. Ralph took hold of it. She hesitated before going below.

'What's the matter?' Ralph said over the clanking of the engine.

'It's weird, but now that I've finally got something from Iris, I'm almost nervous about finding out what this *special task* might be.'

'You think the contents of the box will reveal it?'

'Don't you?'

Ralph adjusted the tiller. 'I don't think we can stand here all day answering questions with questions. Iris has entrusted it to you, Marnie. There's no point putting it off.'

Without another word Marnie stepped down into the cabin. She took her seat at the table in the saloon and stared at the box for a few moments before reaching for the key. It turned smoothly in the lock with the faintest click. Whatever she might have been expecting was not what she found.

The first item made her sit up with a jolt. It was a medal, not just any medal but one which probably anyone would recognise. She picked it up and felt the cold metal against her fingertips. She had seen them in countless films, worn with pride by members of the military deemed to be heroes in their country. But never before had she come into immediate contact with an actual Iron Cross. It was black and edged with silver. At its centre was a symbol universally loathed by all who opposed Nazism: a swastika. Below it was the date, 1939. At the top was a small ring attached to a slightly larger ring, through which was looped a ribbon of red, white and black.

Marnie found herself fingering her *Idle Women* badge which she was still wearing, fastened to her sweatshirt. Iris had called it a badge of honour. The contrast with the Iron Cross could hardly have been greater.

Oh, Iris, she thought. *What is going on? Where on earth did this come from?* She laid the medal on the table beside the box and delved in once more.

The next items were booklets, old and faded, and all in German. The titles meant nothing to Marnie. She grimaced. *What on Earth was this collection? And how did it come to be stored in a London bank vault? Most importantly, how and why did these come into Iris Winterburn's possession?*

As Marnie removed the booklets she saw a number of small ribbons lying in a heap to one side in the box. One was pale blue, another was striped black, red and black, a third was mainly dark red with a thin border on each side in black and white. Marnie guessed they were linked with the Iron Cross.

It was at that point that she made two more surprising discoveries. The first was a notebook, like an old school exercise book, except that it was roughly the dimensions of an A5 pad. The cover was a faded pale green, and she opened it to read the first page. It bore a simple inscription:

Iris Winterburn

Notes in time of war

The handwriting, though unmistakably Iris's, was firmer and less shaky than anything Marnie had seen in the more recent documents. This belonged to Iris as a young woman. Marnie was on the brink of reading the notes when something else caught her eye.

Lying at the bottom of the box was a cream vellum envelope. Marnie breathed in sharply at the sight of the single word written on the front of the envelope staring up at her:

Marnie

****

Ralph pointed ahead as Marnie appeared in the hatchway. She stepped up and joined him at the tiller.

'This is one of my favourite sections of the canal,' he said.

As he spoke, *Sally Ann* advanced onto a broad aqueduct divided in two by a central barrier. Ralph steered into the right-hand lane and they drifted across and above the busy North Circular Road. He and Marnie looked down at the heavy traffic crawling below them. They could see some of the drivers staring up at them as they floated on high.

'I wonder how many of them even know that this part of the canal network exists,' Ralph said.

Marnie chuckled. 'I'm often tempted to wave at the ones who are watching us, but I'm afraid they might crash into other cars if we distract them.'

Within a few moments they had passed over the highway and were now pressing on past modern industrial buildings and commercial estates. Ralph steered into mid-channel and turned to Marnie.

'You've looked in the box?'

Marnie looked troubled. 'Yes. It's rather bizarre.'

'In what sense?' Ralph asked.

Marnie described the contents.

'And the documents are definitely German, you're sure of that?' Ralph said.

Marnie shuddered. 'Beyond any doubt, and littered with swastikas.'

Ralph took a while to absorb this. 'Doesn't sound right, does it? I mean, Iris Winterburn connected to the Nazis? Any idea what the documents are?'

'I didn't examine them too closely. They wouldn't mean much to me, anyway. I thought I'd run them past Donovan to see what he makes of them.'

'What about the letter? Presumably it's why Iris wanted access to the box a month or two ago.'

'I, er ... haven't opened it yet. To be honest, Ralph, this whole business is giving me the heebie-jeebies.'

'So when are you thinking of opening it?' Ralph asked.

Marnie stared into the distance. 'Perhaps when we stop for the night. When will that be?'

Ralph glanced at the cruising guide resting on top of the sliding hatch. 'I think we should make the first lock at Cowley

some time this afternoon, then we could go on to Uxbridge …
maybe tie up for the night after Uxbridge lock, not too close to
the Western Avenue flyover. What d'you think?'

'Fine by me. A good start to the journey.'

****

They decided on an omelette after mooring within reach of
Denham Deep Lock. Both were pleasantly weary after several
hours on their feet, navigating in the open air. It was a warm
evening, and they were able to open the cabin windows to
dispel the odour of cooking. Ralph popped a part-baked half-
baguette in the oven and opened a bottle of Australian
chardonnay while Marnie chopped tomatoes and basil leaves
for a salad. They both knew she was putting off reading Iris's
latest – and Marnie hoped *last* – letter until after supper.

With the saloon seductively lit by oil lamps, and both of
them agreeably relaxed by the meal and the wine, Marnie
finally picked up the envelope which had been lying on the
workbench. She slit it open with her thumb and unfolded the
contents. She read the letter quietly to herself before passing it
to Ralph.

April Cottage
Little Haddon
Herts

My dear Marnie,

By now you must be wondering what you have let
yourself in for. Let me congratulate you on having
succeeded thus far. I trust that at this stage you will not
think of going back on your undertaking to carry out
this, my last wish.

I owe you an explanation for the strange assortment of
items that you have discovered in my box of mementoes.
When I assembled them I was faced with the problem of

what should become of them, if anything at all, when I am no more. For some time I wondered if they were best destroyed and this chapter of my life forgotten, but in the end I found I could not just allow things to be left unsaid. With that in mind my thoughts turned to you. Although we have spent little time together, I knew I could depend on you to do the right thing. I entrust everything to your judgment.

Please let me explain. Try not to judge me too harshly, if you can.

Ralph turned to the second page and looked across at Marnie. She was staring into her coffee cup.

'She's certainly got me wondering what on Earth she's done to warrant all this secrecy,' Ralph said.

'And that letter's only part of the answer, Ralph. There's more to come before her box of mementoes gives up its secrets.'

Shaking his head, Ralph turned to the second page.

You might remember that I visited you at your home a couple of years ago when an archaeological dig was in progress. I told you then that I had been at Glebe Farm myself during the war. Our narrowboat crew was held up waiting for spare parts to arrive for our engine. Like your Anne with an 'e' I too stayed in the attic over what is now your office. What I did not tell you was that I did not stay there alone. The two other girls took the opportunity to go on leave and return to their families. I was unmarried and unattached, so I volunteered to stay and wait for the mechanic to come and repair the engine.

During my stay something rather remarkable happened, something that I have never forgotten and which I thought

I would take unspoken to my grave. Now that that time is approaching, I have had a change of heart. I feel a need to bring into the open, at least as far as you are concerned, my account of what took place at Glebe Farm all those years ago. I think the best way to do this is to share with you the notes I made back then. Instead of casting them into the fire, I am confiding in you, happy in the knowledge that you will act for the best.

There may be more to this story than meets the eye, and much will depend on how far you are able to pursue it. I am beyond its reach now, and I can only refer you to the notes which are my account of events from those troubled times. Make of them what you will, my dear, and try not to think too unkindly of me. I pass the tiller to you now, from one 'Idle Woman' to another.

With fond regards,

Iris

Ralph folded the two pages together and slipped them back into the envelope. He laid it on the table and tapped it twice thoughtfully with a fingertip. 'More delving ahead,' he murmured. He looked across at Marnie. 'Have you started reading her notebook?'

Marnie shook her head and said nothing. Ralph stood and lit the gas under the kettle on the hob.

'Marnie, I know it's easy to say, but try not to let this get under your skin.'

Marnie sighed. 'I am trying, but we've got so much going on in our own lives at the moment … not to mention the small matter of our normal workload. And now this …'

'You know, I think a glass of cognac with our coffee wouldn't go amiss. What d'you say, Marnie?'

'Definitely.' She rose from her seat and cleared the plates from the table.

Ralph occupied himself with the coffee, the cafetière and the brandy glasses. Reaching into the fridge for a carton of cream, he was surprised to hear faint laughter from Marnie.

'What are you laughing at?' he asked.

'You,' Marnie said.

'*Me?*'

Marnie stepped towards him and put her arms over his shoulders. She was smiling.

'Well, thank God for that,' Ralph said. 'I thought for a minute you were falling into the slough of despond.'

'I was.' Marnie pulled him towards her and kissed him lightly on the lips. She released him from her grasp. 'Then the sight of those glasses brought me back to our life. Only you would have thought to bring crystal cognac glasses onto a narrowboat.' She eyed the bottle of Courvoisier VSOP that he had already placed on the workbench. 'I wouldn't be surprised if you'd brought a packet of gold-tipped Russian Sobranies and an ivory cigarette holder.'

'Mock not,' Ralph said, pretending indignation. 'And pray step aside while I fetch my velvet smoking jacket from the boudoir.'

Marnie laughed out loud. 'The *boudoir*! I hadn't noticed we had one until now.'

Ralph scooped coffee into the jug. Like Marnie, he was grinning. He was also relieved. They resumed their seats once the coffee had brewed and raised their glasses of cognac to each other across the table. Sitting in comfortable safari chairs, they fell silent for a few moments before Marnie spoke.

'We'll be going through Denham Deep Lock first thing tomorrow, then they're fairly evenly spaced all the way to the Tring summit.'

Ralph took another sip of brandy and set the glass down. 'So if I deal with the locks, it should give you some space to read Iris's notes. Is that what you're thinking?'

'Would that be all right with you, Ralph?'

'Sure. We should make pretty good time, probably as far as Kings Langley, and we're not under any pressure.'

'No, indeed.' Marnie stared into her brandy glass. 'No pressure.'

Chapter 15

It was Saturday. The morning was cool and still as Marnie pushed *Sally Ann*'s bows away from the bank and walked back to step up onto the stern deck. Ralph pressed on the accelerator, the water churned around the stern, and they were underway. As usual when travelling, they saved their second mug of breakfast coffee for the first stint of the journey.

On the previous evening Marnie had phoned Anne to check on Glebe Farm. There was nothing of importance to report; Anne and Donovan were both engrossed in their assignments, and there had been no further messages from Randall Hughes concerning Sylvia. Nor were there any developments in the media concerning the *Stony Stratford Killer*. Marnie told Anne about Iris's notebooks and promised to let her have more details as soon as she could.

Ralph held *Sally Ann* comfortably in mid-channel, with one hand resting on the tiller and the other holding his coffee-mug. The engine was clanking contentedly beneath his feet, and faint puffs of grey smoke were emanating from the exhaust. For these first minutes Marnie took her place beside Ralph with her coffee-mug, one hand resting lightly on top of his on the tiller. Soon the black and white balance beams of Denham Deep Lock came into view. Marnie finished her coffee, ready to take over the steering from Ralph. She eased the boat towards the towpath and throttled back, bringing *Sally Ann* almost to a halt. Ralph was already clutching the windlass as he leapt ashore and set off at a brisk pace to lock through.

They were in luck. The lock was set in their favour. Ralph only had to climb the steps and swing open one gate, already hanging ajar, to allow Marnie to enter the deep chamber. She advanced slowly in and stopped the boat using reverse gear, with clear water in front and behind. Ralph pushed the gate closed and jogged forward to open the paddles to fill the lock.

Denham Deep Lock had a fall as great as any on the entire canal network, at just over eleven feet. Ralph swung the windlass steadily, and the water began cascading in. Staring down at *Sally Ann* in the chamber, he had the strangest sensation. It was as if Marnie, like Iris Winterburn before her, was lying in her grave. He turned quickly to gaze out over the open land around them so that Marnie wouldn't see his expression, but he knew from hers that she had shared the same thought.

Once clear of the lock, Marnie kept the boat close to the bank so that Ralph could close the gate and step onto the stern deck. He smiled as he hopped up and took over the tiller.

'That was a spot of luck, having the lock in our favour like that,' he said cheerfully.

'I suppose it was.' Marnie's tone was flat. 'I'll, er ... I'll go and get Iris's notebook. I ought to make a start on it. God knows what I'm going to find.'

'Should be interesting.' Ralph hoped he sounded encouraging.

Marnie smiled as best she could and went down into the cabin, taking the empty coffee-mugs with her.

****

Initially the notes were something of an anti-climax and made Marnie wonder why she had been so apprehensive about reading them. The first several pages contained only details of destinations and cargoes, a kind of running account of the missions of the narrowboat pair: the motor *Sirius* and the butty, *Proserpina*. Occasionally names were mentioned: Martha and Alex, no doubt short for Alexandra. These must have been the two other members of the crew. It was all so mundane and workaday that Marnie became absorbed by the technical details of running a pair of working boats in the 1940s. She forgot her anxiety.

'Lock ahead!' Ralph called down into the cabin.

Marnie went up on deck and looked forward. 'Which is this one?' she asked.

'I think it's Wide Water,' Ralph said. 'It's another fairly deep one. If we're lucky it'll be set in our favour again.'

He was right and they were. Marnie took over the tiller while he set off along the towpath. She carried on reading Iris's notes, keeping one eye open for Ralph's signal to advance. To Marnie's surprise, she found the next entries almost amusing. She could at least sympathise with the problems encountered by the three young women. First they had to replace a dead battery – heavy and in an awkward location that gave Martha a crick in the neck – then they had a rope attached round the propeller, which refused to budge until Alex hung over the end with their best sharp kitchen knife. She eventually succeeded in cutting through the rope, only to lose the knife when it slipped from her wet greasy hand.

Marnie was thinking that not much in boating had changed, when she heard Ralph's call and spotted him waving. She returned to her reading when she had safely installed *Sally Ann* in the lock chamber.

The next escapade for the women (Iris routinely referred to them as 'girls') came when ominous black smoke began belching from the exhaust on *Sirius*. The engine began knocking loudly, and it was clear to the *girls* that they had a major problem. It was at the moment when Marnie realised that Iris's pair of boats were by now in Northamptonshire, that the lock gate in front of her swung open and she had to turn her attention back to running *Sally Ann* in the present.

'How's it going?' Ralph asked as he came on board.

'Not bad,' said Marnie. 'At least, it's reminiscent of books I've read before about the so-called *Idle Women*.'

'Good, so nothing too scary,' Ralph added.

Marnie turned to look away as her smile faded, and she wondered what might be in store for her. In her head she heard Iris's voice coming from afar, reading her last letter from beyond the grave: try not to think too unkindly of me. Marnie cleared her throat and tried to sound matter-of-fact as she turned back to Ralph.

'How far to the next lock?'

'It's Black Jack's Lock coming up next. I think you've got about twenty minutes of peace and quiet.'

Marnie settled on the gas bottle container lid and read on. Alex, who seemed to be the senior member of the crew, took the decision to stop the boats out in the countryside where she saw two men, possibly farm workers. They had just dragged out of the canal a sheep that had somehow managed to fall in. It lumbered away, spraying water in its wake.

Alex asked where they were. The answer: Knightly St John. She asked if there was a telephone in the village. Yes, there was. She wondered if she might be able to make an emergency call from it. Yes, she probably could. She asked where it was and was directed to the post office some way away in the high street. The post office contained the local exchange.

Alex had indeed made her call because Iris's next entry described her indignation at being patronised by a mechanic at the nearest boatyard. Without even seeing the boat, he gave the opinion that the problem was no doubt nothing more than an air-lock in the feed-pipe. If they'd checked the system properly the problem would never have arisen. He turned up the next day and was nonplussed to discover that the fault was in fact a split nozzle in one of the fuel injectors, a fault impossible to predict. He grudgingly admitted that Alex had taken a wise decision to stop the boats immediately. The consequences could otherwise have been dire.

As things stood, they would face a wait of several days before the spare part could be obtained. There was nothing for it but to remain in situ until the repair could be effected. After some discussion it was agreed that Alex and Martha would return to their families, while Iris – 'unmarried and unattached' – would stay with the boats. The neighbouring farmer, a Mr Fletcher, offered Iris modest accommodation in a barn. It would be simple and basic, but it was larger than the tiny cabin on the butty, it had a supply of clean fresh water and – its greatest advantage – it did not smell of diesel.

'Lock ahead!' Ralph said.

Marnie was getting to her feet when something on the page caught her eye. She paused just long enough to read the entry.

It was a small stone barn close to the farmhouse, and access to the loft was by way of a ladder attached to the wall. The name of the place was Glebe Farm.

****

Black Jack's Lock was less than four feet deep, and Marnie recalled that it was named after a man in distant times who had badly mistreated his donkey. Or was that in fact the story? No matter. She had enough of a mystery on her hands with the events described in Iris's notes. This was the first lock of the day that was set against them, and she had to wait while Ralph emptied it before she could take *Sally Ann* forward. She used the time to continue her reading.

As she flicked through to find her place in the notebook, Marnie prepared herself for something that Iris had mentioned in her letter.

And there it was.

"During my stay something rather remarkable happened, something that I have never forgotten and which I thought I would take unspoken to my grave."

At this point Iris's handwriting changed. Whereas before it had been neat and well-rounded, now it showed signs of haste. This was no longer the careful account of each day, written at leisure in the evening after a quiet supper. Marnie now faced rushed jottings, almost a scrawl, in a frantic dash to record what was happening, while anxious to be doing other things. The war had come to Glebe Farm in the hitherto peaceful village of Knightly St John.

Iris's first inkling of high drama came in the still hour before dawn. She was woken by the sound of an explosion, at least that was her first impression. Until that moment, she and her crew-mates working their pair of boats were almost unaware of the war; it had little impact on their lives. They had no radio, saw no newspapers. The other boat people were similarly cut off from the outside world, and the majority of them were in any case illiterate. Iris, Alex and Martha heard occasional remarks about faraway battles, U-boat action and bombing raids, but for them it all seemed remote and intangible.

141

Iris quickly threw on some clothes, slid down the wall-ladder and rushed out into the pre-dawn gloom. She raced through the spinney between the farm buildings and the waterway and was confronted by the strangest sight. The accommodation bridge a short distance along the canal was invisible behind an enormous light-coloured shroud. Iris advanced, this time more cautiously, to examine it. Peering from behind a tree at the edge of the spinney, she saw that the shroud seemed to be a parachute. She recognised it as such from newsreels she had seen in cinemas. Then she heard a sound. She recoiled, thinking it might have been a growl. There it was again, and she knew at once what she'd heard. It was a groan.

Someone was on the bridge! It sounded like a man, and he was evidently in pain. Overcome with curiosity, Iris crept forward, wishing she'd had the presence of mind to bring a torch. That thought had barely occurred to her when she stumbled on the rough surface and pitched forward, breaking her fall painfully, extending her hands before her, grazing them on sharp gravel. She gasped, convinced that the sound must have been audible on the Isle of Skye! As she staggered to her feet, another sound reached her ears. It was a metallic click followed by a gruff voice, not much louder than a whisper.

'Who is there?'

The tone was undoubtedly hostile. As her eyes adjusted to the dim light, Iris saw a man in some sort of uniform reclining on the ground, propped against the parapet wall, his features strained. Most importantly, she saw that he was pointing a pistol directly at her.

Somewhere in the background Marnie heard a voice. With a jolt she realised that Ralph was calling her. She waved back in reply, pulled the gear lever towards her and pressed down on the accelerator. *Sally Ann* made smooth progress towards the beckoning lock gate that Ralph was holding open.

Inside the lock, Marnie held the boat steady in the middle of the chamber while Ralph pushed the gate shut behind her.

'You okay?' he asked as he headed for the paddles at the upper level. Marnie gave a thumbs-up. Ralph pointed at the notebook in Marnie's hand. 'Anything happening, anything of interest?'

'Yes, I think so.'

It took only a few minutes for the lock to fill, and Marnie was now anxious to get back to her reading. Nothing that she'd read so far was likely to make her think 'too unkindly' of Iris. But, no doubt, there was more to come. Probably much more.

As the next lock was less than half a mile ahead, Ralph opted to walk on to prepare it. Marnie was confident that she could steer the boat and read at the same time, so she was keen to get back to Iris's story, her encounter with the mysterious uninvited visitor who had literally dropped in on her. But no. The narrative seemed to have come almost to a halt. Only a few sketchy notes covered the next page.

Franz – can't work out his surname

Broken ribs?

No medical help

Disturbed nights

He says fon not von

Garbled story

'Mind your wash!' an angry cry rang out.

Marnie's head snapped up; she was suddenly jerked back to the present. She had come upon a moored boat and failed to slow down. The owner was leaning out of a window, glaring at her. Marnie hastily grabbed the accelerator to reduce speed and raised a hand in apology.

'Very sorry,' she called across, hoping he could hear her over the rumble of the engine.

A short way ahead, the canal curved to the right. With the offended boat tied up on the towpath side to her left, Marnie kept to mid-channel, the engine now barely idling. At that moment the bows of another craft came into view, rounding the curve and heading towards her. It was a beautiful seventy-footer painted a gleaming dark blue with shining brass fittings. The steerer was confronted by a moored boat on his right and *Sally Ann* straight ahead. Running at dead slow, Marnie squeezed *Sally Ann* hard over to the offside to leave space for the oncoming boat down the middle, praying that she had sufficient depth of water to keep from running aground. The manoeuvre worked. The steerer kept his head and guided his boat into the clear water. As he drew near Marnie caught sight of the boat's name: *Mary Jennifer*. Her skipper raised a hand to Marnie and called out.

'Brilliant! Well done! Thank you.'

Marnie smiled back. She had gone from zero to hero in the space of three boat-lengths and felt that she had partly redeemed herself as a boatwoman. Then she thought back to Iris and Alex and Martha in wartime, navigating a fully-laden pair of seventy-foot narrowboats with a cargo of up to fifty-five tonnes, day and night in all weathers. *Idle women*, she thought – huh!

And there was Ralph two hundred yards ahead, waving her on. It was instant karma. Marnie's adept handling of *Sally Ann* had been rewarded. The next lock had been left ready for her by *Mary Jennifer*, and she glided in with ease and precision. Ralph began swinging the windlass, leaving Marnie free to return to Iris's notes, such as they now were. But in fact something had changed. On the next page Iris's account of events had returned to its former style. The handwriting was clear and intelligible; there were whole sentences. Iris was back to writing at leisure.

It transpired that her unexpected visitor was no less than a German airman, an officer of the *Luftwaffe*. The noise that had disturbed her sleep in the early hours of the morning had not been a bomb, but his aircraft crashing in a field between Knightly St John and the village of Hanford, a few miles up the canal. The story of how he came to be flying in that area would not be explained until later.

Sally Ann was now rising in the chamber, and Marnie made sure she kept at least part of her attention on locking through. She wanted no more lapses, no more problems; skippering a fourteen-tonne boat demanded concentration. Ralph was already standing by the top balance beam. As soon as the water in the lock matched the outside level, he pushed the gate open, and Marnie drove through. She held the boat close in to the bank while Ralph closed the gate, but instead of hopping aboard he chose to continue ahead on foot to Springwell Lock. It was a mile or so away, and he relished a good brisk walk, knowing he could be there comfortably before *Sally Ann*. This gave Marnie the chance to resume her reading. She had to admit she had become intrigued by the unexpected direction of Iris's *notes in time of war*.

Chapter 16

Marnie steered a steady course down the middle of the canal. There were no moored craft in sight, only Ralph striding along some way ahead, leaving her behind. She raised the notebook and read on.

Franz is managing to sleep now, thank goodness. At first he seemed very mistrustful, but now I think he knows he is safe in my care. I asked him to write his name for me. It is rather grand. He is Franz von Weidlingen and he pronounces the middle word like fon. He has told me he comes from a small town not far from Leipzig and his family are Lutherans.

I think he broke some ribs when he parachuted down from his plane and collided hard with the bridge over the canal. I have not told him I learnt some German at school. I'm rather embarrassed by my pronunciation, and he speaks quite good English without a strong accent.

Franz has been here for two days now and so far there is no sign of the mechanic or the new engine parts. I don't know what I would do if he suddenly arrived and repaired the engine. A and M and I would have to be on our way with the boats, but I could not abandon Franz and just leave him here. What would become of him? I know he is the Enemy but he is after all an injured man. He is very nervous and keeps his pistol beside the bed at all times.

It was a painful struggle for Franz to mount the ladder to the loft, but he gritted his teeth and persevered. I bundled the parachute together and dragged it up with strenuous efforts before anyone saw it. At least I hope so.

Franz seems a bit better this morning after sleeping for several hours. He has told me a remarkable story. He is an 'Oberstleutnant' in the Luftwaffe. I think that is quite senior. Franz said it was like a Wing Commander in the RAF. I asked him if he was on a bombing raid and if he knew what had become of his crew. He said no. He was flying a fighter plane by himself with extra fuel tanks. He had been hit by Flak (I think that is like Ack-Ack) and crashed when the tanks leaked and he ran out of fuel. I asked tactfully if he could say where he was going. His reply astonished me.

At that point there was a kink in the canal, and Ralph was nowhere in sight. Marnie had to set aside the notebook and focus on steering. On a short straight run she saw Ralph waving again up ahead, standing by the lock, and was glad that no other boat was waiting to lock through with her. The last thing she wanted was to have to make polite conversation with another crew. It seemed that once again *Mary Jennifer* had left the lock ready for her.

After locking through, Ralph suggested the same routine as before. Marnie knew he enjoyed walking in the country, and guessed he was making space for her to read Iris's notes. She brought *Sally Ann* up to cruising speed and read on.

On the third day after his arrival, Franz told me the reason for his dangerous journey to England. He made me promise never to reveal his secret to anyone and I gave him my word. I could scarcely believe what he told me.

He had come to try to rescue Rudolf Hess!

The mission was given to him by Hitler himself. That odious man wanted Hess back safe and sound in Berlin.

Hess had been Hitler's deputy before he flew to England two years earlier. (I had no idea about this at all.) The British had captured him, and German spies believed he was being held under arrest in a country mansion near Rugby. Now Hitler wants the return of his 'loyal and reliable' deputy. Hitler had no faith in Goering, Franz said, regarding him as a 'pompous fool of limited intelligence'.

All of this was news to me. I had no idea about goings-on in Berlin, so I did not doubt what Franz told me. Why would I?

On his fourth day (still no word from the mechanic) Franz said he was still in some discomfort but not in great pain. I asked him what he was planning to do. At first he was reluctant to explain things, but then he relented. He was aiming to locate the mansion in Warwickshire where they believed Hess was being held. He could not explain to me how the rescue would be carried out. They would take a car and drive to an airfield where they would try to steal an aircraft. They were both expert pilots and planned to fly as low as possible to avoid radar and cross the Channel to France or Belgium. It was an audacious plan! I queried it on the grounds that Franz was wearing Luftwaffe uniform. How could he hope to carry out his mission when he was so conspicuous? He said he had brought civilian clothes with him but they were lost when his aeroplane crashed.

I told Franz that I realised that having told me what he planned, I was a threat to him and he could not allow me to live. He laughed and said I was a silly girl. He also said I

148

was very pretty and he had become fond of me as well as grateful. The truth is, I not only found Franz very handsome, but I felt that he was an honourable man, doing his duty as he saw it. Nothing would ever lead me to betray him. He said he believed me and added that he was falling in love with me.

Bloody hell! Marnie was startled by Iris's admission. She tried hard to imagine her as a young woman. Iris was certainly quite striking even as an elderly lady. Yes, it was understandable that a man would have found the young Iris attractive. Marnie was shaking her head with bewilderment when she spotted Ralph at the next lock. A sudden feeling of guilt struck her. He had done all the work that morning, leaving her free to read and drive the boat. The lock was deeper than most of the others, so Marnie threw Ralph a rope to hold *Sally Ann* steady in the chamber as it filled. She went below to make coffee. Ralph joined her on the stern deck for the next pound, and they cruised together through attractive rolling countryside.

'Are the notes enlightening?' Ralph asked. 'Interesting?'

'Certainly nothing I expected. Do you remember she told us once that she had memories of Glebe Farm from staying in the barn in the war when her engine broke down?'

'Vaguely. Was that in Anne's attic room?'

'That's right, but I think you'd better read her account for yourself.'

Ralph grinned. 'Not frolics in the hayloft, was it? I can't imagine Iris Winterburn getting up to hanky-panky with the farm lads.'

'I haven't got to that bit yet, but in a way you may not be too wide of the mark.'

'Are you serious, Marnie?'

'I think it's possible, but not involving farm lads, as such.'

'*As such*? What does that mean?'

'We'll both have to wait and see. Oh look. There's a supermarket on the horizon. Do we need anything?'

149

'Not really. We're pretty well stocked up for the whole journey. Perhaps we can have a short break for lunch in Cassiobury Park. In the meantime you can get on with your reading while I deal with the locks.'

'Okay by me, Ralph, but don't get too tired out. All this talk of frolics and hanky-panky might be giving me ideas.'

Ralph laughed and hopped onto the bank. Marnie thought she noticed a spring in his step as he advanced on the lock, swinging his windlass.

****

Despite Ralph's suggestion, Marnie decided not to spend the afternoon reading Iris's notebook. She needed time to digest what she had already learnt. It had certainly not been anything she'd imagined. She realised she knew very little about Rudolf Hess, and could recall only that he spent the rest of his life after the war in Spandau prison in Berlin. So had Franz rescued him and taken him back to Germany after all? Was this one of the best-kept secrets of the war? Marnie would read on in the hope of finding out, but for now she wanted nothing more than to cruise along peacefully and spend time with Ralph, enjoying the pleasant weather and the fresh air.

They had made good time that day and exceeded their target of reaching Kings Langley. Too fatigued to tackle the succession of Apsley Locks, they tied up for the evening after cruising for over eight hours, not counting their lunch break. While Ralph laid the table in the saloon, Marnie rang home.

It was more or less the same story as on the previous evening. Anne had nothing of importance to report. No one had yet been apprehended for the Stony Stratford Murder, and there had been no further word from Randall about Sylvia in the hostel. All was calm, and the two students were pressing on with their college projects.

'Okay then, I'll phone again tomorrow –'

'Hey, hold on a mo,' said Anne. 'You haven't told me about Miss Winterburn's diary.'

'Diary?' Marnie repeated.

'That's what it is, isn't it?' Marnie hesitated. Anne continued. 'You're not going to say you can't speak about it because it's secret or something, are you? My tongue's hanging out!'

Marnie laughed. 'Fair enough. But the thing is ... I haven't got through all of it yet, and I'd really rather you read it for yourself.'

'Great! But can you at least give me something to go on for now.'

Marnie thought about this, but short of giving a summary of the narrative up that point, she couldn't think of an easy way to précis Iris's story.

'Are you still there, Marnie?'

'Yes, but ... I don't know ... it's sort of complicated. But I will say this, I think I might need some help from Donovan to understand what was going on.'

'Donovan?' Anne exclaimed. 'What's he got to do with ... Oh, hang on. You mean there's a connection between Miss Winterburn and the skeleton in the garden?'

Marnie's cheeks tingled. 'Oh my God ...'

'What is it, Marnie?'

'Of course ...'

Anne said, 'You don't really mean ... What do you mean?'

'Not sure. Look, let's just leave it for now. I want to get to the end of her notes before I say anything else. Then you can read them.'

'And Donovan too?'

'Oh yes, and Donovan too. Definitely.'

They ended the call as Ralph was taking a quiche lorraine out of the oven. 'D'you want to slice the quiche while I see to the wine?' He set it down on the table next to the salad. 'And what was that about Donovan?'

'It's this thing about the German airman in Iris's notes – her *diary*, as Anne calls it – and an apparent connection with Rudolf Hess. I'm guessing that you and Donovan will know more about that than I do.'

'About Hess?' Ralph said, taking a bottle of wine from the fridge. 'My knowledge is rather sketchy.'

151

'Donovan's pretty clued-up about that period, isn't he?'

'True,' said Ralph, undoing the wire cage round the cork. 'There's also a modern European historian I know at Balliol who'd be able to cast light on things.'

Marnie was looking troubled. 'Anne said something that's surprised me. I hadn't thought of it, but she wondered if Iris's story might be connected with the skeleton in the garden.'

Ralph stared at Marnie. 'Is that what you're thinking?'

'I don't know what to think. I'd like to get back to her notes, but not tonight. I've had enough for one day.' Marnie refocused on what Ralph was doing. 'Is that champagne you're opening?'

'No, it's a *Crémant de Limoux*. Experts say it's the area where French sparkling wine began.'

Marnie looked sceptical. 'And you're opening it on a Saturday night in honour of a shop-bought quiche?'

'Not actually,' Ralph said with a mysterious air.

Marnie detected a twinkle in his eye. 'What then?' she said.

'It's rather in honour of something that's been on my mind for much of today, since we both spoke about it.'

'What ... Iris and the Luftwaffe connection?' Marnie suggested, doubtfully.

Ralph popped the cork and smiled at Marnie. 'No. The wine is really in honour of ... what did we call it? ... ah yes, frolics and hanky-panky. May I fill your glass?'

Chapter 17

A quiet Sunday morning. It was always quiet in Anne's attic room, no matter what the weather. The walls were thick, built of solid stone, while the roof had been insulated to Scandinavian standards. Even heavy rain falling was scarcely to be heard. But on that Sunday morning there was no rain; no wind stirred the treetops in the spinney. The only window was a thin double-glazed slit in one end gable through which daylight was penetrating, splashing sunshine over the Oriental rugs covering the floor.

Anne stretched and yawned. She whispered, 'Donovan, are you awake?'

From beside her in bed came a muted sound. 'Mm ...' Definitely a sign of life.

'I've been thinking,' Anne continued quietly.

Donovan squinted one-eyed at the bedside clock. 'Already?'

'D'you feel like going over to Brackley to see Sylvia today?'

Donovan burrowed under the duvet. A muffled sound rose from the depths which Anne interpreted as agreement. With a plan now in place, she slid out of bed and headed for the shower.

****

Sunday was the third day of the voyage of *Sally Ann* on the Grand Union Canal from Little Venice to Knightly St John. After breakfast Marnie and Ralph consulted the cruising guide. They estimated that if they navigated for two full days of eight or so hours each, they should make it back to base some time on Tuesday afternoon. Ralph would carry on working the locks, while Marnie managed the boat.

They slipped their mooring soon after eight o'clock and tackled the Apsley Locks, pausing to take on water after the second. This would be a gruelling day as they made the steady climb up to Cowroast Lock at the start of the Tring summit, but Ralph enjoyed the activity, and he wanted to give Marnie the time and space to finish reading Iris's notebook. In the pounds north of Berkhamsted, in the run-up to Cowroast, Marnie settled into her reading.

In the days since Franz dropped into my life, there is still no word from the mechanic. I'm worried that he might just suddenly turn up with the spare part for the engine and find Franz here with me. I've been able to keep him hidden up in my loft and I've so far been able to smuggle food out for him from my meals in the farmhouse. Even so, we both spend much of our time together feeling hunger pangs. I occasionally raid the apple store and so far no one from the farm seems to have noticed.

Franz thanks me every day for taking care of him. He asks me lots of questions about where we are and what is happening in the war. I answer as best I can from what is reported in Mr Fletcher's newspaper. Franz had always known that he would have to abandon his fighter plane as he would never have enough fuel to make it back to the Continent. He is very brave to have undertaken this mission of mercy. It was believed by the OKW (I think that is the High Command)that the British would torture Hess to extract secrets from him. I was shocked to hear that, but Franz tells me such procedures are carried out over long periods of time and the people involved are very subtle. I worry that they might mistreat Franz, but until I met him I never thought the British would use torture. I still can't believe it.

Another day has passed since my last entry. No mechanic. We are still hungry most of the time. It's good that Franz sleeps quite a lot. His pain is gradually subsiding. I visit the boats each day to make sure that no one is stealing the cargo. Fifty tons of coal would be worth having for the black market!

A strange thing happened this morning. I was rummaging for clean clothes in Franz's kitbag and I found his pistol. He no longer keeps it by the bed. It was underneath the clothes on top of an envelope which I suppose contains his orders. He woke up and when he saw what I was doing he said he was prepared to defend himself in case he was in danger of being captured before he could complete his mission. I said I thought there was more risk if he was wearing uniform. His reply was quite chilling. He said if he was cornered he was certain to die and he would rather die fighting in uniform than wear civilian clothes and be hanged as a spy.

I asked Franz about his life in Germany. He told me he had no family as both his parents were dead. His father was killed in the Great War while serving in Belgium. His mother had died of influenza in 1919. He had a married sister who lived with her children in a small town in the country near Frankfurt. Her husband was in the army in Italy but they have had no news of him for almost a year. I asked tentatively if he was married. He said he had never met the right girl and then he added – until now perhaps.

Still no news of the new parts for the engine. I am trying to pluck up courage to tell Franz that I have learnt some German. I know it's silly, but the right moment never seems to come. He is a very bright person and his English is so good it would put my elementary German to shame. I value our moments of tenderness, sharing the loft together, and I do not want to cause any complications.

Marnie was reading Iris's notes in snatches between locks as they climbed steadily up into the Chiltern Hills. In the times that she couldn't devote to the notebook, she reflected on what she was learning about the woman who had entrusted her with the *special task*. Even now she wasn't clear as to what that task involved. Any diary was presumably private, and some could even be secret, but that was surely no reason for all the legal rigmarole of a confidentiality agreement. No doubt more would be revealed as she read on.

It was now evident that Iris and Franz had become lovers. What else could be inferred from 'our moments of tenderness'? They were after all living together in close proximity and found each other attractive. Iris clearly admired Franz for undertaking a highly dangerous operation as a 'mission of mercy'. Yes, Iris had a German lover – an enemy combatant, no less – but all these years later that could surely not be a subject for secrecy. Marnie was still as puzzled as ever.

Of one thing she was certain: Ralph had remarkable stamina. He seemed able to walk for miles and operate the lock machinery without breaking into a sweat. On the other hand, she was sure he must be fretting at not being able to work, and probably aching to return to his research. That thought drew her back to Anne and Donovan. She wondered how they were spending Sunday and hoped they were enjoying their own 'moments of tenderness' together.

****

'What'll it be?' Anne asked. 'Picnic or pub lunch?'

They were clearing away after breakfast in the farmhouse. Donovan straightened up from putting crockery in the dishwasher and considered the question.

'Can't think of anywhere to picnic in the Brackley area,' he said.

Anne looked thoughtful. 'Nor can I, really. So, pub lunch?'

Donovan agreed. 'Though don't you think we first ought to check with Randall about the best time to visit Sylvia?'

Anne picked up her mobile and pressed buttons. Randall answered promptly, and Anne explained what she and Donovan had in mind.

'Not a problem,' Randall said. 'I won't be there, of course. It being Sunday, I've got a full schedule.'

'Hope I'm not holding you up,' said Anne.

'It's fine. I'm just getting ready to take matins and then I have a baptism.'

'A busy day. Can I just ask how Sylvia's getting on?'

'You'll soon see for yourselves. Oh, it occurs to me I should give you the entry code for the front door. It's one-six-four-eight. Got it?'

'Sixteen forty-eight. Is it significant ... something to do with the Civil War?'

Donovan's head snapped round. 'Treaty of Westphalia,' he said.

Before Randall could reply, Anne repeated the name, quoting Donovan.

'Good heavens, he's probably right,' said Randall. 'You don't think it's too obvious, do you?'

Anne giggled. 'I think you're fairly safe there.'

'Though that isn't the reason I chose those numbers.'

'No?'

'Not at all.' He laughed. 'I wonder if your Cleverclogs boyfriend can work out the real reason.'

Anne was still chuckling after they disconnected. 'Only Randall would think that date might be too obvious.'

'Or Ralph,' said Donovan.

'Yes, or Ralph. Anyway, Cleverclogs, how did you recognise it so easily?'

Donovan shrugged. 'Any German schoolboy could tell you the date of the end of the Thirty Years War.'

'Randall says that isn't why he chose those numbers. Any ideas?'

Donovan concentrated hard then pulled out his mobile and looked at the keypad. A smile spread slowly across his face.

'You're looking terribly smug,' said Anne.

****

For the next few hours the locks followed one after another in unremitting succession, and each time Marnie returned to Iris's narrative she spotted Ralph in the near distance signalling to her to come forward. It was a frustrating morning, though they made steady progress.

While waiting in a lock chamber, Marnie dashed below and dug a pizza out of the fridge. She had it unwrapped and stowed in the oven before *Sally Ann* had risen to the next level. Ralph had been holding the boat steady on a rope and, when Marnie appeared on deck, he threw the rope onto the roof and pushed the gate open for her.

He called across. 'One more lock before we eat?'

Marnie raised a thumb and called out, 'Perfect timing for pizza.'

Ralph closed the gate. He easily out-accelerated the boat and was in position with the next gate open as Marnie lined up to enter the lock. They made a good team, and Marnie found herself wondering if Iris and Franz would have been a good partnership in life. She was becoming desperate to know how their story ended, though she knew not to expect a happy outcome.

When they resumed their journey after lunch Marnie made a determined effort to read the notes in what she thought of as bite-sized chunks.

****

Franz has had a slight relapse today. He complained of a headache and put it down to inactivity. I asked Mrs Fletcher in the farm if she had an aspirin. She found some and gave me a glass of water to take one. I told her I would take it a little later if my head got worse. I don't like being deceitful but I have to be so careful about Franz.

In the afternoon we heard gunfire nearby. Franz became quite agitated and went for his pistol. I explained that lots of farmers hunted rabbits and game birds for

158

food and he calmed down. He said it was the same in Germany. Nobody had enough to eat. The Germans also had shortages and rationing like us.

I wish we could go for a walk to give him some fresh air, but in his Luftwaffe uniform that would be impossible. We might try to go outside for a short time after dark. He will struggle to go down the wall-ladder with his injuries. A worse problem could be the sliding doors to the barn – they make a loud scraping noise when they are pulled open.

There were a few reasonable pounds before *Sally Ann* reached Cowroast Lock, and Marnie was able to read a few more of her 'chunks'.

I'm worried about Franz. His headache is persisting and I think he may have a slight fever. Mrs Fletcher told me she had had a letter from the boatyard asking her to let me know that our spare parts were still delayed. There was no explanation, but with the war going on all sorts of problems arise. I must say I am rather relieved as I could not leave Franz like this. I really don't know what will become of him after the engine is repaired and we have to set off. I have written to Alex and Martha to tell them about the delay. I don't want them turning up out of the blue.

More gunshots this afternoon, quite nearby. Franz was not bothered this time. I think he was feeling rather unwell and could not be roused to react like before.

Marnie was now also beginning to worry about Franz. She was saddened at the thought that his body had been lying in a shallow grave in her garden for so long, the man Iris had grown to love. Yet it was still unclear to her why all the secrecy surrounded these events after so many years had passed. No doubt all would be revealed in the fullness of time. She read on.

159

Franz is worse today. He clearly has a fever and I have been applying handkerchiefs soaked in water to his forehead. I folded a towel under his head so as not to wet the pillow. I'm so worried about him that I said I wanted to send for a doctor. He became alarmed at this and made me promise not to do it. I could see that the bruising on his chest was not as livid as it has been. He has slept for much of the day which is a blessing. I slipped out to spend some time on the boats, tidying and cleaning. Once we get underway and deliver our cargo they will both be covered in coal dust again, but I needed something to occupy me.

So that would be it, Marnie thought. Franz would succumb to illness, probably complications caused by his fractured ribs. But how did he come to be buried in the farmhouse garden? How could Iris possibly have got him down from the attic? Marnie mentally winced at the thought of Iris dragging his body to the hatch over the wall-ladder and tipping him through. She grimaced as she imagined the thud as his body struck the ground. How absolutely horrible to have to do something like that to her lover! Was that the secret Iris needed her to protect? Would Iris's actions have felt so abhorrent to her that she wanted to clear her conscience like a confession before she died?

I could not sleep last night. Franz was tossing and turning for hours. He was moaning much of the time with sudden exclamations. Some of the words he used – just a few – I managed to recognise, like Flugzeug, meaning aeroplane, Hilfe, meaning help, Benzin, meaning fuel or petrol. He fell into unconsciousness just before dawn. His breathing was ragged and uneven. I don't know what to do for the best. I took one of his shirts to Proserpina yesterday to wash it. I hung it up to dry in the cabin on Sirius and to my surprise it was almost dry when I went back this morning. I'm going to take other clothes from his bag to wash for him. The least I can do. Or perhaps the most.

The afternoon was a long relentless slog as *Sally Ann* negotiated a never-ending succession of locks. Once again Marnie admired Ralph for his dogged efforts to have each one prepared and ready. For her part, Marnie was now feeling increasingly troubled by the notebook. She was glad to put it aside; a sad end was imminently in prospect. In her mind she was comparing Iris with those countless women who remained unmarried – *spinsters*, as they were called in those days – for the rest of their lives after losing their men in the Great War.

****

In Brackley Anne easily found a parking space for the Mini, and she and Donovan walked the short distance along the street to Magdalene House. On their way there they had stopped at a supermarket in Buckingham and bought a bunch of flowers and a box of chocolates which Donovan was carrying. At the door they were confronted by the entrance keypad. Anne raised a finger towards the buttons and paused.

'What was that number again?' she said. Before Donovan could reply, she continued, 'Ah yes, one-six-four-eight, Treaty of Westphalia ... *so* obvious. The first thing *any* intruder would think of.'

'Except that isn't why he chose that combination, Anne.'

Anne shook her head. 'I don't get it.'

Donovan stared at her with a solemn expression then did something unexpected and out of character. He crossed himself.

'What was that for?' Anne asked.

'Look at the keypad,' Donovan said. 'Now press the buttons.'

Anne's mouth opened in wonder. 'One-six-four-eight. I made the sign of the cross!'

Donovan nodded. 'I think Randall's idea was that anyone entering Magdalene House would automatically be blessing it.'

Anne was smiling as the door clicked open and they entered the spacious hall. Sylvia was waiting for them. She rose from her chair and walked over to hug them.

'Nice of you to come,' she said. 'It's great to see you both.'

This was a revelation. Once again she was a different person, even compared with the improved Sylvia when Marnie had first brought her to Glebe Farm and offered her use of the shower. Gone was any last trace of the homeless woman, desperate and downtrodden, that they had first met. Now she radiated confidence and ease.

'We got you a few things, a sort of settling-in present,' said Donovan.

Sylvia beamed as she took the flowers and chocolates.

'I'd give you both another hug, but my hands are rather full. Let's go to my room.' She lowered her voice. 'There's a group of old vagrants ... oops, sorry ... I mean other guests in the lounge. They're playing whist and it can get rather rowdy.'

Sylvia's room looked fresh, clean and orderly. Anne had only briefly seen it just over a week ago. Now it seemed a little more cluttered than before. She caught sight of Sylvia's rucksack under the bed. It was hard to believe that until just recently, it had been her most precious possession.

'Are all the rooms in the house like this?' Donovan asked.

'More or less,' said Sylvia. 'This is really a room for two people, but Randall lets me have it to myself.'

'Is there more furniture here than when you arrived?' Anne said.

Sylvia pointed. 'Some. There's that wardrobe – just a single – and the bedside cabinet with a table lamp. Have a seat.'

Anne was offered the armchair while Donovan sat on the bed. Sylvia remained standing.

'I won't be a minute,' she said. 'I know where there's a vase for these lovely flowers.'

Anne and Donovan waited until Sylvia was out of the room and they could hear her walking down the corridor.

'Wow!' said Anne quietly. 'She's really come on, hasn't she?'

'She wasn't doing badly the last time we saw her,' Donovan observed.

'No. But now she's stepped up a gear again. You'd think she owned the place. And with the extra furniture there's no way this can revert to a shared room'

'Am I wrong, or do you think she's wearing new clothes?' Donovan said.

'I think you're right. I don't remember seeing that dress when she was at Glebe Farm. In fact I don't think she had any dresses back then, only two pairs of jeans and a few tops.'

'Are you sure about that, Anne?'

'Positive. I put her things in the washing machine and the tumble-dryer. Come to think of it, that looked rather a nice dress ... pretty good quality, I'd say.'

'Charity shop?' Donovan mused.

Anne nodded. 'Probably. I expect so.'

They heard footsteps in the corridor, and moments later the door opened. Sylvia came in holding a vase filled with their bouquet. She crossed the room and set it down on the bedside cabinet.

'Just what the room needed,' she said. 'They're absolutely beautiful. Thank you both very much.' She sat on the bed.

'So, how's it going?' Anne asked.

'Well, it's not quite home from home, but it's certainly an improvement on a hedge in the park.'

'You do seem in good spirits, Sylvia.'

'I am. Things are looking up. I'm really enjoying helping the others with their literacy and maths. They've started coming to me with other things, too. I've been helping them to fill in forms for benefits, and I even wrote a letter for one elderly lady – what you might call a *tramp* (not a word we use here, of course) – querying her pension.'

'You're becoming indispensable,' said Anne. 'I thought the people in the office helped with that sort of thing.'

Sylvia shrugged. 'There are only one or two of them, and they're part time, so they're glad of a bit of support. I don't mind helping out.'

For a moment it seemed as if Sylvia was going to say something else, but she held back, looking down at her hands folded in her lap. Anne and Donovan exchanged glances.

'Was there something else, Sylvia?' Anne asked.

Sylvia seemed to be struggling mentally with an issue. Eventually she said, 'It's just ...'

Anne sat forward in her chair. 'Anything you tell us will be private.'

'Totally,' Donovan added.

Sylvia looked up. 'Can I ask you something, Anne?'

'Of course you can. What is it?'

Sylvia took a breath. 'I'm still feeling a bit unsettled, to be honest.'

'That's the last thing I expected you to say. You've fitted in very well.'

'I have, really. The thing is ... I don't have any idea how long I can stay here. Do you know if Marnie has any plan for what I'm to do next?' She looked from Anne to Donovan. 'I can see from your expressions that you don't have a definite answer.'

Anne said, 'Well, Marnie and Ralph have a lot on their plates at the moment. It's complicated. I think Marnie just thought this would be a useful solution to your housing problem for the time being.'

'I know I can't stay here indefinitely. That wouldn't be right, anyway.'

Donovan joined in. 'I don't think Marnie has a master plan, as such. I had the impression she was taking things one day at a time.'

Anne added, 'I can see from your point of view, Sylvia, that's not very satisfactory. You must want stability in your life.'

'I do. Being here is great for the time being. Once I'm back on my feet I can start looking around for a job and finding a flat to rent.'

'Okay,' said Anne. 'Leave it with us and we'll talk to Marnie ... see if she has something else in mind. But in the meantime, can we tell her that you're happy here?'

Sylvia smiled. 'Do you need to ask?'

****

In the Mini on the way home Anne and Donovan were so lost in their thoughts that they'd forgotten about a pub lunch.

'Donovan, are you hungry?'

'Ah ... good point. We seem to have overlooked our own master plan. What d'you reckon?'

Anne tutted. 'Well, we can be home in under half an hour.'

'Homemade ploughman's?' Donovan suggested.

'Why not? It seems to be my staple diet these days.'

'Or we can –'

'No, that's fine. I've no objection. Ploughman's would be good.' Changing the subject, she said, 'What did you make of the new-look Sylvia?'

'She seemed quite contented, I thought, even if she feels unsettled.'

Anne said, 'And what about the dress and the general style? Did you notice she was wearing discreet make-up?'

'I can't say I notice that sort of thing, but I did notice her perfume.'

'I noticed that, too. She must have had an outing to a charity shop, like you thought.'

'A charity shop that sells perfume?' Donovan looked doubtful.

'Actually, I'm sure that was no cheap scent or the kind that people give to those shops as unwanted gifts.'

'So what are you thinking, Anne?'

165

'I'm not sure. Then there was that business about getting a flat to rent. She didn't make it sound like a pipe dream, more like a plan. I never thought she could afford to rent somewhere decent around here, and yet ...'

'What?'

'Two weeks ago Sylvia was begging on the street and sleeping under a hedge. Now she's getting back on her feet –'

'Thanks to your intervention and Marnie's,' Donovan interrupted.

'Yeah, okay. But she's become a different person. She's nicely dressed and turned out and making plans for the future.'

'Isn't that a success story?'

'I suppose so.'

'You have every right to be pleased, Anne, even proud. Remember two weeks ago someone was murdered not all that far from where Sylvia was sleeping rough.'

'Blimey, Donovan. Don't remind me.'

****

Marnie knew that sooner or later she would get her second wind, but by the time they tied up in the early evening she'd had more than enough open-air activity. And even Ralph, the seemingly tireless lock-working machine, was ready to call it a day. Neither of them could summon up the energy to find a pub for supper, so they dug the last remaining quiche out of the fridge and slid it into the oven, while on the hob garden peas were simmering with mint. It was a simple impromptu meal, but with a couple of glasses of Chilean red wine, it tasted like a feast fit for ... two weary boat people.

Marnie had read only two more sections from Iris's notebook. She was no closer to learning the fate of Oberstleutnant Franz von Weidlingen, though she thought the second entry might be a clue as to what finally happened to him.

Franz is a dear. He was very touched this morning when I presented him with a clean shirt, though he was not

166

yet ready to wear one. In fact he prefers to lie in bed 'au naturel' as the temperature in the attic is comfortable and he has been feverish for a few days. Thankfully that condition is now improving and he is managing to sleep for several hours at night with the occasional nap during the day. He said I must not worry about caring for his clothes. I think he is concerned that someone might see them and ask questions. Luckily, like all the girls working on the narrowboats, I tend to wear clothes that are normally male, like shirts, jumpers and trousers.

Marnie and Ralph were both yawning when they cleared away after supper, but they had no complaints. The weather had been on their side and seemed fairly settled. Most of the locks had so far been in their favour, and they were making good progress northwards.

Marnie was reading the cruising guide. 'With any luck, we should be home by early afternoon on Tuesday at this rate. That will be our fifth day of travelling.'

'Not bad,' said Ralph vaguely.

'What's that you're reading?'

Ralph held it up for her to see. 'Iris's notebook. She was playing quite a dangerous game, harbouring a German officer. If they'd been caught, she could've been charged with treason. That could lead to a sticky end.'

'Only we know they weren't and it didn't ...' said Marnie. '... at least not for Iris. What do you make of his story that he'd been sent to rescue Rudolf Hess? Wasn't it a bit far-fetched?'

'Well, you could say it was a typically daring German plan, though sending just one officer seems highly peculiar.'

'Typically daring?' Marnie said. 'What d'you mean?'

'There was that time Mussolini was rescued. I think it was in 1943. He was being held prisoner on a mountain-top in Italy ... heavily-guarded. Hitler sent in SS commandos and paratroopers. They got him out and flew him away to safety without a single casualty.'

'Iris's Franz doesn't seem to have been so lucky,' Marnie observed.

Ralph made no reply. He sat deep in thought.

Marnie persisted. 'Don't you think, Ralph?'

Ralph shook his head slowly. 'Something's just occurred to me. There was a big difference between the two missions, wasn't there?'

'You mean only one man involved that time?'

'No ... well, apart from that. The Mussolini rescue involved two sets of soldiers acting separately, with an aircraft arranged for their get-away. Was Franz really expecting to extricate Hess, steal a car, then steal an *aeroplane* that he could fly back to occupied Europe?'

'Certainly daring,' said Marnie.

'No.' Ralph steepled his fingers. 'I would've said implausible. Unless ...'

'What?'

'Unless there was another team sent in at the same time, one we don't know about. That would be more like Hitler's style. Maybe some fifth column agents? I wonder ...'

'One lot backing up the other one?' Marnie said.

'Possibly, or competing with each other for the prize. It was the army that provided the plane to get Mussolini away, but the SS commander, Skorzeny, insisted on going with him to claim the credit for the operation.'

'You think another group was sent as well as Franz?'

'I'm not sure, but the more I think about it, the more odd it appears. I originally thought that Franz died from some sort of infection, and Iris buried him rather than turn his body over to his enemy.'

'Respecting his last wishes or something like that,' Marnie muttered. 'And now you're wondering if he was picked up by other Germans who got him away, even though they failed in their rescue mission?'

'I'm not sure of anything any more, Marnie.'

'Are you thinking that the skeleton in the garden might *not* be his remains, then?' Marnie asked. 'I'd been wondering if perhaps he *was* discovered and fought to the end.'

'If that's the case, then why is he buried in the garden? By whom? And in what circumstances?'

Marnie stood up. 'Thoughts like that have been going through my head for the whole of this journey. I think I need to put it down for now. How about you?'

Ralph yawned again. 'Yes, time for bed.' He chuckled. 'D'you realise it's only nine o'clock? What night-owls we've become!'

That night they fell asleep in each others' arms with unanswered questions floating in their minds.

Chapter 18

They made an early start on Monday morning. *Sally Ann* slipped her mooring just before eight o'clock as the sun was nudging its way through light clouds. Marnie and Ralph had slept soundly and awoke feeling refreshed. They stood together on the stern deck, with no locks to interrupt their passage over the Tring Summit. The banks of the cutting rose on either side of them, and there were no other boats about at that time of day. The clanking of the engine drowned out any birdsong. Only a solitary heron eyed them suspiciously as they chugged by.

Marnie decided not to make a start on Iris's notes for a while. Her story gave rise to depression or at least morbid introspection. It would do no harm to set it aside and enjoy the freshness of the morning, while the boat chugged along at modest speed and its wake scarcely ruffled the water's edge.

It came as a surprise when after only cruising for a short distance, Marnie's mobile began trilling. The phone's tiny window revealed that the caller was Anne.

'Everything all right?' Marnie asked.

'No probs,' came the almost inevitable reply. 'I was half expecting you to phone last night. I guessed you were out clubbing till the early hours.'

'Wrong,' said Marnie. 'Ralph had entered for a karaoke competition and we stayed late. He reached the semi-finals.'

Marnie held the phone away from her ear as a sound suspiciously resembling a raspberry came through the air.

'Glad you're in fine fettle,' Marnie began. 'Have a good weekend?'

'We went to visit Sylvia yesterday.'

'How's she getting on?'

'Great, but she's wondering if you have any thoughts about what should come next.'

Marnie sighed. 'Can't say I've given it much thought at all. Doesn't she have any suggestions?'

'She knows the hostel's just a stop-gap. She's talking about trying to get a job and a flat to rent.'

'That makes sense, at least in theory, but she'd need a decent wage to afford a flat.'

'That's what we thought,' said Anne. 'But there was something about her yesterday. She was wearing a nice dress and what we both thought was quite a good perfume. At least I think it wasn't some cheap old stuff.'

'I don't remember her having a dress in her things,' Marnie said.

'Nor do I. Donovan thought she might've got it at a charity shop. Oh ... I've just realised something else.'

'What is it?'

'Her hair! I think she'd been to a hairdresser. She looked quite smart, you know, well turned out. Marnie, had you given her any money?'

'I gave her twenty quid so that she had something to go on. It wouldn't pay for a hairdresser, let alone a dress and perfume, even from a charity shop.'

'Oh ...'

'Something else occurred to you?' said Marnie.

'No. A car's arrived and two of our old chums have got out.'

'What chums?'

'I was being ironic, Marnie. It's Marriner and Lamb, our two friendly neighbourhood detectives.'

'Wonderful. Give them a big hug from me.'

'May not be a good idea. They're not smiling. I'd better hang up and put on my cheerful face.'

****

Marnie disconnected and slipped the mobile into her back pocket, looking pensive. At the tiller, Ralph raised an eyebrow. Marnie told him about Sylvia and the arrival at Glebe Farm of the two detectives.

'That's good news about Sylvia settling in well,' Ralph said. 'And there's probably a simple explanation about the new clothes and perfume. After all, we don't know everything about her circumstances.'

Marnie looked thoughtful. 'I wonder ...'

171

It was Ralph's day for raising eyebrows. 'What?'

'Well, I've assumed she was destitute since she was sleeping rough and begging in the street. It's just occurred to me … perhaps she had some money left over from selling her mother's house and paying the charities.'

'Then why beg?' said Ralph.

Marnie shrugged. 'I don't know, but she must've got some money from somewhere if she's bought new clothes and perfume and had a hair-do.'

Ralph said, 'I can't imagine Randall lending her any, though perhaps there's a charitable fund for guests, as he calls them, without money.'

'I'll ask him some time. Ralph, changing the subject …'

'Go on.'

'What about Marriner and Cathy Lamb? What's got them up and about first thing on a Monday morning?'

'I expect they've got the results back from forensics about the skeleton in the garden.'

Marnie looked glum. 'Their visits usually mean they think I've got a skeleton in the cupboard.'

Ralph laughed. 'Unfortunate choice of words.'

Marnie grimaced. 'No joke intended.'

'Well, they've got nothing on you this time.'

'For once, perhaps,' said Marnie. She had a sudden afterthought. 'That's curious … Why Marriner? What's happened to Sergeant Binns?'

'He did say he was moving to London.'

'I hadn't realised it was so imminent.'

'I expect Anne will ring to fill us in.' Ralph paused. 'Marnie, I've been thinking …'

'That sounds ominous.'

'It's about Franz and Iris … mainly about Franz. There's much more to that business than meets the eye. I can't believe he was part of a crazy mission to rescue Rudolf Hess. I can't believe he'd fly a fighter plane to the middle of England, knowing that he wouldn't have enough fuel to get back. Where was he going to land it? Why would he risk a German warplane falling into the hands of the enemy?'

'Presumably he was expecting to crash it so that it wouldn't be of use to anyone.'

'Think about it, Marnie. He could hardly sneak in unnoticed by crashing a Luftwaffe fighter plane in the middle of the country. Rather conspicuous, don't you think?'

'So what d'you think he was doing?' Marnie asked.

'Frankly, Marnie, I'm baffled. There may have been a plot to get Hess away. I'm no expert, but I know a few historians who are. I'll see if I can find out if there ever was such a rescue operation.'

'So what part do you think Iris's Franz might have played?'

Ralph's brows furrowed. 'I'm wondering if he might have been some kind of decoy. That might make sense.'

They were approaching the first lock of the morning, and the black-and-white balance beams were coming into view. Ralph offered the tiller to Marnie and stepped forward to pick up the windlass from the lid of the gas bottle container.

'Downhill from here on,' Ralph said.

Marnie gave a wry smile. 'In more ways than one, I expect.'

****

Anne did her best to look cheerful as DS Marriner and DC Lamb entered. She stood up and smiled brightly.

'Good morning. Would you like coffee … or tea, perhaps?

'Thanks, Anne.' Marriner didn't return the smile. 'That would be nice. Coffee, please.'

'Milk with one sugar,' Anne said. 'And for you, Cathy, your usual? Black without?'

'You know us too well, Anne,' said DC Lamb.

'Pull up chairs while I put the kettle on.'

For the next few minutes Anne was occupied in the kitchen area while the detectives made themselves at home. They had been to Glebe Farm too often for her liking in the past few years. Though they were generally pleasant enough, she knew it was never wise to drop your guard where the police were concerned, and the CID were not known for making social calls. She brought the drinks and a plate of biscuits – plain digestives, not chocolate. She didn't want to seem to be trying too hard.

'No Marnie?' Marriner said, as Anne took her seat.

'She and Ralph are in London on business, Mr Marriner. They went down by boat.'

'We'll need to take statements from them both some time.'

'I'll let them know,' said Anne.

'Donovan not about?'

'He's around somewhere.' Anne knew perfectly well that he was in her attic room, no doubt listening to every word. 'What can I do for you?'

'Your boyfriend owns a pistol, doesn't he? A 9mm German Luger.'

At the other end of the office there was the sound of feet on the wall-ladder and Donovan descended at his usual rapid rate.

'I do,' he said, 'and it's licensed, as you'll recall, sergeant.'

'And where is it now, precisely?'

'In its secure, locked container on my boat, as required by law.'

'What brought you down from up above so promptly?' said Marriner.

Donovan smiled. 'The smell of coffee, of course.'

Anne stood up and turned towards the kitchen area. 'I can take a hint.'

Donovan said, 'Do you want to inspect my security arrangements for the Luger, sergeant? My boat's up here. I'll give you the key.'

'That won't be necessary. Not just now, thanks.'

'Do you mind me asking why you're suddenly interested in my pistol?'

Cathy Lamb looked pointedly at Marriner. After a few seconds he replied.

'The skeleton. We now know how he died.'

'So it was a *he*,' Anne said, putting a mug of coffee on the desk beside Donovan.

'Yes, it was.'

'And he was shot with a 9 mm bullet, no doubt,' Donovan added.

'Yes, he was.'

'So how long has he been dead?'

Marriner shook his head. 'It's not like on the telly. We don't get the results back as fast, and we don't get everything neatly bundled together at the same time. We have to be patient.'

'Sorry, Mr Marriner,' Anne began. 'But have you come here specially to ask Donovan about his gun?'

'No, Anne. We've come to cordon off the garden as a crime scene. Our officers are doing just that as we speak.'

Without hesitating, Anne reached for the phone.

'Who are you calling?' said Marriner.

'Two calls. Marnie, to tell what's happening, and the gardeners to let them know they can't do any more work until further notice.'

****

Marnie dropped the mobile back into her pocket and guided *Sally Ann* smoothly into the next lock chamber. As Ralph closed the gate behind her, Marnie gave him the latest news from home.

He said one word. 'Franz.'

Marnie's reply was equally succinct. 'Yeah.'

A breeze was picking up. Marnie had to concentrate on steering to keep *Sally Ann* in mid-channel. It also meant she had less time for reading, and that suited her quite well. She knew there was no happy ending to the story of Iris and Franz. And yet it was difficult – impossible – to keep them out of her thoughts.

The descent from the Tring Summit involved several locks in succession. Some of them were set against them, and Ralph had to fill them before beckoning Marnie on. This doubled the time it took to lock through, leaving Marnie holding station in the middle of the canal, leaving Marnie lost in her thoughts.

Her mind kept straying to Iris's situation and Franz's daring plan, if that's what it was. Ralph had thought it was implausible, and Marnie suspected he was right. But then what was the real background to his mission? How was he really going to rescue the Nazi who had been Hitler's deputy? If in reality he'd been a decoy, surely there would be a record somewhere of an attempt by others to extricate Hess. Was Hess in fact being held as a prisoner in a country mansion near Rugby?

Going over and over these quandaries in her mind, Marnie suddenly realised that she was hazy as to why Hitler's deputy was in Britain at all. Everything about that whole episode seemed improbable. She resolved to read up about him.

She was exiting another lock when she succumbed to her curiosity. Ralph was striding ahead as she reached down to the chart table and grabbed the notebook. Gripping the tiller under her arm, Marnie kept one eye on the water as the breeze buffeted *Sally Ann* across the canal. She struggled to give her attention to the next episode in Iris's narrative.

Good news today! Franz is feeling so much better, though I fear my efforts to cheer him up are not fully appreciated. He said not to try to make him laugh, for the sake of his aching ribs. Last night he managed to climb down the ladder into the barn. I checked that no one was about (on the farm they tend to retire early as they rise soon after five o'clock). We crept out and walked through the spinney in the dark. I took him to see Sirius and Proserpina. He seemed very interested and asked all sorts of questions about how far I travelled on them, what cargoes we carried and how many of us worked on our pair. He said in his part of Germany the barges were much bigger and travelled on the great European rivers like the Rhine, the Meuse and the Moselle.

****

'Can I ask you a question, Mr Marriner?' Anne said. 'How do you know the garden is a crime scene if you don't know how long the skeleton has been there? I mean, is it certain that the man was definitely murdered?'

'That's two questions, Anne.'

'But you take my point.'

'You know we don't give out information. All I can say officially is that we have reasonable grounds for suspicion that the man whose body was buried did not die from natural causes.'

Donovan joined in. 'I'd have thought that was fairly obvious, sergeant.'

Marriner narrowed his eyes. 'So you're a forensic expert, are you?'

'No, but I think it must be clear that if he'd died from what you call natural causes, he wouldn't have a 9 mm bullet hole in him or be buried in the farmhouse garden.'

Marriner cleared his throat. 'Quite. I was simply giving the official answer to Anne's question. There's a limit to how much information we can divulge.'

Anne struggled not to smirk at the thought that only the police use words like 'divulge'. She guessed that Marriner and Lamb both noticed her lips twitching.

'Can I make coffee or tea for your people outside, Mr Marriner?' Anne asked hastily.

'No, you're all right, Anne. Thanks. They won't be staying long. Now I've got a question for you.'

'Oh yes?'

'When are you expecting Marnie and Ralph back?'

Anne shrugged. 'Well, I expect it will be before the end of the week. It's a long way to London by boat, and there are loads of locks to get through.'

'What do you think, Donovan?' Marriner asked.

'I agree. It's hard to be precise. A lot depends on how much traffic they meet on the way, how the locks are set, how many hours they travel each day, not to mention –'

'Fine, thanks,' said Marriner. 'I get the picture.' He put his mug on the tray and stood up. 'Thanks for the coffee, Anne. Will you ask Marnie to contact me as soon as she gets back.' He reached into his wallet for a card.

Anne raised a hand. 'No need for that, Mr Marriner. We've got your number on speed-dial.'

It was the detectives' turn to smirk as they left the office.

****

One advantage of playing leap-frog with the locks was that it gave Marnie time to catch up with Iris's notes while she waited for each chamber to fill. The next entry in the journal brought some amusement.

Franz slept longer than usual last night. I think this was on account of the fresh air of our excursion to the boats yesterday. I was pleased that it gave me the chance to attend to his clothing. Unfortunately I was the cause of some pain. He awoke while I was rummaging once again in what I call his kitbag. At first I thought he was going to be angry, but he sat up while I was pulling out a vest and pants. He asked what I was doing and I told him I was going to wash his (I could not think of a polite word, so I said) undergarments. At this he started laughing. I asked what was funny about a pair of knickers and he almost collapsed in hysterics. Then, he was seized with a sharp pain from his damaged ribs and he fell back on the pillow groaning and laughing at the same time. I felt guilty but my main concern was that someone from the farm might hear him.
He is much more relaxed now than before. Even the sound of shotguns does not bother him. He suggested that we try to find some more food. I told him the farmers had dug up their garden to grow vegetables and he said we should

explore it. It would be like an adventure. I was worried that we would be discovered. Also I don't like to steal from our hosts who have been kind to us, or rather to me, as they would see it. But we are often very hungry, sharing my rations between the two of us. We decided to go out after dark to see what we could find.

It was time to drive *Sally Ann* forward again. Ralph noticed the change in Marnie's expression as she eased the boat into the lock. He raised both hands palms-up as a question. Not wanting to delay progress, Marnie called out.

'Tell you later!'

Ralph bent to his task and swung the windlass to open the paddles and empty the chamber. He jogged on his way, keen to prepare the next lock. It was going to be a busy and arduous morning.

****

DS Marriner and DC Lamb were driving back to their base in Towcester, hoping that more forensic results were awaiting them, both mulling over what little information they had obtained at Glebe Farm.

'You know, Cathy, I always get the impression whenever we visit that place that we only get half the picture.'

Cathy Lamb negotiated a roundabout before replying. 'What d'you have in mind, sarge?'

'Don't get me wrong. I like Anne, but somehow ...'

'Too much influence from Marnie Walker?' Lamb suggested.

'Wouldn't be surprised.'

'Anything in particular?'

'Well, just how long does it take to get here from London on one of those boats?'

Lamb considered this. 'No idea.'

'So they could spin us any old yarn and we'd have to swallow it.'

Lamb fought to control her features at the mixed metaphor. She would have turned her head away but she needed to concentrate on the road. Oblivious, Marriner persisted.

'Don't you agree, Cathy?'

'I do, sarge.'

They turned in at the police station and Lamb found a parking space near the entrance to the building. Marriner made no attempt to get out of the car. Lamb switched off the engine and looked at him.

'Must be a good fifty miles or more to London from their place,' he mused. 'And what speed do they go at in a boat?'

Lamb shrugged mentally. 'When I've seen canal boats they seem to be going at something like walking pace.'

'Yeah.' Still he remained immobile. 'Cathy, I want you to get onto the waterways people and find out how long that journey should take.'

'Mind me asking what's on your mind, sarge?'

'Dunno. It's just, I felt that Anne was trying to stall us. They both were.'

'You think Marnie might know more about the skeleton than we think?'

'Wouldn't surprise me, Cathy. And it wouldn't be the first time.'

****

The canal meandered on its descent from the summit, and Marnie lost count of the locks, keen as she was to get on with Iris's story. She knew there could be no happy ending, but if the skeleton found in the garden at Glebe Farm really was the earthly remains of Franz von Weidlingen it would be a tragedy for Iris.

Ralph was trying his best to prepare the locks in advance, but they were conspiring to thwart him. One after another had to be filled before Marnie could bring *Sally Ann* forward. She steered the boat round a sweeping curve and up ahead Ralph was advancing on the next lock. She saw his shoulders slump and he turned to raise both arms in the air, waving them across each other, the signal they had devised to indicate a lock needing to be filled. Marnie throttled back and drifted slowly along. Time for another short episode of Iris's notes.

First thing this morning Mrs Fletcher came across with another letter from the boatyard. I tried to look disappointed as I read it in front of her and explained that our spare parts were still subject to delay. I told her I would be writing to Inland Waterways to bring them up to date and also to my fellow crew-members. They would no doubt be pleased to have some extra time with their families. Mrs Fletcher said I could stay on in the barn as long as necessary. I had handed over my ration book on arrival and she told me that on a farm they could live better than townsfolk. I know she keeps chickens and rabbits and the government permits them to keep a pig for personal use. She told me she could see I was losing weight and would do her best to build me up. She smiled and said it would be part of her war effort. We both laughed and I wondered what she would think if she knew that some of my rations were feeding a Luftwaffe officer who at that very moment was resting in the attic above her head!

****

DC Lamb walked across the office to DS Marriner's desk.

'Result, Cathy?'

'Sort of, sarge. Anne and her boyfriend were telling the truth. The bloke at British Waterways talked about lock-miles – whatever they are – and said it all depended on how the locks were set – whatever that is – and how much traffic there is at any given time.'

'Couldn't he be more precise?'

'Apparently not. He also said it depended on how many hours a day anyone would want to spend travelling.'

181

Marriner looked despondent. 'Okay. Good job, Cathy.'

'Sarge? Why are you bothered about this? It's not as if we want Marnie for anything. She didn't even know there was a skeleton in her garden. And it's not exactly a live case ... nothing to do with her.'

'Instinct, Cathy. Whenever something suspicious turns up, Marnie Walker always seems to be involved. There's always more than meets the eye.'

'Right, sarge. I'll chase up Forensics.'

'Good. We need to know what that archaeologist has turned up.'

'No stone unturned, sarge,' Lamb said lightly.

'Good girl.'

Lamb tried not to wince as she headed back to her desk.

****

Ralph suggested an early lunch. Marnie was more than happy to agree. At the next village they passed they found a pub that had been a favourite stopping place for boaters for two hundred years. They tied up close to a bridge and crossed it to an inn that offered a friendly welcome and hearty food.

They both opted for 'scampi in a basket'. Ralph confessed it had been his choice because the basket option ruled out what he described as the 'tasteless accoutrement of the dreaded salad garnish'. Marnie laughed at his confession.

'Ralph, I do believe you're becoming something of a gastro-snob.'

'*Moi?* How dare you!' He tried valiantly to keep a straight face, studying the wine list. 'D'you think the *Viognier Vendanges Nocturnes* would be a safe bet?'

Marnie rocked in her chair with laughter. 'I rest my case, m'lud.'

'Well, I'm jolly-well going to order a bottle. All right with you?'

'Not if you want me to steer in a straight line this afternoon.'

'Okay, a glass each. That's a decision ... my final offer.'

'You're on, guv'nor,' Marnie said.

'That's settled, then.' He headed for the bar and placed their orders, returning with two large glasses of white wine.

They toasted each other and the good ship *Sally Ann*. Marnie murmured appreciatively and gave Ralph's choice her approval. He put down his glass and asked for a summary of that morning's reading of Iris's diary. They both laughed at the 'undergarments' episode.

Ralph said, 'Any idea yet why Iris was so secretive about her notes?'

'Nothing has jumped out at me so far.'

'No clue as to why she insisted on a confidentiality agreement?'

Marnie shook her head. 'Whatever the reason, I haven't come across anything remarkable.'

'Apart from the fact she'd rescued a German airman and was hiding him in her attic, you mean?'

Marnie conceded the point. 'Well, apart from that small detail. Though, come to think of it, there might be a fairly simple reason.'

'Such as?'

'She'd given her word not to reveal anything about him. People felt strictly bound by their word in those days. Perhaps she regarded it as a commitment for life. Perhaps it was no more than that.'

Ralph's brows furrowed. 'I think it could be rather more than that.'

Further elaboration was interrupted by the arrival of scampi in baskets. They set about their meal, pleased by the absence of any salad garnish.

****

After lunch they opted for coffee on the boat as they travelled, both of them keen to keep up the momentum of the journey. Marnie took the tiller as they stood together on the stern deck and set off, refreshed and revitalised with mug in hand, aiming to get as near to Leighton Buzzard as conditions allowed. The next pair of locks were close together and in their favour. Once cleared, Ralph strode off to the next lock which was well over a mile away. He said he wanted to walk off lunch, but Marnie guessed he was giving her space to get back to Iris's notes.

She read on.

A mechanic arrived today and we had an incident. He came on a motorcycle and told Mrs Fletcher in the farmhouse that he was passing our way and wanted to see if there was anything he could do to our boat's engine to enable us to limp to a workshop at Yardley Gobion. This is a few miles south where they have a dry dock and a workshop. I was on Sirius when he arrived and I got back to the little barn just as he was starting to climb the ladder to the loft, looking for me. He stopped when he saw me and I showed him to the boats. I left him looking at the engine while I went back to see Franz. I had quite a shock. I found Franz in the loft kneeling near the ladder opening. He was holding his pistol and his expression was hostile. I wondered what would have happened if I had not returned when I did. I told him I would keep the mechanic away and he seemed placated. When I went back to the boat the mechanic shook his head and said there was nothing to be done until the injection nozzle was delivered. I did not let him see how relieved I was to hear that.

Later that night we had what Franz called our 'adventure'. By the light of my torch we explored the garden behind the farmhouse and came back to the loft for a midnight feast. We had radishes, cauliflower and spring onions, all things we could eat raw. It was a primitive meal but we were very much in need! With luck, no one will notice the absence of the few things that we took.

After our impromptu supper Franz surprised me. He presented me with a single primrose and asked me for a slip of paper. I tore one from my notebook and he wrote on it for me. He explained that it was a line from a poem by the greatest German poet. It is very beautiful and I shall always treasure it.

The mention of the poem made Marnie's cheeks tingle. She read the whole passage twice more. It brought home to her how precarious the situation was for Iris and Franz. If the mechanic had climbed to the loft Franz would surely have shot him. That would give rise to dire consequences resulting in Franz's capture or probably his death.

The reference to the garden behind the farmhouse sounded an ominous note. Marnie laid the journal aside and spent the rest of that day concentrating on steering the boat through the gently rolling Buckinghamshire countryside.

Chapter 19

Tuesday would be the last day of their journey. *Sally Ann* had not made such good time as they hoped, but they expected to reach Knightly St John before dusk. The previous evening they had passed through Grove Lock and tied up for the night on the edge of Linslade and Leighton Buzzard. The sky was overcast and the air was cool as they passed through the town that morning, resisting the opportunity to visit the vast Tesco supermarket.

As usual Marnie and Ralph were clutching their second mugs of coffee as they cast off. A journey that by train would take barely half an hour took a good four days or so on a narrowboat and required a deal of physical exertion. A mile out of town they found Leighton Lock set against them. Once through it, they faced a long pound before the trio of locks at Soulbury. Ralph took the tiller for that section, giving Marnie an opportunity to sit on the lid of the gas bottle holder and read on. She was getting close to the end of the narrative.

After our midnight feast I knew we had only a short time together before a major decision had to be taken. Soon the mechanic would arrive with our spare parts, and the engine would be repaired. Alex and Martha would return and we would complete the journey to Limehouse with our precious cargo. Franz was tired following our late night – he still has not regained full health and strength – so I decided to clean all his clothes and tidy his kitbag so that whatever path he chose he would be well prepared.

I must confess that while going through his kitbag I became curious about the envelope concealed under his clothes. It was not sealed. I do not know why I opened it, but it gave me quite a shock. Inside was headed paper from the office of the Reichsführer-SS, no less a person than Heinrich Himmler. That was a name I had heard many times. The document was of course all in German and much of it was a mystery to me. However, even with my limited command of the language I could understand the gist. Franz's orders were not what he had told me. He had lied.

His mission was to find Rudolf Hess – and assassinate him! He would then have to make his way as best he could to the coast of North Wales where a U-boat would be waiting at a certain hour each day to take him back to its base in Kiel in Germany. There really was no plan to steal a car and an aeroplane for the escape with Hess. I must have been a fool to believe this improbable story. My head was spinning. What should I do? What could I do?

When Franz awoke he suggested we find some more food in the garden despite the risk of being found out. I agreed to go with him but I think he noticed how disturbed I was. I told him that I was worried for his future and he said I should not be concerned. He would somehow succeed.

For Marnie the situation was becoming clear. Franz was prepared to take risks, anything necessary to achieve his goal. Marnie wondered if Iris had no choice but to reveal him and his plans to the authorities. It would be an unbearable act of betrayal on her part. Or perhaps those last days were one risk too far, and Franz was in fact discovered. That could explain why his remains – if in fact that was his skeleton in the garden – were hastily buried in that shallow grave. Nobody would want it known that a German officer had actually penetrated into the heart of England on such a daring mission.

Marnie was roused from her reading and her thoughts by Ralph pointing at a milestone on the towpath.

'It's about half a mile to Soulbury Locks from here. If you'll drop me off I'll go on and get them ready.'

Marnie agreed and took over the steering while Ralph set off at a great pace and *Sally Ann* gently returned to her modest cruising speed. Far from being upset at having to stop reading, Marnie was now only too pleased to take a break. Iris's story was nearing its end and it was never in doubt how sad that would be. Soon she saw Ralph in the near distance waving her on. She acknowledged, and he disappeared from view to tackle the next lock and the next after that to ease her way. Marnie knew they were passing through some of the most delightful country on the whole waterways network, but she had spared it not a second glance. Now, every time they passed that way by boat, she would think back to Iris and Oberstleutnant Franz von Weidlingen of the Luftwaffe and their ill-fated stolen season together at Glebe Farm.

Despite her curiosity, Marnie felt reluctant to resume her reading that morning. It was only after lunch, nearing the outskirts of Milton Keynes, that she could bring herself to pick up the notebook and learn how the story ended. But she was to be disappointed. There were no further episodes to bring Iris's narrative to a conclusion. When she turned the page for the next and final entry she found that it contained only one sentence.

When she read it, her blood froze.

****

After locking through at Soulbury, Ralph remained on board for the rest of the journey and settled on the lid of the gas bottle container. Marnie handed him the notebook. There would be no more locks all the way around Milton Keynes and beyond as far as Cosgrove, and he would probably be able to read all of Iris's diary notes at one sitting while Marnie took charge of *Sally Ann*.

It seemed to be a feature of that late spring that Marnie's head would be a jumble of thoughts. She couldn't get Iris and Franz out of her mind. The diary notes had not in fact told the whole story, and left much to the imagination. What had become of Franz? Had Iris betrayed him to the authorities? Had he been discovered and gone down fighting? Had Iris

188

simply left him behind and gone on her way after a tearful farewell, leaving him to fend for himself? Each and every scenario would have left Iris devastated.

Then another thought persisted in Marnie's mind. Had she really come upon the reason for Iris demanding confidentiality? On balance, Marnie thought not. In that case, was she missing something? Or was there still more to be revealed and, if so, how and when? It was all very confusing.

'I think that's yours.'

'What?' Marnie was aware that Ralph was speaking, but it took her a moment or two to rise to the surface.

'Your mobile, I think,' Ralph added, indicating her jeans pocket.

'Oh, thanks, yes.'

Marnie pulled it out and pressed a button. 'Anne? Any developments?'

'Not really,' came the reply. 'The garden is now officially roped off as a crime scene and the scene-of-crime people have left. So have our two detective chums. Marriner wants you to contact him when you get back.'

'So it's all quiet on the Glebe front.'

'Yes. But that's not why I'm ringing. I was wondering when you expect to get here. Still on target for this evening?'

'We're rounding Milton Keynes, so we expect to arrive in good time.'

'I thought I'd do pasta for supper – simple and quick – with yogurt or fruit for dessert. Is that okay?'

'Perfect.'

'Ralph will no doubt choose an appropriate wine.'

'No doubt about that,' said Marnie.

'Any more news about Miss Winterburn?'

'I've finished reading her journal notes, and Ralph has them now.'

'And?'

'Not really much the wiser.'

'But you do know what happened to her German bloke, presumably?'

'That's just it; she doesn't really let on what became of him.'

Anne sounded dubious. 'But surely we do. I mean, his skeleton in the garden is a pretty good clue.'

'Yes, but how did he come to be buried there ... if in fact it really is him?'

'You think there's some doubt about that?'

'Quite frankly, Anne, I don't know what to think. Let's see what Ralph makes of it all, then you and Donovan can have a go. That way, we might get somewhere.'

'I can't wait to read her notes,' Anne said. 'Oh, there's something else I wanted to tell you.'

'Please make it cheerful,' Marnie said with feeling.

'Cheerful ... not sure. But it's certainly interesting.'

'That's what I feared. Is this still Skelly or have we moved on?'

'Skelly? Oh, him. No, it's not about the bones, it's Sylvia.'

'What now?'

'Randall phoned with some more news about her. She asked him if there was a bank nearby and was glad when it turned out to be the one she uses. I forget which one it is, but apparently she has a fair amount of money. She wanted to enquire about her account and access to her funds.'

'Are we talking about the same Sylvia? By that I mean the one who until last week was sleeping rough and begging?'

'The very same,' said Anne. 'Also the same one who is now wearing nice clothes and perfume and wanting to find a flat to rent.'

Marnie shook her head, causing Ralph to look up and ask if she was feeling all right. Her reply to Ralph was a shrug.

To Anne, Marnie said, 'I'm now permanently programmed to confused. It's my default setting. Where did she get the money for the clothes and all the rest of it?'

'From a cashpoint at a building society in the high street. That's what Randall told me.'

'A hole in the wall?' Marnie said. 'You mean she has a bank card?'

190

'Must have.'

'Did she get to see the bank manager or whoever's in charge?'

'They told her what her balance was and noted her temporary address care of Magdalene House. They're going to send her a bank statement there.'

'Any idea how much she's got in the account?' Marnie asked.

'No. She didn't tell Randall and, of course, he didn't like to ask.'

'Wow ...'

'That's what I thought.'

'Blimey,' Marnie added.

'That too,' said Anne.

'What with Iris and her estate and Sylvia and her situation, we're never short of things to talk about.'

'Lucky us,' said Anne.

****

About one thing Marnie was proved to be right. They made good time passing Milton Keynes, and even the last lock of their journey at Cosgrove was set in their favour. A last hurrah! Somewhat fatigued from their efforts, their spirits rose at the sight of the familiar accommodation bridge just beyond *Thyrsis*, and the spinney that told them they were arriving home. Marnie lined *Sally Ann* up for the entrance to her dock and guided her in with customary precision.

Ralph left Iris's notebook on top of the hatch while he attended to the mooring ropes, and Marnie dealt with the engine. She turned the knob to lubricate the stern gland while he tied up fore and aft. Together they replaced the centre panel of the stern decking, grabbed the notebook and their travel bags and set off through the spinney.

They opened the front door of the farmhouse to be greeted by a welcoming aroma of spicy sauce and cooking pasta. The travel bags were deposited in the hall, and Marnie pushed open the kitchen door. She gave the traditional boatman's greeting when confronted by a meal being prepared by someone else.

'Bliss,' she murmured.

'Arabbiata?' Ralph suggested, as Anne embraced him.

'Got it in one,' she said.

Donovan appeared from the pantry clutching a bottle. 'I hope I've made the right choice.'

'A late vintage dandelion and burdock?' Ralph suggested.

Donovan sighed. 'You've spoiled my surprise,' he said, uncorking a bottle of *Valpolicella*.

****

After the meal they settled in the living room for coffee. Anne wasted no time in tackling Iris Winterburn's notebook, and Donovan quizzed the travellers on their journey. Marnie was curious to know how he managed to complete the trip from London to Knightly St John so quickly. His answer was simple: long hours; he kept going until well after darkness had fallen. In so doing, he could comfortably cover the distance in a mere four days … and nights.

'Any more news about Sylvia?' Marnie asked.

Donovan shook his head. 'Nothing since her trip to the bank.'

'A beggar with a debit card and a healthy bank balance,' Marnie mused. 'Not what I expected.'

'I've been thinking about that,' Ralph said. 'She could have had a serious breakdown after the shock of losing her home. I believe it's possible in such cases for people to go to pieces and not be able to cope with anything.'

'Even when they actually have some money in the bank?'

Ralph shrugged. 'I have the impression they can't connect with reality.'

Marnie absorbed this. 'And the change is brought about by …?'

'Suddenly finding a measure of security again, finding the time to take stock of oneself and regain a degree of self-confidence. Your intervention in her life could've made all the difference, Marnie.'

Anne looked up from her reading. 'I suppose the skeleton in the garden really is this Franz von Wotsit, is it?'

'We're assuming so,' said Ralph.

'Are you having doubts?' Marnie asked.

'I am starting to wonder.'

'We've got the dog-tag to go on,' Donovan said.

'And I've got more than that,' said Marnie. 'There were other things passed on by Iris ... documents. I think they're quite explicit. I'd like you to take a look at them, Donovan.'

'But you're sure they belonged to Franz von thingy?' said Anne.

'Pretty certain.'

'Okay.' She went back to her reading.

'What about these documents, Marnie?' Donovan said. 'When d'you want me to look at them?'

'I'll let you have them tonight. Perhaps we can discuss them tomorrow.'

'Do you have other plans for tomorrow?' Ralph asked.

Marnie said, 'For a start, I think you need to get back to your own research. You've been away from it too long. It's been great doing things together, Ralph, but I know you must be aching to get on with your work.'

'Well ... there is that, and I've got some postgrad students to see.'

'Good,' said Marnie. 'That's settled then. Coming back to your question, Ralph, I think I'd better get over to see Sylvia, and Randall if he's about. We need to get things clarified so that she can move on.'

Donovan said, 'I can check those documents you mentioned and man the phone while you and Anne go to Brackley, if you like.'

Marnie smiled. 'The dynamic duo ride again?'

'Sure.'

'Thanks,' said Marnie. 'We have a plan.'

'And you'll speak to Sergeant Marriner?' said Anne.

'How could I forget when I've got you to remind me?' Marnie smiled.

Anne smiled – sweetly – and put out her tongue.

Chapter 20

Anne looked up from studying the road atlas and read a sign as they swept past. She looked down and ran a finger over the page.

'Now we've cleared Buckingham it's just straight on all the way to Brackley on the A422.'

'Got it,' said Marnie. 'But we knew that anyway.'

'Sure, but I like seeing it all on the map, like we used to do.'

They were cruising the next morning in the Freelander at a steady fifty on the country road. Driving conditions were pleasant: dry, a clear sky, no wind, light traffic. Before setting off, Marnie had phoned DS Marriner. He confirmed the results from Forensics: the skeleton in the garden had been buried there for at least fifty years. He'd added that he'd be visiting the site in the near future.

Anne looked across at Marnie and said, 'This is like *déjà vu* all over again.'

'Ha-di-ha,' Marnie said slowly. 'That's an old one.'

Anne grinned. 'It wasn't, when he said it the first time.'

Marnie groaned.

Anne continued. 'Wasn't it a football manager who coined that phrase?'

'No idea. You're very perky today, Anne.'

'I like being on the road again. Oh, here's the Water Stratford crossroads. About five miles to go.'

Marnie speeded up a little 'I like the A422. It's a nice road to drive.'

They were in open country, the road bordered by trees and hedgerows, with fields of wheat and oilseed rape stretching away on either side under a broad sky. It was the kind of easy-riding highway that Marnie liked best. Within a few minutes they reached the A43 by-pass round Brackley and crossed it to enter the charming old market town. Marnie found the side street in which Magdalene House was located, and they parked nearby. Anne pressed the familiar buttons on the keypad by the front door and they went in.

The first surprise of the morning came as soon as they entered the building. At the reception desk, they were welcomed by the smiling face of Sylvia Harris. She stood to greet them both with a hug, and yet again Marnie and Anne were struck by the transformation she had undergone, even since their last visit. She was wearing navy slacks and a cream shirt that looked like silk. Her make-up was discreet, and Anne noticed that light perfume again.

'Wow, Sylvia,' Marnie said. 'You look really ...*great.*'

'Thank you. So do you, Marnie, but then you always do.' She turned to Anne. 'So lovely to see you ... radiant as ever.'

'I was hoping we might have a chat,' Marnie began. 'But it looks as if you're busy. No ...' She grinned. 'It looks as if you're *in charge.*'

'Not a problem, Marnie. Let's go into the lounge and have coffee.'

Sylvia turned and stood a sign up on the desk: All Enquiries to the Lounge. Marnie noticed a vase of pale yellow freesias beside the phone, and then came the second surprise: a black nameplate with gold lettering bearing the inscription:

SYLVIA HARRIS, Bursar

In the lounge a new coffee machine had been installed, and it wafted a rich, inviting fragrance towards them as they entered. Sylvia indicated a low table surrounded by armchairs, and she operated the machine while Marnie and Anne took their seats. A 'Reserved' notice stood in the middle of the table, which was well advised, as most of the other tables were occupied by guests. Some of them were reading newspapers while others played board games. Sylvia brought the coffees over.

'This is really good coffee,' said Marnie.

'Glad you like it. I think it's an Italian roast ... comes with the machine.'

'Quite an innovation.'

Sylvia shrugged. 'Well, our tea lady left for a job in school dinners, so I persuaded Randall that this was better quality and more economical.'

'In your capacity now as *bursar*, presumably.'

'Oh that,' Sylvia made a self-deprecating gesture. 'I think that was Randall's idea. Anyway, it keeps me occupied.'

Marnie set her cup down. 'Sylvia, I really came here today thinking we might talk about your future. I don't have a master plan in mind. Bringing you here was a sort of stop-gap measure. It was Anne who brought you to my attention. We couldn't leave you there on the street, especially with a murderer on the loose.'

'Have the police made any progress?' Sylvia asked, suddenly serious.

'Not so far,' said Anne. 'But they're making a big effort.'

Marnie pressed on. 'Seeing you now with new clothes and a new job title, Sylvia, it seems to me that you're already well on your way. And Randall tells me you've even sorted out a bank arrangement.'

'It's no secret, Marnie, and no mystery. I was such a mess that I couldn't cope with anything. I just fell apart, but I do have some funds left over from the sale of mum's house. It's a tidy sum, but obviously not enough to buy a home of my own. I'm hoping that with a position here – with a small income – and some collateral in the bank, I might be able to rent a flat somewhere nearby. I like Brackley and ...' She looked around the room. '... I like this place. It's given me a sense of purpose.'

Marnie and Anne followed her gaze. The guests looked relaxed, safe and contented.

Marnie smiled. 'It does me good to hear you say that. I'm *so* pleased for you, Sylvia.'

'And I'm so grateful to you, Marnie – and you, Anne – for not abandoning me in the street. I can never repay your kindness.'

'No need. Let's stay in touch, and if there's anything we can do for you, just let us know.'

'Er ...' Sylvia hesitated. 'Well, there is one thing.'

'What is it?' Marnie asked.

197

Sylvia looked around again. She lowered her voice. 'The system here is that all the clothes go in the washing machine together. Some of the items, when the guests first arrive, haven't been washed for … you know.'

'Since the Romans were in charge?' Marnie suggested.

Sylvia smiled. 'Just about.'

'You're thinking of your nice new clothes?' said Anne.

Sylvia nodded. 'Look, I'm not a snob but –'

'It's okay,' said Marnie. 'We get the picture. Would you like us to take some things and put them in our machine at home?'

Sylvia made a face. 'It's an awful imposition and I really don't like to ask, but there isn't a launderette around here. It would only be one more time.' She lowered her voice to a whisper. 'I'm getting a second washing-machine installed.'

Marnie wasn't surprised. 'It's fine, Sylvia … really.'

****

Anne rang Donovan from the Freelander on the way home from Brackley. On the back seat a black bin-bag was lying. It contained a quantity of Sylvia's clothes, including a smattering of designer labels. Sylvia had been on a spending spree. Marnie guessed that she had probably visited the Bicester Village outlet centre where top brands were sold at greatly reduced prices.

Donovan confirmed that there had been no problems for Walker and Co during their absence. He had a small stack of phone messages but had otherwise devoted the morning to Iris's notebook and Franz's documents.

They agreed to eat together shortly after noon, a simple meal of cheese rolls and fruit.

Marnie interjected. 'Tell Donovan the main course will be his views on those documents.'

His reply was ominous. 'Okay, but be prepared for indigestion.'

****

198

There was an air of expectancy when they adjourned to the living room in the farmhouse for coffee after their modest lunch. Donovan laid out the German documents on the coffee table. He cleared his throat and took a sip from his cup.

'Okay, so what we have here is a collection of actual wartime documents of the German military.'

'Had you ever seen anything like them before?' Marnie asked.

'No, but I don't doubt they're authentic.'

Beside the documents he'd laid out the Iron Cross and his photograph of the dog-tag from the grave.

'Oh, the dog-tag,' Marnie said. 'I'd forgotten about that.'

'With all the running around, so had I,' said Donovan. 'Anyway, I've sort of cleaned it up on the computer, and I've been able to make the markings clearer.'

'And it belongs with the rest of the stuff I found in Iris's box?'

'I'm pretty sure it does.' Donovan picked up the Iron Cross. 'You all recognise the medal, I'm sure, probably the most easily recognised medal in existence.'

'So does it mean Franz won that medal in 1939?'

'Not really, Marnie. All Iron Crosses from World War Two that I've seen have that date on them. I think it was the year Hitler reinstated the award.' He pointed at the next item. 'And this is the photo of the dog-tag from the garden. I've enhanced it. There's no question it is a military dog-tag. You can now just make out its markings: Nr 144 ... 9./JG 41.'

'From the Luftwaffe, presumably,' said Ralph.

'Yes, though it's not as straightforward as that,' said Donovan. 'I'll come onto that in just a moment.'

'But we know from Iris's journal that he was a senior Luftwaffe officer,' Marnie said.

'Ye-e-s ... sort of ... It's not the whole picture.'

'What else could it be?' said Anne.

'Let me explain.' Donovan gathered his thoughts. 'Franz von Weidlingen was a qualified Luftwaffe pilot. That much is clear.' Donovan lightly touched the first document in the row. 'This paper is entitled *Verleihungsurkunde*. It confirms his

199

appointment as a pilot – in German, a *Flugzeugsführer* – and is signed by a Luftwaffe general and dated 4 October 1938. The crest at the top, an eagle with outstretched wings clutching a swastika in its claws, is the emblem of the Luftwaffe. He was certainly a Luftwaffe pilot. At that time his rank was *Leutnant*, equivalent to Second Lieutenant.'

'You said *sort of*,' said Marnie.

'Yes. This next item confers on him his badge as a pilot. There's our eagle again.'

'*Sort of?*' Marnie prompted.

Donovan nodded. 'I'm getting there. I want to go through the story as it evolves so that the picture is clear in your minds. The next document confers on him his Iron Cross, second class.'

The single sheet was headed with an Iron Cross emblem and began with:

IM NAMEN DES FÜHRERS
VERLEIHE ICH DEM

Beneath this was typed the name and rank: Oberstleutnant Franz von Weidlingen together with the abbreviation: 9./JG 41. Then came the award itself:

DAS
EISERNE KREUZ
2. KLASSE

This document was dated Berlin, 15. Mai 1942 and signed by another general.

Donovan added, 'That abbreviation is his wing in a fighter squadron. You see it's the same as on the dog-tag. And by then his rank was equivalent to Lieutenant Colonel or Wing Commander, so in all senses he was a high-flyer.'

'So what's the problem?' Marnie said. 'Franz was a high-ranking and decorated pilot. Or not?'

Donovan ignored the question and tapped the next item. It was a small faded grey-blue booklet bearing the eagle-and-swastika emblem and the name Luftwaffe. Its main title was *Soldbuch*.

'This was his pay book and personal identity document, his ID.'

Marnie, Ralph and Anne were concentrating.

'All seems clear so far,' said Marnie.

Donovan took a breath before speaking. 'Okay. At this point I started to wonder if these papers actually related to two people.'

'*Two* people?' Marnie said. 'I'm bewildered.'

'So was I. You see, here is where it gets more complicated.' He laid a finger on a very small booklet entitled: *Soldatenehre.* 'This relates to the honour code of the German soldier ... yes, *soldier.* Every one of them would have been issued with this. It deals with questions like obedience, duty and comradeship, and it was produced under the name of the army's Vicar-General, Georg Werthmann. On the back cover there's the *Fahneneid,* the oath of allegiance to the flag of the Third Reich.'

Ralph said, 'Could it not just relate to anyone serving in any branch of the military?'

Donovan shook his head. 'I've read through the whole thing, and it really does relate specifically to being a soldier. And there's more than just that.' He tapped a card and turned it round for the others to see. 'This is where it gets more than complicated and rather sinister.'

'Sinister?' Marnie said. 'In what way?'

'Just look. This is really creepy. What you're looking at is part of another ID.'

The ID was a little smaller than a postcard. It included a photograph in profile, the head and shoulders of a man in uniform, a diagonal blue stripe and the title: *SS-Ausweis.* The name and rank it gave was:

SS-Standartenführer Franz von Weidlingen

'What's that bottom line?' Ralph asked.

Donovan said, 'It gives his unit as 1./Ecs.-Batl. SS "Westland". It's the title of his regiment in that SS division.'

'And that rank?'

'I think it's equivalent to a full Colonel.'

'Franz was a Colonel in the SS?' Ralph muttered.

The room was silent for several seconds before Marnie spoke.

'I don't understand. In her notes, Iris said Franz was wearing Luftwaffe uniform.'

'He was flying a Luftwaffe fighter plane,' Donovan pointed out.

'So was he an airman or was he a soldier?'

'Both, I think,' said Donovan. 'It looks as if he transferred at some point from the Luftwaffe to the SS. I think such movement to an elite unit was not uncommon.'

'Any idea why?'

Donovan shook his head. 'There could be all manner of reasons but I don't know the answer to that.'

Marnie turned to Ralph. 'Any ideas?'

'Not offhand, but I can check with an expert on the history of the time.'

'I was wondering ...' Anne began. 'Perhaps there might be something in the local press about his plane coming down. Worth looking into?'

'Good idea,' said Marnie. 'Why not?'

Anne said, 'So where do we go from here?'

Ralph said, 'I can talk to a colleague at the university. In fact I can make a few phone calls this evening.'

'I'd like to read Miss Winterburn's notes,' Anne said. 'I'm the only one who hasn't read them yet.'

****

Later that evening the four of them reassembled in the living room for a nightcap and to review their progress. Ralph had lined up a meeting the following day in Oxford with a colleague at All Saints' College. Dr Archie Gilchrist, was Senior Fellow in modern history, an expert on Germany. Marnie had set up preparatory meetings with three potential new clients.

Donovan had made good strides with his college dissertation. Only Anne was less than satisfied with her efforts. Reading Iris's notes, she had expected to understand the task set for Marnie, but instead she was left with a series of questions, but no answers.

'Now you know how I feel,' said Marnie.

'And not just you,' Ralph added. 'I don't think any of us feel enlightened by those journal notes. I had hoped they'd reveal what the mystery and the special task entailed.'

'Perhaps we're meant to deduce what it all means,' Marnie mused.

Donovan laughed. 'For once I can't say I would have thought it was all rather obvious.'

Marnie grinned at him. 'That's a relief.' She looked across at Anne. 'What about you, Anne? You've gone very quiet. Any thoughts?'

Anne's expression was serious. She looked down at the notebook on her lap. 'Nothing of any use. To be honest, I can't get that last sentence out of my mind. It's sort of spooked me out. I was expecting her to round off her story with a summing up that explained everything. Instead, she's left me full of doubts.'

They all fell silent. Each of them had had much the same reaction to the ending of Iris's notes. Anne opened the book and turned to the last page to stare down once again at Miss Winterburn's parting words.

It would be better if I had never lived.

Chapter 21

On Thursday Ralph left straight after breakfast. He had arranged to see three of his postgraduate students for individual tutorials that morning before meeting Archie Gilchrist for lunch in college.

Donovan settled himself comfortably in Anne's attic room to re-read Iris's notes, hoping for enlightenment. Later he would phone his relatives in Germany. Any information they had on Rudolf Hess might be helpful. Marnie insisted that he used the office phone. The call would be part compensation for managing Walker and Co in her absence.

For her part, Anne had prepared herself for a visit to the local newspaper offices in Buckingham, hoping to consult their archives of past editions. Her first task of the morning was to fold Sylvia's freshly-washed, dried and ironed clothes for Marnie to take back to her in Brackley. As it turned out, both would find the day sent them in entirely different directions.

While Marnie caught up with correspondence, Anne phoned the local newspaper. She was surprised and impressed to learn that they had computerised everything back to 1921. The service had not yet gone public, but she was welcome to access it online free of charge on condition that she provided feedback on the system.

Anne found the procedure simplicity itself to operate. With a click of the mouse she opened up the search function, then typed into the box: *Luftwaffe fighter plane crash 1943*. One result appeared.

A short article reported that a Focke-Wulf 190 fighter plane of the Luftwaffe had crashed in a field near the village of Hanford. Anne's pulse quickened. Hanford was just a short distance north of Knightly St John. She had found Franz's plane! On impact it had exploded and been completely destroyed by fire.

Despite an extensive search by policemen and local volunteers, no trace of the pilot had been found. A farmer reported a possible glimpse of a parachute some time around sunrise, but he couldn't be certain; he'd been helping a cow through a difficult labour at that time. There were no further references either to the aircraft or its pilot and it was suspected that he may have been vaporised in the fireball. Anne printed the article from the screen, then phoned the newspaper office to report that the system was user-friendly and worked well.

'A good result for all concerned,' she called across to Marnie while putting down the phone.

Marnie looked up. 'You found an article?'

'Yeah, but it doesn't tell us anything we didn't know already.'

'Oh well, one more piece of the jigsaw.' Marnie stood up. She looked at the neat pile of clothes on Anne's desk. 'Are those all Sylvia's things?'

'Yes, it's the lot.'

'I'll bring the car round. Don't want to risk dropping them on –'

She was interrupted by the phone ringing. Anne took the call, and their plans for the day changed completely.

****

The Freelander was running well, but its route was not taking it to Brackley. Anne was consulting the road atlas on her lap beside Marnie. Once again, they had left Donovan in charge of the office.

'What was that I said about *déjà vu* all over again?' Anne said.

Marnie groaned. 'I'll not dignify that statement with a comment, even an expletive one,' she said.

Anne grinned and changed the subject. 'Mrs Allen sounded really distressed on the phone.'

'I'm not surprised,' said Marnie. 'It's lucky she went in to check that the cottage was all right. Must've been quite a shock to find the kitchen flooded like that. You did the right thing, Anne, telling her to turn the main water supply off at the stopcock.'

'It's what my dad always says: first thing to do where water's concerned.'

'Quite right. Is this our turn?'

205

'Yes. Follow signs to M1, then it's southbound to junction 9. The car should be able to take itself there by now.'

****

Ralph had never had much contact with Dr Archie Gilchrist, but he knew he had the reputation of being very sound in his field, if a trifle pedantic. They had agreed to meet in the senior common room at All Saints' before lunch at one o'clock. Ralph arrived promptly to find Gilchrist already ensconced in a leather armchair, armed with a glass that Ralph guessed was probably a dry sherry. He rose as Ralph approached and offered a hand.

'Good of you to see me at such short notice, Archie.'

They sat.

'Not at all. It's a pleasure, and I have to say I'm rather intrigued after our phone conversation yesterday evening. What can I get you, Ralph?'

Ralph raised a hand. 'Nothing for now, thanks. I'll be driving.'

Gilchrist held up his glass. 'An advantage of living in college.' He sipped his drink.

The two dons differed markedly in style. Ralph tended towards the formal when in college. On that day he was wearing a charcoal grey double-breasted suit with a white shirt and dark red silk tie. Gilchrist wore a black academic gown over a tweed jacket and corduroy slacks with a yellow waistcoat and a check shirt, finished off with a paisley bow tie. His suede shoes were Hush Puppies.

'You wanted to talk about Rudolf Hess, Ralph. I'm curious to know why an economist of your standing would be interested in him. He was never in your league.'

'I'll come straight to the point,' said Ralph. 'In the war was he ever held in captivity in a country house near Rugby?'

Gilchrist's eyes twinkled. 'Ah … that old chestnut.'

'He wasn't?'

'No, never, though it was one of the rumours put about in case Adolf ever decided to attempt a rescue.'

'And did he?'

206

Gilchrist sat back in his chair and stared at Ralph appraisingly. 'You know something.'

Ralph shook his head. 'Nothing much. It's mostly just questions. Perhaps you could tell me more about his time in Britain?'

'I'll paraphrase. Well ... I'm sure you know, Ralph, that he flew single-handed to try to make contact with the Duke of Hamilton to arrange a peace deal. That was in May 1941. When low on fuel over Scotland, he parachuted out and injured himself in so doing. He was arrested and shortly thereafter taken to the Tower of London.'

'The Tower?' Ralph found it hard to conceal his surprise.

'Oh yes. That place has housed all sorts, and not just in mediaeval times. Anyway, from there he went to a mansion, not in Warwickshire but in Surrey. The following year he was sent to a secure hospital in Wales near Abergavenny. There he stayed till the end of the war before being flown to Nuremburg to stand trial. I can provide much more detail if you'd like it, but I'm really curious to know why you're asking about him.'

'Forgive me for answering your question with a question, Archie, but to your knowledge did Hitler try to get him out?'

A smile spread across Gilchrist's features. 'You *do* know something. What can you tell me?'

'Now you're answering my question with a question. We could go round in circles all day, but I'd be grateful for an answer, Archie.'

'Very well. To the best of my knowledge there never was an attempted rescue.'

'But?'

Gilchrist shrugged. 'Over the years there have been ... let us say suggestions ... perhaps more than just rumours ... that Hitler wanted Hess back in Berlin. His nominal deputy by then was Hermann Goering, but Hitler found him boorish and unsubtle. He felt the lack of his former deputy. Hitler himself was quirky and unpredictable. Perhaps he realised that if there were two fruitcakes in command, things would probably not go well. Though I suppose Hitler's own ego would never allow him such a self-image.'

'If the British government was putting out disinformation they must have thought an attempt might be made,' Ralph suggested.

Gilchrist sipped his sherry again. 'Of course. In 1943 you know the Germans sprang Mussolini from a mountain-top hotel where he was held after being deposed by the Italian king.'

'That's the time when the British circulated rumours about where Hess was incarcerated?' Ralph said.

Gilchrist nodded. 'Disinformation, old boy.' He finished his sherry and put down the glass. 'Are you going to tell me what's on your mind, Ralph?'

They adjourned to the refectory for lunch and were waiting to be served before Ralph replied.

'Some information has come my way by a route that I have to keep confidential, at least for now. I've learnt that an officer of the Luftwaffe – with SS connections – may have tried to get to Britain either to rescue Hess or to assassinate him.'

Gilchrist looked astonished. 'How reliable is your information?'

'Original documents and a first-hand account.'

Gilchrist lowered his voice almost to a whisper. 'My God, Ralph ... You said *may have tried.*'

'He actually did come ... in the summer of 1943.'

Ralph could virtually see Gilchrist's mind racing. He knew what the next question would be.

'Do you have a name for this officer?'

'Do I have your word that this is confidential?'

'I give you my word that I would do nothing with whatever you tell me without your permission. But, Ralph, can you assure me that I will be the first person to have access to anything you may be able to provide?'

'That's entirely reasonable, Archie, but the information must for the time being be treated in confidence. This may be something new but, let's face it, it isn't an earth-shattering scoop. It won't change the face of military history or scholarship, but it is of importance to certain parties. I know I can rely on your discretion.'

Gilchrist nodded slowly. 'I understand, and I stick to my promise.'

Ralph looked Gilchrist in the eye. 'Oberstleutnant Franz von Weidlingen.'

Gilchrist quickly took out a pen and notebook and wrote rapidly. He turned the paper to show Ralph. 'Like that?'

Ralph read and nodded. He saw the glint in Gilchrist's eyes and knew that this was not the last he had heard from his colleague on that subject.

****

There were two cars parked at the side of April Cottage when Marnie drew up, so she positioned the Freelander across the entrance to the drive, leaving enough room for cars to pass down the narrow lane. Marnie carried the toolbox to the house while Anne unloaded mop, bucket, rubber gloves and J-cloths. When Marnie opened the front door she heard three voices coming from the kitchen, all talking at once. They stopped when the door closed with a click.

The kitchen was buzzing with activity, and Marnie was surprised to see that the flood, such as it was, had been brought under control. The three voices belonged to Mrs Allen, another younger woman and a man, only the rear half of whom was visible. All of them were on their knees. Seeing Marnie in the doorway, the two women stood up.

'Mrs Walker ... er, Marnie. This is Jenny, my daughter. I asked her to come round to help. Hope you don't mind.'

Marnie put down the toolbox and held out a hand. 'Nice to meet you, Jenny. Good of you to come.' As they shook, she added, 'I take it, that is Duncan down there?'

The rear end of Duncan Grisewood protruded from a cupboard under the sink from which he emerged slowly, not without some difficulty.

'Don't get up, Duncan, please,' Marnie said.

'Morning, missus,' he said. 'Seems to be a leaky joint down here. I've tightened it up and it's stopped now.'

'That's brilliant.' Marnie swept her gaze around the kitchen. The floor was damp but no longer under water. To the three stalwarts she said, 'You are the heroes of the hour. I'd like to take you to lunch at the pub, my treat.'

Mrs Allen looked at her watch. 'Lovely idea, Marnie, but a bit early. Pub's not open for another hour.'

'Then let me suggest a plan. If you three can finish off down here, Anne and I will make a start upstairs.'

Mrs Allen tried not sound offended. 'I think you'll find everything neat and tidy ... and clean.'

'Absolutely. I want to see what books I might want to keep and what might go to a charity shop.'

With the cleaner placated, Marnie and Anne climbed to the first floor and went into Iris's bedroom. Marnie closed the door behind them.

Anne said in a hushed tone, 'Did you really mean that, Marnie, about the books?'

'I want to see if there are any German books that might have letters or notes or anything tucked into them. Also, I want to have another thorough search of the bureau in the study.'

'What are you looking for?'

'No idea ... any clues about what happened to Franz, I suppose. We still don't know how he came to be buried in the garden or got shot ... if those really were his remains.'

Anne pulled a face. 'He met a sad end, we know that much, and Miss Winterburn was involved somehow. Tragic for both of them.'

Marnie nodded. 'Now that we've come this far, I'm determined to get to the bottom of things.'

Anne looked around the room. 'Mrs Allen was right about it being neat and tidy. Shall I sort out the glass and the bottle on the bedside table? It makes me sad to see them. They were there in her last hours.'

'Good thinking, Batman.' Marnie knelt in front of the bookcase.

Anne looked down at the plastic mineral water bottle on the bedside table. It still contained a small amount of water. She picked it up and unscrewed the top.

'Marnie, would it be sacrilegious to finish off the water in Miss Winterburn's bottle?'

'I don't think so.'

Anne drew the bottle to her lips and closed her eyes.

Across the room, Marnie was opening a fourth German book and shaking it without result. There was nothing tucked in between the pages. This was starting to feel like a fool's errand, she thought. Suddenly from behind her came a strange noise. It was somewhere between a gasp and a cough and was followed by a blast of expletive.

'Bloody hell!' Anne coughed and gasped again, holding a hand against her throat. 'What the hell is this?'

In seconds Marnie was beside her, patting her firmly on the back. 'What happened, Anne? Are you all right?'

Anne held out the bottle and said hoarsely, 'It says still mineral water on the label. I think it's blown my tonsils inside out.'

Marnie sniffed the bottle. 'Can't smell anything.' She cautiously touched the inside of the neck where it was damp. 'Doesn't sting.' She licked her fingertip. 'Ah ...' She poured a few drops into her palm and lapped them with her tongue like a cat. 'A little water.'

Still hoarse and coughing, Anne spluttered, 'Not like any water I've ever drunk.'

'No, I said a *little* water. Ralph once told me the Russian for water is *voda*. The diminutive – *little water* – is ... vodka.'

'*Vodka?* Is that what it is?'

'That's what it is, unless I'm very much mistaken.'

'So why does it say mineral water on the label?'

Marnie made no reply. Her mind was in overdrive.

'Marnie?' Anne persisted.

Marnie looked at her with a vague expression. 'You know, Anne, if Donovan was here now he'd probably say that isn't the right question.'

'I'm sure he would. So what is the right question?'

'Why did Iris have vodka in a bottle by her bed at all?'

'And would he have an answer? He usually does. Do *you*, Marnie?'

'I'm starting to think of one.'

Just then, a voice called up the stairs. Marnie crossed the bedroom and opened the door.

'Say again.'

Mrs Allen said, 'I think we've done everything down here. It's still too early for lunch. Do you fancy a cup of tea?'

'Can you turn on a tap without a disaster?'

'Kettle's on already.'

'Then we'll be with you direct.' She turned to Anne and lowered her voice, 'We'll not mention this. Let's take the bottle and that glass downstairs. Put them in the bucket and take them straight out to the car. Okay? I'll see you back in the kitchen.'

Minutes later they were sitting round the table sipping the last of Iris Winterburn's Earl Grey. Mrs Allen had had the foresight, not only to enlist the support of her daughter and the gardener-handyman, but also to bring a pint of milk.

'I think the cottage is in good hands when you're about, Shirley,' Marnie said.

'I wanted to keep an eye on it for Miss ... I mean for you, Marnie.'

'It's all right, Shirley. I think we all feel we're looking after Iris's home. We want to do the best for her.'

Mrs Allen's eyes welled up, but she spoke in a firm, clear voice. 'That's how I feel, too.'

'Good. Can I ask you something, Shirley? Did Miss Winterburn drink at all?'

'Drink? Alcohol? No, I never saw her touch a drop.' The answer brooked no discussion. 'Why d'you ask, Marnie?'

'Oh, I just wondered. I think she once had some Champagne when she visited us. It was a pleasant memory, that's all.'

Mrs Allen held up her cup of Earl Grey. 'This was *her* Champagne ... her favourite.'

Marnie raised her cup. 'To Iris ...Miss Winterburn.'

They all raised their cups and repeated the toast.

It was when they were gathering their things together that Duncan sidled up to Marnie.

212

'Don't take this the wrong way, Miss ... Marnie ... but I don't think anyone's done the bins since Miss Winterburn ... you know.'

'You mean the bin in the kitchen?' Marnie said.

'No, I mean the dustbins outside. There's the general bin and the bin for the recycling. This week it's the general bin.'

'And they've not been touched since she ... left, you mean?'

'No. You see, that was something she always did herself. She never asked me to do them, and they weren't part of Shirley's jobs. I was wondering if you'd like me to come round on Wednesday – ready for dustbin day on Thursday – and put the black bin out.'

'That would be very kind, Duncan.'

Marnie led the way to the pub in the Freelander while the others followed in their cars. As soon as they set off, Marnie glanced across at Anne.

'I know,' Anne said. 'We're coming back after lunch?'

Marnie nodded. 'That's just what I was thinking.'

****

Back at Glebe Farm Donovan replaced the phone after speaking with his uncle in Germany. Everyone at Glebe Farm referred to him as *Onkel Helmut*, and Donovan was very fond of him. Contrary to popular opinion – perhaps fostered by Basil Fawlty and other cultural icons – Donovan never found any difficulty in talking about the war with Germans. Onkel Helmut was no exception, and they chatted for a few minutes, covering everything that Onkel Helmut knew about Rudolf Hess, which was not a great deal.

****

As they walked out to the pub car park after lunch, Mrs Allen's daughter Jenny thanked Marnie and said she had to dash off to collect her youngest from nursery school. Duncan Grisewood thanked Marnie and assured her he would put the dustbins out the following Wednesday. Shirley Allen thanked Marnie and assured her she could walk the short distance home

'I live just round the corner. It's no trouble. And you'll be wanting to get home, I expect.' Mrs Allen suddenly stepped forward and gave Marnie a brief hug. 'I'm glad Miss Winterburn left the cottage to you, Marnie. She knew you'd care for it.'

'With your help ... and Duncan's,' Marnie said. 'Oh, there is one thing I meant to ask you. Did Iris ever go to a bottle bank?'

Mrs Allen look surprised. 'Now, there's a thing. It's funny you should ask that. Miss Winterburn asked me that same question just a few weeks ago. I offered to go for her, but she said no bother. She'd be going that way herself. Did you want something taken, Marnie?'

'No, I was just curious.'

'I expect you're thinking of the bottle on the bedside table. You do know you can't take plastic bottles to the bank, don't you? They only accept glass.'

'Ah, yes. I'll deal with it. In fact I'm going to pop back to the cottage to make sure I've locked it up properly.'

Mrs Allen smiled at her. 'And you're wondering if there's any more water on the kitchen floor, I expect. Miss Winterburn would've done the same.'

Marnie drove the short distance back to April Cottage and parked on the drive.

Before they climbed out, Anne said, 'We're not here to check you've locked up, are we, Marnie?'

'Not exactly.'

'Or that there's water leaking onto the kitchen floor,' Anne added.

'No, though it's not a bad idea to make sure.'

'What was all that about the bottle bank? You've had an idea, haven't you?'

Marnie pushed open the car door. 'We'll see. Can you bring the rubber gloves from the boot.'

They stood for a few moments in silence in the hall. No sound reached them, not even the ticking of a clock. Anne

214

recalled that this was a habit of Marnie's on entering a building. She wondered if Marnie was letting the house communicate with her in some way, but dismissed the idea as fanciful. Even so, she did nothing to interrupt Marnie's thoughts.

As they walked towards the kitchen, Anne pulled on the rubber gloves.

'What are we doing here, Marnie?'

'Duncan said the dustbins hadn't been emptied since Iris died.'

Anne looked at her gloved hands. 'You want me to rummage in the dustbins?'

Marnie was already kneeling by the sink. She opened an underbench door to reveal a bin bag fitted to a light frame. As the door swung open the lid popped up, and Marnie looked inside the bag. It was empty.

'I'm guessing that Mrs Allen would routinely replace this bin bag with a new one as one of her jobs.'

'But not put out the dustbins?' Anne said.

'No. You remember when we first met her, she said she came every Tuesday and Friday. Duncan said the bins here are emptied on Thursdays, probably quite early in the morning. That means they have to be put out on Wednesdays. Mrs Allen said she found Iris in her bed. I'm not sure now which day that was, but I'm guessing Iris died either on a Monday or a Thursday night.'

Anne sat on a chair at the table, struggling to come to terms with Marnie's reasoning. 'I'm trying to see the connection with the bottle bank.'

'So am I,' said Marnie. 'Let's check the bins.'

The dustbins were the latest form of wheelie bin, one black, one blue, and they stood together outside the kitchen door. Marnie pulled open the lid of the black bin. Duncan had been right; the bin contained a number of white plastic bags, the same size as the bag in the kitchen. Marnie pulled out the top bag and undid the knot in the drawstring.

'Shall I rummage in the black bin?' Anne asked.

'Please,' said Marnie. 'It's not unsavoury … no nasty smells.'

Anne pulled out the bags and passed them to Marnie, who ran her hands round the outsides before turning her attention to the blue bin.

'Am we looking for anything in particular?' Anne said.

'Just see if anything strikes you as out of the ordinary.'

'Apart from those bags, there are just odd bits and pieces, various wrappings, yogurt pots … stuff like that. What about you? Anything interesting?'

Peering in the blue bin, Marnie said vaguely, 'It's interesting to see what isn't here.'

'Marnie, you're getting more like Donovan every day.'

'What d'you mean?'

'Speaking in riddles. What isn't there, that you find interesting? If you see what I mean.'

'No bottles in either bin. Have you finished with yours?'

'More or less. There are just a few of these bubble-pack things.'

Marnie held out a hand. 'Let me see.'

She was holding a used strip that had contained some sort of tablets. They had all been pressed out, leaving only the plasticised card and a dimple where each tablet had been ejected. Marnie turned it over and tried to read the wording on the back. It was difficult to decipher anything, as the surface was punctured all along its length, leaving only fragments of words intact.

'Are there many of these, Anne?'

'Eight or nine. Why?'

There was no reply. Anne looked across at Marnie who was straining to decipher whatever was printed on the reverse.

'This is hopeless,' she said eventually. 'Anne, gather together all the strips. We'll take them home and examine them thoroughly.'

'So has this been a wasted journey?' Anne asked.

'Not entirely. I've discovered what wasn't in the rubbish bins.'

'What wasn't in the rubbish bins that you discovered?' Anne frowned. 'Do I really mean that?'

'Surely it's obvious,' Marnie said. 'Oh God, I am sounding like Donovan again.'

Anne laughed. 'I think we're both talking rubbish … literally. So are you going to tell me what you mean?'

Marnie turned to face Anne. 'I've checked both bins. There's no trace of any sort of glass bottle in either of them.'

Anne understood at last. 'So Miss Winterburn did go to the bottle bank.'

'Yes, I'm sure of it, and I'm pretty sure that what she disposed of … was a vodka bottle.'

****

At close of business at Glebe Farm there was unanimous agreement. Everyone wanted to share what they had learnt during the day. They gathered round Marnie's desk in the office barn, each of them armed with a glass of white wine. Donovan was invited to go first and gave an account of his phone conversation with Onkel Helmut.

'Did you learn anything new?' Ralph asked.

'Not really. My uncle's knowledge of Hess was sketchy – he was born just after the war ended – but it was interesting to find out how much or how little he knew.'

'Are they taught about that time in school?' Marnie asked.

'Not very much. They prefer looking to the future. Being on the losing side in two huge wars, they had to focus on rebuilding their country. That's Germany's priority.'

Ralph said, 'They lost the wars but have done well in peacetime.'

'Okay, so what about Rudolf Hess?' said Marnie.

'I asked Onkel Helmut if he'd ever heard of any attempt to rescue Hess. He had no idea about that. He vaguely knew Hess had flown to Britain to sue for peace, had been arrested and held by the British, but he didn't know where. He knew Hess had been tried at Nuremburg, was sentenced to life imprisonment and held in Spandau prison in Berlin. He recalled that Hess had committed suicide there in his nineties and thought his ashes had been scattered at sea.'

'That was quite normal for top Nazis,' Ralph observed. 'They didn't want any graves that might become places of pilgrimage for the far right.'

'Was that everything?' Marnie said to Donovan.

'That's pretty knowledgeable compared with most Germans nowadays, Marnie. But there was just one other thing that he said he half-remembered. He'd read in a magazine some time an accusation that Hess had been killed by the British, but he thought no one believed that. He said why would they wait till he was over ninety? They could have bumped him off at any time during or after the war.'

Marnie said, 'Did your colleague mention that, Ralph?'

'No, though I'd read about that conspiracy theory. I agree with Onkel Helmut; no evidence was ever produced to support the idea. In fact Hess tried to kill himself more than once, but he received medical treatment from the Brits and survived.'

Marnie continued, 'So how did you get on with your colleague, Ralph?'

'Archie Gilchrist knew nothing of any attempt to free Hess during the war. In fact, he was genuinely surprised when I asked about that. He got quite excited.'

'Is that as far as you got, then?'

'Well, actually ...'

'You told him about Franz?'

'I did mention the name. Would you rather I hadn't, Marnie?'

Marnie shook her head. 'I don't think it makes much difference, frankly. Perhaps best not to give much else away, nothing about Iris and her involvement.'

'No,' said Ralph. 'I think Gilchrist will see what he can find out about Franz, if anything. And that will be that.'

'Will he want to publish something, Ralph?'

'Inevitably, but nothing without my agreement. We don't have to go into detail about Iris or the time he spent with her here.'

'Talking of Iris ...' Anne said.

'Oh yes,' said Ralph. 'How did you get on with the great flood of Little Haddon?'

Marnie said, 'It was more or less sorted by the time we got there. Mrs Allen, the cleaner, had roped in her daughter as well as Duncan, the handyman-gardener, and everything was under control.'

'So not much to do.'

Marnie hesitated for a few seconds while the others looked at her expectantly. Eventually she said, 'I think I'm starting to see a pattern.'

'Iris's secret?' Ralph said.

'It's just an impression, but I think it hangs together.'

'What did you find?'

'Where to begin?' Marnie paused again. 'There was a mineral water bottle beside the bed – a half-litre bottle – and an empty glass. But there was also a water jug, and that got me thinking.'

'Why have both?' Ralph said.

'Exactly. Then Anne took a mouthful of water from the bottle to finish it off –'

'And it almost finished *me* off,' said Anne. 'It certainly wasn't mineral water. It was more like *fire water!*'

'Vodka,' Marnie said.

'*Vodka?* Ralph and Donovan choroused in unison.

Anne nodded. 'I wasn't expecting it ... practically blew my head off.'

Ralph and Donovan began to laugh and then just as suddenly fell silent.

'Wait a minute,' said Ralph. 'Why vodka? Was she a vodka drinker?'

'According to Mrs Allen, Iris didn't drink at all.'

'Why in a plastic water bottle?'

'There's more,' Marnie added. 'The dustbins hadn't been emptied since Iris died. We checked and found no empty vodka bottle in either bin. Mrs Allen said Iris had asked about a bottle bank shortly before she died.'

'You think she'd been planning something.'

'I'm sure of it, Ralph. Just like those letters she gave the solicitor for me. Everything was thought out. And there's something more. What we did find was some strips – you know those bubble-packs – for tablets that you push out.' Marnie turned to Anne. 'You've got them?'

Anne produced the strips. There were six in all, each one containing compartments for fourteen tablets. Marnie gave two strips each to Ralph and Donovan, sharing the others with Anne.

'I was trying to read the names on the reverse side,' said Marnie.

They all studied the strips intensely.

'Not easy to read,' Ralph murmured. 'Too broken up.'

Donovan said, 'Looks like *diaz* something ...'

'Diazepam!' Marnie exclaimed. 'It's a benzodiazepine.'

'Valium,' Ralph muttered.

'Yes. Do you remember Anne found a tablet tucked behind the leg of the bed, and I took it to a pharmacist? She identified it as diazepam.'

They stared at each other as the implications sank in.

'Let me just get this straight in my mind,' said Marnie. She spoke slowly. 'Iris had a bottle filled with vodka by the bed. If she drank half a litre of vodka and took a large dose of diazepam, being an elderly person ...'

'Suicide,' said Ralph. 'Even if she left some, that's still quite a quantity.'

'Why vodka?'

Donovan said, 'It's colourless like water and has little or no odour.'

'That's what fooled me,' Anne said, feeling her throat.

Marnie went on. 'She disposed of the vodka bottle in advance and emptied the tablets from their strips, thinking that it would look as if she simply died in her sleep. She didn't want anyone to think she'd committed suicide.'

'She wanted everything to be secret ...' Ralph said, '... her death, the episode with Franz ...'

'She wanted to draw a line behind that aspect of her life,' said Marnie. 'But she also felt the need to get it off her chest.'

'Which is what she entrusted to you, Marnie.'

'So that was her secret,' said Marnie.

The others nodded in agreement. Iris Winterburn had had a German lover in wartime and had eventually committed suicide. That was her secret.

But they were all wrong.

Chapter 22

It was Friday morning. Breakfast was over and life was gradually returning to normal at Glebe Farm. Marnie and Anne were busy getting Walker and Co back on track. Ralph set off for Oxford for the next round of postgrad tutorials, followed by lunch with Archie Gilchrist. Donovan was re-reading his project dissertation for university, though he was aching to go through Franz's orders and translate them into English. Dolly the cat sat under the desk lamp on Anne's desk and surveyed proceedings with equanimity.

Eventually Anne called across the office. 'Ready when you are, Marnie.'

Minutes later they were on their way to deliver freshly-cleaned clothes to Sylvia in Brackley. This time they had no need of the road atlas. Anne sat watching the scenery go by until a thought occurred to her.

'Marnie, did you let Sylvia know we weren't going to make it yesterday?'

Marnie gasped. 'I didn't! The flood in the cottage put it right out of my mind. Damn!'

'I don't suppose it'll be a problem,' said Anne. 'We'll probably still find her running the place.'

Wrong again.

****

Donovan carefully took the papers out of the envelope from Iris's safe deposit box. This was partly out of respect for their antiquity and partly with a feeling of revulsion. He almost shuddered at the sight of the heading: *Amt des Reichsführers-SS*, Office of the Reich Leader-SS. The thought that the document he was handling might have been held by no less a monster than Heinrich Himmler filled him with disgust.

He began reading aloud in German the orders assigned to Colonel Franz von Weidlingen of the SS. They left no room for doubt. The plan that Donovan read was a model of simplicity. Franz was to fly to England in a fighter aircraft, land where he could and locate the house known as Crandon

Abbey between Dunchurch and Rugby. There he was to assassinate 'the traitor Rudolf Hess', destroy the aircraft and make his escape. The documents included an open-dated travel warrant – no doubt a forgery – for the Irish Mail train from Rugby to Holyhead on the island of Anglesey in Wales. He was to alight at Bangor where the train made a brief stop. An agent would meet him there and drive him to a rendez-vous point where a U-boat would wait at an appointed time each night for a week.

The words 'suicide mission' floated through Donovan's mind. There was so much in these orders that depended unrealistically on precision, on perfection. The thought of Franz's bones lying in a shallow pit not forty metres from where he sat was ample proof of that.

Donovan began his translation, this time reading the English version out loud. When he finished, he silently read through the original text again. In German he said aloud, 'He must have known he had only a remote chance of getting away alive, even if he had been able to kill Rudolf Hess.'

He looked up, realising that the office was empty.

'I'm talking to the cat,' he said, also out loud but in English, turning his head to stare at Dolly.

She stared back with her big amber eyes, unblinking, indifferent.

****

Sylvia was not sitting at the reception desk in the entrance hall of Magdalene House. Instead, they were met by Randall Hughes. He stood as they entered and greeted Marnie and Anne with a kiss on the cheek and a hug. As usual he was wearing his full-length black cassock, buttoned down the front from throat to hem. He invited them to join him for coffee in the office behind reception. Anne was carrying the black plastic bin-bag filled with Sylvia's things. She set it down on the floor as they took their seats. Marnie looked embarrassed.

'Randall, I'm really sorry we didn't manage to get here yesterday or even let Sylvia know we couldn't make it. We had to deal with an emergency and –'

Randall raised both hands. 'It's fine, Marnie. Don't worry about it. We guessed there was some problem keeping you away.'

'Yes, but I should've –'

'No. It's okay, really. Have some coffee.'

Anne said, 'We've brought Sylvia's clothes back, and I think she has some more for us to take away.'

'Okay,' said Randall. 'You know her room. Do you want to take them up while I organise coffee? Here, take my key.'

Anne climbed to the first floor and walked to the end of the corridor to Sylvia's room. She noticed that it was the only room to have a lock, apart presumably from the bathroom opposite. Inside, everything was tidy and well-ordered, with a vase of pink and white carnations on the beside table. Anne laid the bin-bag on the bed, but there was no sign of Sylvia's dirty washing. The only place in the room where it might be kept was the wardrobe. Anne opened it to find a further stack of clothes in the bottom, all folded and ready to take away. She was about to empty the bag onto the bed when she had another idea. Under the bed was Sylvia's rucksack. She pulled it out and looked inside. It was empty apart from some newspapers folded at the bottom. Anne filled the rucksack with the clothes to be washed and left the room, carefully locking it behind her.

When she returned to the office, Randall and Marnie were discussing Sylvia's future. Randall was explaining Sylvia's absence that morning. She had made an appointment with a lettings agent to view a number of properties for rent in the area. Most of them were flats, but one was a charming little house in a Victorian terrace on the other side of town. Sylvia was not expected back until some time that afternoon.

They agreed to keep in touch about Sylvia, pleased that she was settling into a new life that would be safe and secure after so many hardships. Marnie explained that they had to get back to Glebe Farm to give statements to the police about the skeleton. They thanked Randall for the coffee and took their leave. Anne heaved the rucksack onto the back seat of the Freelander, and they were on their way with nothing more on their mind than a light lunch.

****

As soon as Ralph saw Archie Gilchrist enter the senior common room, he knew from his gait and the gleam in his eye that he'd found something. This impression was reinforced by the fact that Gilchrist didn't even spare the sherry decanter a single glance in passing. He took his place in the armchair opposite Ralph with a flurry of academic gown and an elaborate adjustment of that day's bow tie. He leaned forward.

'Do I take it,' said Ralph, 'that your research has borne fruit?'

'You do indeed, old boy.'

Ralph made a gesture with one hand. 'I'm all agog.'

'And well may you be. First, I've scoured all my sources and I can assure you no known rescue attempts were made on Rudolf Hess. The Nazi High Command – and we're talking Heinrich Himmler here, no less – had no certain knowledge of where the British were holding Hess. Without verified certainty they would never have attempted a rescue. The British put out numerous rumours of where he might have been, all of them intended to cause confusion.'

'That would include the country house near Rugby, presumably.'

'Yes, Ralph, it did, plus various other locations in Shropshire, Westmorland, Lancashire and so on.'

'So you're *absolutely* certain that no attempt was ever mounted.'

Gilchrist looked uneasy. 'Well ... nothing documented that has come to light.'

'I know,' said Ralph reassuringly. 'One can never be dogmatic about such things.' He might also have added, *and no academic likes to stick his neck out for fear of being discredited.*

'Quite. I know you appreciate that, Ralph. After all, who knows what might turn up out of the blue?'

'Who knows, indeed?'

For a brief moment Gilchrist's composure faded. Did he wonder perhaps if Ralph had something up his sleeve? What had Ralph said about *original documents and a first-hand account?* He continued.

'No attempt at rescue, then, Ralph, unless you know of ...'

Ralph shook his head briefly, though he thought to himself that the German intelligence service – the *Abwehr* – and its spy network was better informed than Gilchrist realised, but not with a rescue in mind. He gestured to Gilchrist to continue.

Gilchrist narrowed his eyes and said, 'Of course a lot of records were destroyed by the SS at the end of the war, and Berlin was heavily bombed and ravaged.'

Ralph sensed that there was more to come; that gleam was still there, albeit now a little more subdued. 'Well, Archie, thank you for clarifying that point. I'm grateful to you for looking into this matter.'

The gleam was rekindled. 'Ah, but Ralph, there's more.'

'Really?'

'Oh yes. That name you mentioned, Franz von Weidlingen.'

'You found him?'

Gilchrist nodded. 'I knew just where to put my finger on him.'

Ralph thought of Franz's lonely grave in the Glebe Farm garden, the bones buried in the earth, the bullet hole, the dog-tag covered in dirt.

'And where was that, Archie?'

Gilchrist tapped the side of his nose. 'In my own archive. I had the feeling that I'd come across that name before. I searched and I found. Our friend started out as a pilot in the Luftwaffe just before the war and on active service rose to the rank of colonel. He must have been an excellent pilot. He earned rapid promotions, but there might have been another reason, too.'

'Political?' Ralph suggested. 'He was a party member?'

'Indeed. The fact that he requested a transfer to the SS is a sure sign of his inclinations. It's clear that von Weidlingen was a staunch Nazi. Transfers of that kind were granted but not all that common. Having said that, I must admit that his SS career is not well documented – all those destroyed files, no doubt – but it's known that he served as an assassin.'

'Atrocities against Jews?' Ralph asked.

'No. The SS took the view that anyone could massacre civilians, burn villages, execute prisoners. That would be all in a day's work to them.'

Ralph felt a sickening wave of revulsion. He said nothing. Gilchrist went on.

'Our man was a specialist. It's recorded that he carried out a number of assassinations. One of his victims was the leading Belgian socialist, Jacques Aliot. He was in hiding in Holland, but somehow the SS located him and sent von Weidlingen to kill him. It was a daring mission. Aliot was heavily guarded in what he thought was a safe house. Then there was the Austrian political philosopher, Heinz Wagner. He was in hiding in the south of France. No one had the foggiest idea where he was, but von Weidlingen tracked him down.'

'The same fate as Aliot?' Ralph said.

'Exactly. This chap seems to have specialised in such killings. His motto might well have been: making the impossible, possible. He really was one nasty bastard, old boy.'

Ralph nodded slowly. 'I get the picture.'

'What I don't get, Ralph, is how you came to know of him. I'd be interested in anything you have on this man. You see, he just disappeared from the records some time during the war, and was never heard of again. There was some suggestion that he'd made it to Argentina …' He shrugged. '… but that's the standard assumption where the SS was concerned.'

'Archie, I'm grateful to you for what you've found out. I've learnt things in confidence and I don't know when or what I can reveal, but once that becomes clear, I'll pass it on to you.'

'And no one else?'

'And no one else. That's a promise.'

****

227

Marnie was approaching the Buckingham ring road when her mobile rang. Anne took the call. It was Donovan.

'I'll be quick. The police have been here, wanting statements from Marnie and Ralph. They've just left but they're coming back later on. Where are you now?'

'Ten minutes away. No idea when Ralph will be back. Hang on a sec. I'll see if Marnie knows.'

Anne explained the situation to Marnie who was none the wiser. After Anne disconnected, Marnie asked her to ring Ralph at college and get him to call in at the supermarket in Stony Stratford. They needed some provisions. Anne got Ralph's voicemail and she left a message. Marnie was amused – but not surprised – to hear that it consisted of a shopping list.

They sped on, and Anne's estimated time of arrival proved to be accurate. Marnie was surprised – but not amused – when a uniformed policeman stepped in front of the car as she turned into the entrance at the top of the field track. She hit the brakes and narrowly avoided running him down.

'Deep breaths,' Marnie muttered to herself as the policeman stared at the number-plate and waved her on.

Anne said, 'I think you handled the self-control thing there very well, Marnie.'

'So do I. I was comforting myself with the thought that next time he pulls that stunt I might not be so quick on the brakes.'

Anne laughed, certain that Marnie was joking. She stopped laughing as they drew nearer to the house and another constable stepped forward and waved them towards the small barns. Marnie turned at a sedate pace and drove the Freelander into its regular space in the garage barn. They climbed out. Anne tugged Sylvia's rucksack from the back seat and followed Marnie round to the office barn.

The welcoming party comprised Donovan backed up by Dolly the cat. Marnie dumped car keys and mobile phone on her desk while Anne crossed the office and planted Sylvia's rucksack on hers.

'Anyone for coffee?' Anne asked.

Donovan declined the offer.

'Gasping,' said Marnie. She turned to Donovan. 'Did they ask you for a statement?'

'They did. It was about three sentences long.'

'Mine will be about the same, something along the lines of not having set foot in the garden –'

'Jungle!' Anne called out from the kitchen area.

Marnie nodded, 'Okay, jungle … since we came here roughly three years ago. Ralph and I were at a meeting in London when Anne phoned and told us about the skeleton. That's it, really. Not much more I can add.'

Donovan said, 'You think they'll believe you really hadn't been in the garden in all that time?'

'I think the clue was in Anne's name for the place. I've devoted all my energies to getting this office up and running, the cottages renovated for letting and lastly the house refurbished as a home. All that in addition to starting a business. No wonder the garden was overgrown like a jungle.'

Anne brought a mug of coffee and handed it to Marnie. She perched on the corner of the desk and said, 'David Attenborough thought there was a rare species of gorilla living in there.'

Donovan sniggered, even though he'd heard it before.

Marnie said, 'Did they say if they'd had it confirmed how long the skeleton's been in the ground?'

Donovan nodded. 'They said the forensic archaeologist settled on fifty years or so, which ties up with the dog-tag.'

'Nineteen-forties,' Marnie muttered. 'At least it's nice to know I'm not a suspect.'

'Actually,' Donovan said, 'They were chattier than usual. I asked if they had any ideas about who the skeleton might be. I didn't expect an answer, but Marriner said they had wondered if he might've been a pilot who got shot down.'

'He can hardly have buried himself,' said Marnie.

'I made that same point.' He grinned. 'They said they had worked that out, but those were dark days, all sorts of things going on, not much investigation, few records kept.'

Marnie sipped her coffee. 'Interesting,' she said.

Donovan went on. 'There was something else. I made a comment that the skull seemed intact, and Marriner said he wasn't shot in the head. The bullet hole was in a rib. He was shot through the heart.'

'You seem to have got a lot out of him. He never gives anything away to me.'

'I think the reason is rather obvious,' Donovan said.

Anne rolled her eyes.

'I'm serious. I got the distinct impression the police don't think they're ever going to get to the bottom of this. They just don't have the resources to mount an investigation of that sort, not after so many years.'

'Did they say that?'

'More or less.'

'So they'll never find out about Franz?' said Anne. She got down from Marnie's desk and crossed the office.

'No. I don't think they ever will.'

Anne began undoing the rucksack on her desk. 'Glebe Farm has had more than its fair share of tragedy.' She looked up at the hook in a beam from which a young woman had hanged herself hundreds of years earlier.

Something suddenly occurred to Marnie. She said, 'They've still got uniforms on site. Why's that?'

Donovan said, 'When Marriner and Cathy left, they did say their team would be packing up. They've probably gone by now.'

On the other side of the office Anne began pulling clothes out of Sylvia's rucksack. To speed up the process she lifted the rucksack, turned it upside down and shook it. Clothes tumbled onto her desk, some of them spilling onto the floor. The newspapers that were lining the bottom joined them, and there was a muffled thump on the carpeting.

'Let me help you with that, Anne,' Donovan said.

Reaching the desk, he gathered up the clothes and newspapers from the floor. Something wasn't right. 'That's strange,' he murmured.

'What is it?' Marnie asked. She went across to join him. Anne leaned forward to peer over the desk.

Lying among the clothes was a hammer. Marnie stared at Anne.

'Did that fall out of the rucksack?' she asked.

'Yeah.'

'Did you know it was there?'

Anne looked blank. 'I had no idea.'

Donovan knelt down and reached for it. Before he could touch it, Marnie laid a hand on his shoulder.

'I don't think you should do that.'

The atmosphere in the office chilled as they absorbed the implications of what Marnie had said.

****

For the second time that day Marnie and Anne were on the road to Brackley. The difference was that this time they had a greater sense of urgency than when they had made the same journey that morning. Both were in a state of turmoil. Both had seen the hammer close up and been disturbed by the sight of it. Neither of them spoke until they had cleared Buckingham and were on the straight run of the A422 to Brackley.

Eventually Anne said, 'D'you think we could have got the wrong impression back there, Marnie?'

'No.'

'But ...'

There was a long silence.

'But what?' Marnie said.

'I don't know. I just think we both jumped to the same conclusion. Now, I'm not sure if we were right.'

'Anne, you saw the head of the hammer ... those stains and ... well, the other stuff.'

Anne shuddered. 'Yes, I suppose so.'

'I've got my doubts, too,' Marnie said, 'but I think there's nothing for it but to talk to Sylvia.'

'She'll think we're accusing her of ... something.'

'I know. I'm trying to work out what to say. To be honest, Anne, my mind's in a spin.'

'Mine too. I just can't believe that Sylvia ... It doesn't make sense. Sylvia Harris ... the Stony Stratford killer? When

231

I think how feeble she looked that day on the pavement, begging. She was utterly pathetic. It made me want to cry, just looking at her. That's why I told you about her, Marnie.'

'And you did the right thing. Hang on ... have to concentrate.' Marnie slowed as they approached the Water Stratford crossroads, and a tractor was hovering at the junction, waiting to turn onto the main road. They passed the crossing, and Marnie accelerated away.

Anne said, 'But then I thought why was she carrying a hammer in the rucksack in the first place?'

'I suppose she carried it for protection. I've heard of women doing that. And don't forget, Anne, she had a better reason than most. She was sleeping rough. Can't say I blame her, really.'

'Oh, I see ...' Anne began, enlightenment dawning. 'You think she might've hit that man in self defence.'

'Anne, I don't *think* anything. I'm kinda hoping it might be that. The question on my mind is, if she hit him to defend herself, why didn't she report it to the police?'

****

Donovan heard the sound of tyres rolling over the gravel at the side of the farmhouse. He knew that it wasn't Ralph returning home from Oxford. He would have driven round to park in the garage barn. From Anne's desk he could see across to the full-width, full-height plate glass frontage of the office barn and he waited to see who came past on their way to the door. His joy was not unalloyed as he recognised DS Jack Marriner and DC Cathy Lamb. Donovan stood and rounded the desk, hoping that he might block their view of the hammer. It had been left on the floor at Marnie's insistence

'Hello,' he said, hoping that his cheerfulness was not obviously forced. 'If you're wanting to see Marnie and Ralph I'm afraid I have to disappoint you. They're still not back yet.'

Marriner looked at his watch. 'So when do you expect them?'

Donovan shrugged. 'Hard to say, really. Ralph's tied up in meetings at the university.'

'And Marnie? She was in the car when she rang me this morning.'

'That's right,' Donovan said. 'She had to go out … also a meeting.'

'So where's Anne?' said Cathy Lamb. 'They don't usually go together, leaving you in the office, do they?'

'No, not usually, but as I was here …'

'Yes?' Marriner's body language was clear; he was not going to let go.

'I believe they were looking in on a place in Brackley.'

'What's in Brackley?' Marriner stepped closer.

Donovan hesitated, wondering if he could plead ignorance, but he knew it would be inadvisable to lie. It would probably be worse for all of them in the long run, so he opted for the truth.

'They're visiting Magdalene House. It's a hostel for homeless people, vagrants, rough sleepers … that sort of thing.'

'Why? And why does it take two of them?'

'They've been helping a homeless person who's staying there for a while. They wanted to see how she's getting on.'

'Do you have an address for this place?' Marriner asked.

Cathy Lamb took out her notebook and walked towards Anne's desk. Donovan was outflanked, and there was nothing he could do about it. As she passed him, Cathy glanced at the floor.

'What's this?' She crouched to examine the hammer. 'Sarge?'

Marriner joined her. The two detectives stared at the hammer; neither of them touched it. Marriner wheeled round to face Donovan who was looking as if he would rather be anywhere but in that office.

****

When Marnie and Anne walked into the hall at Magdalene House they found Sylvia and Randall in conversation at the reception desk. Sylvia seemed to be in high spirits. She looked animated, excited. When she turned and saw the new arrivals her expression faded, the light went out in her eyes. Randall's face lit up when he saw the visitors, but the sight of their serious demeanour warned him of a problem.

'Marnie,' he said, 'twice in one day. Lovely to see you. Is everything all right?'

Sylvia said, 'Sorry I missed you earlier.'

'Can we talk in your office, Randall?' Marnie asked.

There were only two chairs in the office, so they remained standing.

Randall looked at their worried faces. 'What's happened, Marnie? Do you want to speak to Sylvia in private?'

'No.'

Before Marnie could elaborate, Sylvia broke in. 'You want an explanation.'

Randall said, 'Am I missing something here?'

Marnie nodded. 'I think you are.'

'You found it,' said Sylvia. 'I was going to put my washing in a carrier bag, but I was buoyed up at the thought of looking at flats, somewhere to live. Stupid of me to overlook it.'

'You're right, Sylvia,' Marnie said. 'We found it.'

Randall's brows furrowed but he said nothing.

'I found it by accident,' Anne said.

'By accident?' Sylvia repeated.

Marnie continued. 'Anne was sorting the clothes when the hammer fell out of your rucksack.'

'Hammer?' Randall looked bewildered. 'Can someone please tell me what's going on.'

'I think Sylvia's the only one who can do that.' Marnie looked Sylvia in the eye. 'But only if you want to.'

'What are you going to do, Marnie?' Sylvia asked.

Marnie sighed. 'What am I going to do? Sylvia, I'm at a complete loss to know what to do. I've never been in this position before.'

They all looked at Sylvia expectantly. When she spoke, her voice seemed to come from far away. She had relocated to a place somewhere in her memory.

'I saw him one afternoon and nearly fainted with the shock. It all came back to me. I was walking down the high street in Stony Stratford, and there he was, just coming out of

234

a shop. For him it was a normal day. He looked as if he hadn't a care in the world, just going about his business. And there I was, homeless, alone, my life in tatters. I had to stop and lean up against a lamp-post to get my breath. My head was spinning.'

Randall was beginning to understand. He walked round the desk and dropped onto the chair.

'Oh my dear Lord ...' he muttered.

Sylvia continued. 'I watched him walk up the road. He turned into the path by the church, and I followed at a distance. When he came out of the churchyard he headed down towards the park. I was about thirty or forty yards behind him, and he had no idea I was there. He never looked back. I didn't follow him into the park. It was too open. I'd be exposed. He was just going for a walk in the spring sunshine, enjoying life. It was a Saturday, and people were walking their dogs. Children were playing. He walked right past the place where I'd been sleeping rough and didn't spare it a glance.'

Sylvia fell silent, lost in her memory.

'The hammer?' Marnie prompted.

'Oh yes ... the hammer. I bought it at the hardware shop and, yes, I'd made a plan. If ever I saw him again ...'

'Which you did,' Marnie said.

'I did.'

Sylvia drifted off again, her expression blank, staring unfocused ahead. No one dared speak. It was as if she was sleep-walking, and the others feared to jolt her awake. When she resumed her story it was in that dreamy faraway voice.

'It was the next Saturday that I saw him. He was coming out of the pub late in the evening. I was wandering around aimlessly, killing time, as usual. It was a fine evening and he went for a walk in the park.' She smiled faintly. 'A walk in the park ... Yes, that was life for him. No matter that he'd trampled on my life and more or less destroyed it.'

'Trampled on your life?' Marnie said. 'How did he do that?'

Sylvia's eyes regained their focus, and she gazed at Marnie.

'Don't you realise, that's what this is all about? Hadn't you worked it out, Marnie?'

Marnie's was racing. The hammer, the bloodstains, the fragments of skin, the hair ... would could it all mean? How could she work it out, apart from the obvious, that the hammer was a murder weapon? She shook her head slowly.

'I saw the hammer ... the condition of it. That's all I know. How could I understand?'

'But I told you, Marnie. I thought you realised.'

'What did you tell me?'

'When my mother died, she left money to a charity. I told you that.'

'Yes. The charity demanded its share of your mother's estate. That's how you lost the house ... your home.'

'No, Marnie, not the *charity*. I told you a *firm* acted for the charity. When I went to their offices and spoke to them, they turned me away.'

Marnie was beginning to see the light. 'The man who was murdered. In the press they said he worked for a charity. It was really on *behalf* of a charity, you're saying.'

Sylvia nodded. 'Yes. You've got it. He was the man I spoke to in their office. I told him that our house had been my only home all my life, that I'd given up my job to look after mum. I said I was sure she never meant me to be thrown out on the street, that she thought I was secure for the rest of my life. Do you know how he reacted, Marnie?'

'Not sympathetically, I'm guessing.'

Sylvia scoffed. 'He just shrugged his shoulders and said he was sorry but the money had to be paid to the charity. It was their money, not mine.'

'That's dreadful.'

'Sorry!' Sylvia exclaimed. 'I'd lost my mum, the roof over my head, everything ... and he was *sorry* but that was that. Too bad. Tough.'

'Was there no room for exercising discretion?' Marnie said.

'Huh! When I protested, he said mum should have taken more care when she wrote her will. Then he stood up to show that the meeting was over. He said: *is there anything else I can do for you?* I was numb, didn't know what to say. He buzzed for his secretary to show me out. I was given six weeks to pay them. Marnie, I had to borrow the money and pay interest on it till I sold the house … my *home.*'

'And you saw him that day by chance,' said Marnie.

'Yes.'

'And you decided to kill him.'

'No, not at first. I was too shocked at the sight of him in the street like that, living an ordinary life while I was sleeping under a hedge, with winos and druggies groping at me in the night.'

'You had money in the bank left over from the sale of the house. Couldn't you have found somewhere to rent?'

'Of course I could, if I'd been in control of myself. Any normal person would've done that. But Marnie, I had a total breakdown. I was an utter mess. I didn't know what day it was, didn't even know who I was some days. You have to be organised to get a flat, meet a bank manager, sort out your finances, sort out your life. I could do none of those things.'

'Was there no one you could turn to for support?'

'I'd been the support, Marnie, supported my mum to the end. It didn't leave any room for friends. There was just the two of us. I didn't have any work colleagues any more; I'd lost touch with them. I hardly knew the neighbours. It was as if the world had given up on me after mum died. I had to cope with that grief, too. Don't you understand what I was going through?'

'I'm so sorry, Sylvia.'

'That's why I did it. I watched him in the park. He was out for a walk that evening. There was no one around. He never saw me. I came up behind him …'

Sylvia's narrative was interrupted by the sound of loud banging on the front door. Randall stood, excused himself and went out quickly, leaving the office door open.

Sylvia said, 'This happens sometimes. Some of the *guests* turn up drunk, rather the worse for wear.' She turned to look towards the open door. Suddenly her eyes grew wide.

Marnie and Anne also turned to see Randall standing in the hall. Around him were police officers in full combat gear. Randall raised both arms outstretched. For a second, Marnie thought of the crucified Jesus. The police were pointing assault rifles into the office, at Sylvia. She turned her gaze on Marnie.

'You've betrayed me,' she said.

****

It was late afternoon when Ralph remembered to call into the supermarket on the way home. He found a parking space in the Stony Stratford high street and climbed out of the Jaguar. He was pressing a button on the key fob to lock the doors, when he became aware of movement up and down the road. Nearby, a woman was unpicking the sellotape that fixed a police poster to the window of her shop. Ralph saw similar bustle in all directions. Shopkeepers were working on their windows, others were taking down posters displayed on lamp-posts. He stepped across to the woman.

'Excuse me. Can you tell me what's going on ... all this activity.'

The woman quickly looked Ralph up and down. 'It's the killer,' she said. 'The police have told us we can get rid of the posters.'

'The killer's been apprehended?' Ralph said, justifying the woman's appraisal of him.

'Yes, apprehended,' she repeated, never having used the word before.

'Have they said who it was?' Ralph asked.

'Not as far as I know, but it's definite that they've caught him.'

Ralph thanked her and set off at a brisk pace for the supermarket. He was looking forward to giving Marnie the good news.

Chapter 23

Marnie had a restless night. On Saturday morning she had dark smudges under her eyes and yawned all through breakfast. For the umpteenth time she glanced up at the wall clock and had to be asked three times by Anne if she wanted more toast or coffee before she managed a reply. There was little conversation at the table. When everyone had finished eating, Donovan stood and began gathering up the crockery.

'I'll clear away,' he said. 'Marnie, I'm sure you have things to do. I'll press on here. If you want me to do anything in the office, you just have to say.'

Marnie got to her feet. 'Thanks,' she said. 'The truth is, I'm not sure what to do … what I can do.'

Ralph said, 'Last night you did mention going to the police station to try to see Sylvia, in case she needed anything.'

'The more I think about it, the more I wonder just what we *can* do, or what Sylvia would trust me to do. She thinks I called the police to come and arrest her in Brackley. I didn't get the chance to tell her that was nothing to do with me. I'll never forget the way she looked at me when they arrested her and carted her off.'

'D'you think the police will let you talk to her?' Anne asked. 'More to the point, would she even be willing to see you?'

'No idea. I tried phoning Roger Broadbent last night for his advice.'

'No luck?' said Donovan.

Marnie shook her head. 'No reply. I just left a message on voicemail.'

Ralph said, 'Perhaps they're away. Didn't Roger say they were going off for a long weekend about now?'

'Damn! You're right. He did say that. But …' Marnie waved a finger in the air. 'He did say he could link up with the answering machine. With any luck he might pick up my message and get back to me.'

'In the meantime, Marnie?'

Marnie reflected for a brief moment. 'I can't just sit around and wait for him to call. I'm going to the station.'

'I'll come with you.'

'No, Ralph. You have a lot to catch up on. I'll go on my own, unless ...'

Donovan grinned. 'I can take a hint. Anyway, there shouldn't be many calls on a Saturday morning. I think the dynamic duo are needed. Dolly and I will mind the shop.'

'You're an angel, Donovan. And if Roger phones ...'

'I know. I'll tell him about Sylvia and get him to ring your mobile.'

****

Marnie turned off the high street in Towcester and swung into the police car park. This was by no means her first visit, and she mused on the idea that they might soon allocate her a reserved space. As she lined up to park, her mobile began warbling. With Marnie manoeuvring in reverse, Anne picked up the phone. She checked the screen.

'That's strange. It says SOLICITORS.'

'It'll be Roger ... good timing.'

'No, just a mo, it looks like BHL SOLICITORS.'

'Probably B for Broadbent ... maybe a new name for the company. You'd better answer it before he hangs up.'

'Hello? Marnie's phone. Roger? It's Anne.'

The voice was familiar, but it was not Roger Broadbent. It was a solicitor, but not Broadbent and Partners.

'Good morning. If you're expecting another call, I can ring back later.'

It was the upper-class drawl of Seymour Lang of Burnett, Haydock and Lang, BHL SOLICITORS.

'Mr Lang, good morning. This is Anne Price. I'll pass you over to Marnie.'

Marnie pulled on the handbrake and switched off the engine.

'Marnie here. What can I do for you, Mr Lang? I didn't expect a call from you on a Saturday morning ...or in fact ever.'

'Quite. Had to come into the office to work on a case. Checked the post and there's another letter.'

'Another letter?'

'From Miss Winterburn ... for you.'

'I thought that was all over once I'd dealt with the estate.'

'So did I, Mrs Walker, but it appears not. The letter has come via Gresham's Bank. It enclosed another letter addressed to you.'

Marnie paused. 'Handwritten?'

'Oh yes, and it's Miss Winterburn's writing.'

'I see. You knew nothing about this, and the bank had separate instructions. Is that what you're saying?'

'Indeed. The branch where Miss Winterburn banked had instructions to send me this latest letter once her accounts had been closed.'

'Are you phoning to let me know you're posting her letter to me?'

'I'm afraid not. It's as before. My instructions are to hand the letter to you in person.'

'Can't it be sent by recorded delivery or whatever that's called these days?'

'Mrs Walker, I'm bound to follow my late client's instructions ... to the letter, as it were.'

'Even though they're instructions from beyond the grave?'

'Even so, I'm afraid.'

'Well, I'll have to –'

Marnie jumped at a sharp tapping on the window beside her head. She snapped round to find a police officer staring in at her, gesturing at the mobile. Anne reached forward and pressed a button; the window wound down.

Marnie began, 'Sorry, I'm just –'

'You can't use a mobile on police premises, madam. I have to ask you to hang up at once.'

'Okay.' Into the phone she said, 'Mr Lang, I'll have to phone you back.'

Marnie pressed the red button. 'I'll make my call from over there on the pavement. Is that all right?'

The officer shook his head emphatically. 'You can't leave the car here unattended.'

Anne leaned over. 'I can stay with it, if that's all right.'

'That's not all right. That's not how it works.' To Marnie he said, 'I must ask you to state your business or leave right now.'

'I've come to see DS Marriner or DC Lamb in CID ... or DI Binns.'

'Detective *Sergeant* Binns has left the county. Do you have an appointment?'

'No. As a matter of fact I –'

'Then you'll have to leave. You can phone for an appointment and –'

To his horror, Anne suddenly opened her door, jumped out and shouted, 'Cathy!'

Across the car park DC Cathy Lamb stopped in her tracks and stared in the direction of the Freelander. She recognised Anne and veered off towards her.

Marnie said, 'That's the person we've come to see. I'm sure she'll vouch for us.'

Tight-lipped, the constable watched as Cathy Lamb drew near.

'It's okay, Gary,' Lamb said. 'I'll deal with our visitors. They've come to give a statement.'

'I told them –'

Lamb cut off his protest. 'Yeah, that's fine. You can leave them to me.'

He walked away without another word.

****

It had been a fruitless morning. They had been kept waiting in separate rooms for ages, waiting for DS Marriner to be found. When he eventually appeared, Marnie explained that she had no further statement to give. She had seen the hammer fall from Sylvia's rucksack and that was that. Cathy Lamb had posed the awkward question of why she'd then driven down to

Brackley to see Sylvia. Marnie explained that she was helping Sylvia to rehabilitate herself. She cited her dirty washing in evidence. Marriner asked if Marnie realised that the hammer was potentially a murder weapon. That was surely a question for a forensic expert, Marnie had said.

In an adjacent interview room Anne gave a similar account of events in her own words. Lamb was satisfied with both stories, though she suspected that DS Marriner felt short-changed, as usual. There had been no question of an interview being granted between Marnie and Sylvia, who was being held at the station pending an appearance before magistrates on Monday morning.

Marnie practically bolted from the police station as soon as her meeting with Lamb was concluded. Anne was still fastening her seat belt when Marnie turned onto the high street.

'What's the rush, Marnie?'

'I need to be somewhere I can use the mobile to phone Seymour Lang. I thought I'd finished with Iris's affairs, but it seems I was wrong.'

To add to Marnie's frustration, the traffic lights turned to red just as she was changing gear to accelerate through. She braked heavily.

'Did you hear that sound, Marnie?'

Marnie cocked her head on one side and listened intently to the engine. It was idling and barely audible in the well-insulated cabin.

'Sounds okay to me,' she said. 'I'll concentrate on it when we pull away.'

'It's not the engine. It's me, or rather my stomach. It's well past lunchtime. I'm *ravenous*. I could eat a horse.'

'You're a vegetarian,' Marnie pointed out in a reasonable tone.

'A vegetable, then ... a large one.'

'Will you survive till we get home?'

'Touch and go.'

There was a supermarket not far away. Marnie drove in and found a parking space. She grabbed the mobile and pressed

243

the recall button. At the other end it rang five times before the answerphone cut in. Marnie gave a loud sigh before leaving a message.

'This is Marnie Walker. Sorry I couldn't get back to you, but I was –'

'Hello?' A slightly breathless drawl heralded the arrival of Seymour Lang. 'Mrs Walker? Just on my way out.'

'Sorry for my abrupt departure. I was having to give a statement to the police on a different matter. I couldn't break away.'

'You do seem to move in interesting circles, Mrs Walker.'

'So I'm told. Talking of which ...'

'Ah, yes, the letter. It was quite a surprise, not something I expected. Do you feel able to look in some time? It's tiresome, I know, but ...'

'From my point of view, I'd like to get things settled as quickly as possible. Would you have a window some time soon, perhaps?'

They agreed to meet late in the morning on Monday, and Marnie drove home with questions – but few answers, if any – swirling around in her mind. Not for the first time she recognised that it had become her default setting.

****

That evening after supper there was a strained atmosphere around the kitchen table at Glebe Farm. The events concerning Sylvia had stunned them all. The only sounds to be heard were the rattling of the electric kettle and the clinking of crockery by Anne, while Donovan filtered coffee.

'Shall we take it in the sitting room?' Marnie said.

'I'll bring the tray,' said Anne.

They settled in their usual places on deep-cushioned sofas while Marnie turned on the table lamps that bathed the room in a soft glow. Donovan brought in the coffee pot, and for a few minutes no one spoke while he poured and Anne served.

Ralph said, 'We've got a fair amount to talk about. Where to begin?'

244

'Well,' said Marnie. 'Why don't you tell us about your meeting with Gilchrist? We haven't done that justice.'

'Okay, though I can't help thinking the information I got from Archie Gilchrist has been rather swamped by subsequent developments.'

Donovan said, 'What Gilchrist told you is backed up by what I found in Franz's papers. I've made a translation of his orders from SS High Command. I can print copies for you all.'

'I'd be interested to see that,' said Marnie.

Ralph said, 'I'm interested first to know how difficult the German was.'

'Quite straightforward, really. Why d'you ask?'

'So would someone with a modest grasp of the language be able to understand it?'

'They'd probably get the gist, I think.'

'I've seen some of it,' Anne said, 'and I didn't find it too hard.'

Marnie said, 'So presumably if Iris read his orders she could have understood them.'

'She learnt he was an officer in the SS and an assassin,' said Ralph. 'He was a fanatical Nazi sent not to rescue Hess but to kill him. He didn't mind risking his own life to do it.'

'It really was a suicide mission,' Marnie said. 'It must've broken Iris's heart when she found out. And then, if that wasn't bad enough, I suppose she had to leave him and go on her way with Alex and Martha on their boats.'

'And we'll never know for certain how it all ended,' said Anne, 'how Franz came to be shot and buried in the garden.'

'There are so many unknowns,' Marnie said, despondent.

Donovan eyed Marnie speculatively but kept his thoughts to himself and drank his coffee.

Chapter 24

Roger Broadbent phoned on Sunday morning. He was initially in high spirits, travelling on his beloved narrowboat *Rumpole*, enjoying the freedom of the waterways. His mood changed as Marnie explained about Sylvia, the hammer and her incarceration.

'Roger, I know you're going to tell me you're not a criminal lawyer, but I have no one else to turn to for advice.' She heard him take a deep breath before replying.

'How can I put this, Marnie? Given your various shenanigans over the past few years, I think I've gained a little experience in this field. I'm going to give you some advice both as a solicitor and as your friend.'

'That sounds ominous, and I've heard it before, but I'm grateful ... I think.'

'Legally, the position is somewhat awkward. I've never met Sylvia, and she's never heard of me. For all I know, she may well have a solicitor of her own.'

Marnie said, 'There is one who dealt with her mother's will and the sale of the house.'

A sigh. 'I take it you mean the solicitor who drafted her mother's will.'

'Yes.'

'That document, Marnie, is the root of all her problems. That solicitor failed to warn them of the consequences of leaving such a large sum to charity. Am I right?'

'So it seems. I'm guessing, Roger, that you don't think that would be the best person to advise her in this current predicament.'

'There's no excuse,' Roger said. 'Every solicitor knows that charities employ firms to scour the wills announced in the press. We know they can be aggressive in pursuing legacies left to them. That's how they earn their percentage; too bad about the consequences. Sylvia's mother should have been advised of that risk when drafting her will.'

'Sylvia certainly knows about it now,' said Marnie. 'She's learnt the hard way.'

'And she probably has enough sense not to go down that particular path, so I'll say no more. Then there's the other factor: the police may well have offered her a duty solicitor. Do you know if they have?'

'No. I haven't spoken to Sylvia since her arrest, and my only contact with the police was when I gave a brief statement.'

'Very well. As far as Sylvia's concerned, my guess is, they've already got her some legal representation. But there is another dimension to all this – more important to me – and it's you, Marnie.'

'Me? What dimension do you mean?'

'We have to be very careful here. You've told them that when you saw the hammer you drove to Brackley to see Sylvia. You said you went because you've been helping her to get back on her feet?'

'That's right.'

'Not quite right, perhaps,' said Roger, slowly.

'Well ...'

'I think they'll press you on this. Why did you in fact go to see her?'

'I suppose I was being impetuous. I wanted to confront her about the hammer ... to get at the truth.'

'Mm ... The police may not see it that way.'

'What d'you mean?'

'It could be construed that you went to warn her.'

'But ... that's not how it was.'

'Marnie, you'd been helping and supporting her for a while. It would be logical – or at least understandable – to regard your action as an extension of that help. You see what I'm getting at?'

Marnie swallowed. 'You mean they might see me as a kind of accessory?'

'It's by no means certain what they might think, but there's something I have to say to you, Marnie. Be very careful what you say to the police. In fact, if they start asking any questions at all, even just by popping in to the office for a chat, you should say nothing. Don't make a big deal of it. Just say you don't want to say anything in case you cause problems for Sylvia.'

'I should deflect questions away from myself, you mean?'

'Exactly what I mean. Then if they persist, you should say you don't wish to say anything more without your solicitor present. It would be good if someone else was in the room when you said that.'

'A witness?'

'Just having someone around would mean they wouldn't press you further.'

'That's when I call you?'

'Yes, but only if they want to interview you again.'

'Blimey, Roger! This is all sounding a bit heavy.'

'You need to be prepared for any eventuality.'

'Could they charge me with anything?'

'Honest answer … I'm not sure. In theory, they could, but it could depend on what Sylvia said when interviewed under caution.'

'Roger, when she saw the police come to arrest her, she said I'd betrayed her.'

'Did she now? That's interesting.'

'Is it a good or a bad sign?'

'No way of knowing for certain. It depends what else she said. For the moment, Marnie, my advice is to sit tight and await developments.'

'There is one other thing, Roger. The solicitor in London dealing with Iris Winterburn's will. I've arranged to see him. Another letter from Iris has turned up … it's addressed to me.'

'I thought you'd dealt with all that.'

'So did I, but apparently not. I've agreed to go to London to see Seymour Lang on Monday. Could that be a problem?'

'Not unless the cops have told you not to skip town.'

'Skip village in my case, Roger.'

He chuckled. 'Quite. No, there's no problem, but it might be as well to let the police know you'll be away that day. I seem to recall you know some of them personally.'

'Know them? I'm practically on their Christmas card list.'

'Then it will do no harm to keep them informed. Let me know if you need me, Marnie ... at any time.'

Anne walked into the office a few minutes after Marnie hung up.

'Roger phoned,' Marnie said.

'Any joy?'

'Not quite the word I would've used.'

'Metaphorical joy, then.'

'Well, among other things he said I could be treated as an accessory to murder. At least he thought it might be a possibility.'

'Blimey!'

'That's what I said.'

'So is he coming up here, Marnie?'

'No, not unless they drag me down to the 87th precinct and get the thumbscrews out. In fact, he thought it was okay for me to go to London to see Seymour Lang. I seem to spend half my life these days whizzing up and down to London.'

'*Whizzing* ... including the trip on *Sally Ann* ... at three or four miles an hour?'

'Metaphorically whizzing then, if you're going to be pedantic.'

Anne gave that some consideration before saying, 'I'll put the kettle on.'

'Good idea. I'll phone the 87th precinct.'

Chapter 25

Ralph offered to go with Marnie to see Seymour Lang on Monday. In fact, he insisted. They travelled down by train as soon as the morning rush hour was over and caught the tube to Holborn. They presented themselves at the premises of Burnett Haydock and Lang and were ushered into the office of Seymour Lang.

They had neither expected to find themselves in that place again, but now they were confronted by much that was familiar: the immaculate if slightly old-fashioned suit, the upper-class drawl, the tidy desk. Seymour Lang seemed pleased to see them again and wasted no time in handing over one more envelope.

'As I said on the phone, Mrs Walker, this arrived out of the blue in the post on Saturday morning. Totally unexpected.'

Marnie took the letter and at once recognised the high quality brand of envelope. 'And your instructions?' she said.

'Well, apart from handing the letter to you in person, I was to bear in mind Miss Winterburn's earlier requirements.'

'You're not to be informed or consulted on the contents of the letter?'

'Precisely. I know you are respecting the confidentiality agreement that you signed, and you know that it applies even to contacts with me, her solicitor.'

'Yes. And I think I understand why Iris made that condition. I'm wondering now how best to proceed with this new letter.'

'In the sense ...?'

'It's probably not appropriate to open it and read it here, but I'm asking myself what if I need to seek your advice on anything arising from it.'

Lang consulted his watch. 'I'm due in court with a client, but that's not until two o'clock.'

'And you don't normally take a lunch break, as I recall,' Marnie said.

'That's correct. I have a mug of tea here in the office at about one o'clock. If you wish to go away and read the letter somewhere in private, I'll be here until about one-thirty.'

****

Marnie and Ralph made their way to the pub where they had discussed Iris's first letter. The pub had just opened and, they even occupied the same table as before. Marnie thought briefly of Anne's quip – *déjà vu all over again* – and she smiled to herself while Ralph went to the bar to order coffees and sandwiches. She flipped open the envelope and was not surprised to find the usual cream vellum notepaper and Iris's familiar handwriting.

They had agreed that Marnie would read the letter first, then pass it on to Ralph.

> April Cottage
> Little Haddon
> Herts

My dear Marnie,

I promise that this is the last letter that you will ever receive from me, and when you read it you will understand why that is so. First I owe you my thanks. If you are reading this letter it means that you have fulfilled the duties of executrix and have closed my bank accounts. It also means that you have retrieved my 'notes in time of war' and you know my story and the account of the time I spent at Glebe Farm in 1943, caring for the only man I ever loved. How ironic that must now sound.

I want you to know that the only reason I opened Franz's order documents was that I was desperate to know everything about the man who I thought, hoped, dreamed, would be my life partner. I have lived to regret my curiosity. You know that I had learnt some basic German,

251

and this enabled me to understand most of what I read. To my dismay I discovered that that wonderful man was not a heroic idealist but a Nazi assassin. His mission was nothing less than murder. He had deceived me about that, and I wondered what other lies he had told me. I took his bag while he rested, solely with the intention of washing his clothes. I read the documents at the edge of the spinney just behind the small barn where we were staying, which is now your office. He must have woken up and wondered where I was and, most importantly, where his belongings had gone. It was early in the morning when he found me reading his papers. I will never forget the look in his eyes. He told me I had deceived him, and I ran off round the barn and into the farmhouse garden. He cornered me at the furthest end and in my distress and fear I pulled out his pistol. Even the sight of it did not deter him and he rushed at me. I held out the pistol, closed my eyes and squeezed the trigger. When I opened them, for a second I saw in his face the kind of man he really was. Then he fell at my feet.

No one came to investigate the gunshot. Bird-scarers and shot-guns were in common use at that time. I found a shovel leaning against a wall and dug a shallow grave in the corner behind the compost heap. There I buried him and never returned to that place. I took the pistol and threw it in the canal beside Sirius. The next day the mechanic arrived to repair the engine. Two days later Alex and Martha joined me and we went on our way to deliver our cargo to London.

There you have it. I asked you to treat this whole matter in confidence and I know you will honour my wishes. As I have grown old I have found myself needing to unburden myself of my secrets with a sympathetic person. I can think of no one better than you, dear Marnie.

If Franz's remains are ever found, perhaps you could perform one last service for me and for him. If it is possible to locate his family and let them know that he died in England on active service, that would be a kindness to them that neither he nor I really deserve.

Thank you, my dear. I have no time for religion or prayers, but perhaps you might spare me a thought once in a while. You will I'm sure have uncovered my final secret concerning the ending of my life. Please do not judge me harshly.

Live well and be happy,

Iris

Marnie read the letter a second time. She looked up and found Ralph gazing at her.

'Your coffee's getting cold,' he said quietly. He nodded towards the letter. 'Interesting?'

Marnie passed it to him 'See what you think,' she murmured.

****

Marnie and Ralph caught the next train back to Milton Keynes Central. Before leaving, they had called in on Seymour Lang to inform him that no further action was required. Marnie was certain that she would never see him again. She told Ralph that she was glad finally to draw a line under that whole episode. As on so many occasions that year she was proved to be wrong, not once but twice.

Comfortably installed on a West Coast mainline express, Marnie read the letter from Iris for a third time. When she'd finished, she handed it back to Ralph.

She said, 'Iris seemed very keen that I shouldn't think badly of her. Why would she think I'd be judgmental?'

Ralph looked thoughtful. 'For people of her generation, I suppose committing suicide carried a certain stigma, not to mention the fact that she'd killed someone. I'm not surprised she wouldn't want either of those facts to be known. And she may have felt some shame at having been in love with an enemy, and not just any enemy but a committed Nazi, who was even an officer of the SS.'

Marnie shook her heard slowly. 'Who'd have thought it? She looked like a harmless little old lady, yet she had those dark secrets and kept them to herself for so many years.'

'And she entrusted them to you, Marnie, because she valued your judgment and discretion.'

'So no pressure there,' said Marnie.

'Certainly none to worry about. You've completed all the tasks she set you. You've more or less finalised the executrix role. I expect there'll be some accounts to settle, but that's about it. And you've become custodian of what you call her *dark secrets*. Iris wanted you to decide what was for the best, and I think you've acquitted yourself admirably.'

'Really?'

Ralph smiled. 'I think you've shared her concerns, so she finally got them off her chest and able to rest in peace. That's what she wanted, isn't it? I don't see there's much more you can do.'

Marnie turned her head to look at the countryside flashing by the window. She turned back to Ralph.

'There's that other thing she wanted. I think she left me all Franz's military documents so that I might be able to locate his family and let them know what became of him.'

Ralph nodded. 'That's true. Will you try?'

'I think I should at least give it a shot.' She grimaced. 'Unfortunate choice of words.'

Ralph chuckled. 'There's no one here likely to be offended.'

Marnie relaxed. 'I suppose not. Perhaps Donovan will be able to help with enquiries.'

'I'm sure he will.'

The train raced through a station at high speed.

Ralph said, 'Nearly there. I think that was Leighton Buzzard. Just a few minutes to go.'

****

As they drove down the field track at the end of their journey Marnie was pleased to see the van of the gardening contractors parked near the house, but she was surprised to see another vehicle alongside it.

'What's he doing here?' Marnie muttered and swung the Freelander past the parked car, round to the garage barn.

Ralph twisted in his seat to look back through the rear window. 'That Volvo. It's Roger Broadbent's, isn't it? You weren't expecting him, were you Marnie?'

'Not at all.'

They found Roger sitting on a visitor's chair, armed with a mug of tea and a plate of biscuits. He rose as they entered to kiss Marnie on both cheeks and shake hands with Ralph.

'Excellent timing,' he said. 'I've only been here a few minutes and, as you see, Anne has made me feel at home.'

At the rear of the office Anne waved the kettle in Marnie's direction. Marnie and Ralph shook their heads.

'Always delighted to see you, Roger,' said Marnie. 'I didn't realise you were coming.'

'No, well, it's like this. After we spoke on the phone yesterday I started fretting. I was worried about your position and I didn't want Sylvia landing you in trouble. I couldn't rest. so I cancelled a couple of meetings, got in the car and made straight for the police station.'

'You've seen Sylvia?'

'I have indeed, and it's just as well I did. She'd refused the offer of a duty solicitor and opted for silence. I announced myself as her legal representative and was shown in. After her initial surprise she agreed to talk to me. I must admit I, er ... well, to be perfectly honest, I let her think you'd asked me to come, Marnie.'

'But she thought I'd betrayed her,' Marnie protested.

'No, at least not any more. She's had time to think about things and she realises that you'd only acted in her best interests. Naturally, I warned her not to say any such thing to the police.'

'You really think they could regard me as an accessory?'

Roger shrugged. 'Let's not take any chances.'

'Did Sylvia seem cooperative?'

'She told me everything that happened, how she'd almost lost her mind when she suddenly saw the man who'd destroyed her life. A kind of red mist descended on her, she said, and she lost control.'

Ralph said, 'If you're advising her, Roger, is that the line you're planning to take?'

'Obviously I have to take more legal advice myself and probably talk to a barrister friend, but I think it might be worth looking at diminished responsibility in the circumstances ... even temporary insanity.'

'Could you make that stick?' Ralph asked.

'It's all to play for.' Roger looked thoughtful. 'There was one other thing. Sylvia asked me to pass on a message. Tell Marnie and Anne, thanks for everything. That was it.'

'That sounds rather valedictory.'

'I don't think she'd want you to see her in prison, Marnie. And visiting her might compromise you.'

Ralph said, 'We're really grateful to you for intervening like this, Roger.'

'Yes, thanks for all you're doing,' said Marnie.

'My first consideration was – and still is – to keep you from being involved, Marnie. I'll do everything I can.'

****

It was a day for unexpected visitors. Marnie was tackling an ever-increasing workload. She was checking availability of Zoffany fabrics when Anne called up the wall-ladder to invite

Donovan down for coffee. His feet had barely touched the floor when the sound of a vehicle was heard rolling to a halt on the gravel drive next to the farmhouse. Marnie braced herself for the arrival of the local CID officers. All eyes turned towards the plate glass window in time to see the burly figure of George Stubbs passing. He was in full tweeds, including cheese-cutter, despite the warmth of the day. Anne automatically reached for an extra mug and checked the level of water in the kettle.

'Good afternoon, everyone. Am I disturbing?'

It was George's standard greeting, and Marnie had often felt tempted to offer a witty reply. As usual, she resisted.

'George, nice to see you. Do come in. Coffee?'

'Thank you, Marnie, but I can't stop. On my way to a party meeting.'

George was chairman of the local Conservative Association. He respectfully removed his cap.

'What can I do for you, George?'

Marnie suspected that all manner of creative possibilities crossed his mind, but he too resisted temptation.

'Just remembered something that might be of interest … or might not.'

'Oh?'

'Yes, you know, in relation to the, er …' He inclined his head to one side. '… bones and such … over in the garden … the, er … German chappy.'

George made it sound as if Oberstleutnant Franz von Weidlingen had just dropped by for a chat, but his words certainly grabbed the full attention of everyone in the office.

'Really?'

'Well, it may be nothing, but I remembered an incident from a long time back. It must've been in the fifties. I'd not long started in the family business when there was some sort of damage to the canal.'

'Damage?' Marnie said.

George waved a hand vaguely. 'Er, some sort of leak, I think it was … towpath crumbling … that kind of thing. Anyway, it had to be repaired so the waterways people came and drained the canal all the way down from somewhere north of here to as far south as the lock at Cosgrove. *Hell* of a big job. Oh, pardon my French.'

Marnie suppressed a grin, wondering if George expected her to blush with embarrassment at his choice of words to her delicate ears.

'Sorry about that,' he continued. 'So, a few of us went down to have a look at the canal with no water in it. Surprising how shallow it was.'

'The incident?'

'Ah, yes. They found a number of strange things in the mud at the bottom. There were one or two pots and pans, a set of false teeth, some spectacles, a spanner or two and ...' George paused for effect. '... a pistol.'

'Do you know what kind?'

'How d'you mean, Marnie?'

'A revolver, perhaps?'

'Oh, I get you. No. It was one of those ... automatics. You know the kind. You see them in war films.'

Donovan spoke for the first time. 'You mean a Luger?'

George nodded. 'That's the sort of thing.'

'Did you see any markings on it?' Donovan asked.

'No ... covered in mud. They took it away. I only saw it for a few moments.'

'But you're sure that's what it was,' Marnie said.

'Pretty sure. Can't really mistake those bloody things. Oops. Oh dear ... French again ... sorry about that. Just slipped out.'

****

Preparing supper they brought Ralph up to date with George's news. While Marnie fried garlic, onions, chopped tomatoes and aubergines she told Ralph about the finding of the Luger in the drained canal.

Anne was weighing out *fusili* pasta while water boiled. She looked up and was about to ask a question when Marnie changed the subject.

To Donovan she said, 'Can you see any way of getting in touch with Franz's family to let them know he died here?'

258

Donovan looked thoughtful. 'Well, we have quite a few documents to go on. Then there's the dog-tag. Not sure how I'd pursue that. I'll have to make some enquiries.'

'Not a common name,' Ralph observed.

'No, that should help. And I think the phone book for the whole of Germany has been computerised, so I'll probably start there.'

Ralph offered to check with colleagues in Oxford in case they had any ideas. Marnie reminded them that they knew Franz came from the Leipzig area. Donovan said that might help, but it was in part of Germany that had seen fierce battles between the Wehrmacht and Soviet forces late in the war. He was not optimistic about tracking down members of the von Weidlingen family.

Anne was still wondering about the Luger, and how it had come to be in the canal. A host of questions floated in her brain, but she didn't want to interrupt the flow of conversation. Her moment had passed. It would keep.

****

After supper Ralph and Donovan went off to use the showers. It was the turn of Marnie and Anne to clear away. It had been Anne's idea to operate a rota, and it fell to her to organise it. That particular evening she was pleased at how it turned out.

'Marnie?'

'Uh-huh?'

'There's something I'm still not sure about.'

'Tell me.'

'In Miss Winterburn's letter, what was all that about cleaning the house *carefully*? Did we ever resolve that?'

'I think I've worked it out.'

'So what's the answer?'

'I think *you* resolved it, Anne.'

'*I* did? How?'

'When you found that tablet behind the leg of the bed.'

'I don't follow.'

'You remember Mrs Allen saying Iris didn't drink alcohol?'

'Of course. That's why I couldn't understand the water bottle filled with vodka.'

'I think Iris knew that if she drank a lot of vodka she might get clumsy trying to swallow all those tablets. You know how careful she was about detail. Think of how she planned the letters.'

'I'm with you so far,' said Anne.

'I think she guessed she might fumble and drop some, especially towards the end when she'd be really befuddled. She wanted us to make sure no one else found anything.'

'Wasn't there always the risk that Mrs Allen might find something?'

'She didn't know that Mrs Allen would decide to clean the whole house. That happened after she died.'

'I see what you mean. Yes ... that must be it.'

'I can't think of any other explanation for it, Anne.'

'No, I'm sure you're right. Marnie, there's something else I want to ask you about.'

'Go on.'

'It's about the letter from Seymour Lang.'

'Okay.'

'Were you going to show it to me, or do you want to keep it private? I'm not pressing you to –'

'Of course I'm going to show it to you. It's just that I wanted to read it again tonight. I'll let you have it tomorrow. Is that all right?'

'Absolutely. Does it tell you any more about what happened?'

'Yes, it does.'

'Had you guessed already?'

'No.'

'It's a sad ending, isn't it? It had to be.'

Marnie hesitated. 'I'll let you have it after breakfast.'

Chapter 26

Donovan wasted no time. On Tuesday morning he phoned his uncle in Germany and talked to Onkel Helmut about tracing Franz's family. His uncle's suggestions included the German Red Cross.

Donovan rang their offices in Berlin but initially drew a blank. A very helpful young-sounding woman explained that many records were lost or destroyed in the chaos at the end of the war. Her computer only produced a von Weidlingen family owning a small estate between Leipzig and Dresden. She could find no other details.

'May I ask, is this part of your family, Herr Schmidt?' she asked.

He had given his name as Nikolaus Schmidt, as normally in a German context, rather than Nikolaus Donovan Smith.

He said, 'It's the family of an acquaintance. When she died she left a note asking us to try to trace the family in Germany to find out what happened to their relative Franz von Weidlingen.'

'Did he possibly serve in the military?'

'In wartime he was a pilot in the Luftwaffe.'

'In that case, are you aware of the *Deutsche Dienststelle?*'

'Afraid not.'

She explained that this was the Military Search Service, located in Berlin-Wittenau and gave him a phone number. He thanked her and rang the number. A not-so-young-sounding woman agreed to check their records. The result was the same.

'I'm sorry but we have no records of an Oberstleutnant Franz von Weidlingen killed in action.'

'May I ask, do you have any records under that name?'

'There is nothing for that name at all. Are you sure it's correct?'

Donovan then spent a fruitless time online consulting the German phone book. He wasn't surprised to find the whole system uploaded to the Internet, but there was no trace of anyone with Franz's surname currently living anywhere in Germany at all.

He reported back to the others at coffee time. It seemed hopeless. The von Weidlingen family was extinct.

Ralph had made some enquiries of his own in academic circles but had fared no better.

At that point, they gave up. Marnie was satisfied they had done all they could to fulfil Iris's request. Like Franz, his entire family had disappeared from the face of the Earth.

****

Anne had been unusually quiet all morning. She had dealt with the post, brought all the filing up to date, emptied the waste-paper bins and tidied the office while Donovan occupied her desk and phone. She had accomplished all the mundane tasks, including making coffee and washing up. The office was immaculate, and Marnie reflected how much she relied on the thorough, efficient, positive contribution that Anne made to running Walker and Co. From time to time she watched Anne at work. Over the past three years of working together they had grown as close as sisters, and Marnie could read Anne's state of mind like an open book.

After coffee Donovan had announced that he had things to do on *XO2*. Ralph was heading back to his study on *Thyrsis* to continue his own work, so the two of them walked out together. When they were left to themselves, Marnie spoke to Anne.

'Are you okay?'

Anne sat at her desk and picked up a pen. 'Sure.'

'Only you seem a bit subdued, Anne.'

Anne chewed the end of the pen and looked across the office at Marnie. 'I've been reading Miss Winterburn's last letter.'

'I know.'

Anne sighed. 'We always knew there wouldn't be a happy ending to their story.'

'We've known that from the start, haven't we?'

'Yes, but I hadn't thought it would turn out like that.'

'Neither had I.'

Anne's tone was flat. 'She killed him.'

'Yes.'

'Even though she loved him.'

'At the end, Anne, when she found out what he was, she was scared for her life. She acted out of an instinct for self-preservation.'

'I suppose. But even so, it must've been a horrible thing to do. And she never found anyone to take his place ever again, did she?'

'I doubt if she ever tried,' said Marnie.

****

Ralph was feeling restless. For him, it was an unfamiliar state of mind. His powers of concentration were usually exceptional. But on that day his head was filled with images of Iris Winterburn squeezing a fateful trigger with her eyes closed, of Sylvia Harris swinging a heavy hammer into the skull of a man who had robbed her of her home, her inheritance and her dignity.

Normally he valued the quiet privacy of the canal where Marnie and the others left him in peace to pursue his work. For a world-class authority like Ralph no interruptions were welcome, which was understood and respected by all. And so it came as a surprise when he heard a tap on the study window, followed by a knock on the boat's central door. It could only be Marnie. When he opened the door to her, she was taken aback by the reception she received.

'Oh Marnie, I'm *so* glad to see you.'

'That's a relief,' she said. 'I was worried that I might be disturbing you.'

'Marnie, you've disturbed me from the first day we –'

'I didn't mean it like that.'

'I know,' Ralph said, stepping back. 'Come aboard.'

He gave her a hand down into the cabin.

'I'm really not being a nuisance?' Marnie asked.

Ralph shook his head, leading the way to the study. 'Not at all. I'm finding it really hard to concentrate ... can't help thinking of ... you know.'

'Me too. That's why I'm here. I wanted a breath of fresh air, but then I had an idea. Anne's feeling the same, ever since she read Iris's last letter. And Donovan's feeling frustrated at not tracking down the family of our local skeleton.'

'Does your idea include a break from work?' Ralph said.

'It's almost lunchtime and it's a beautiful day. How about a tootle? We've got some pizzas in the freezer, some wine in the cellar – or the cupboard if you want to be pedantic – and two melons that should be perfectly ripe for dessert. How say you, good sir?'

'I say yeah, thrice verily, fair maiden.'

Marnie grinned. 'Okay, don't get carried away. Your boat or mine?'

Before Ralph could answer, there came another tap on the window. They saw Anne pointing in the direction of *Sally Ann*. Ralph reached across and slid open the window.

Anne said, 'Donovan's just putting the pizzas in the oven. I defrosted them in the microwave.'

'It seems we have a decision,' said Ralph.

Marnie muttered, 'I swear she's a witch, that girl.'

'Did you bring wine?' Ralph asked.

'*Valpolicella.*'

Ralph turned to Marnie and murmured, 'I agree with your previous statement.' To Anne he said, 'That's it, then. We sail on the next tide.'

Marnie gave him The Look, but was glad to take to the waterway.

****

The air was warm, and the water smelled fresh and clean. There was little breeze; a still day with wispy clouds high up in the sky and the sun poking through. They headed north, aiming for a spot where they could tie up far from any likely contact with the outside world. It felt remote, with fields all around, flocks of sheep scattered across the landscape and distant views of wooded rolling countryside.

Ralph was at the tiller with Marnie beside him on the stern deck, one hand resting lightly on his arm. Below in the cabin, Anne and Donovan busied themselves with setting the table, keeping a watchful eye on the pizzas through the glazed oven door, and opening the bottle of wine. Four bowls were already standing on the workbench, each holding half a cantaloupe melon. It was a Tuesday, by common consent a strange day to be escaping for a picnic lunch on the boat. It felt like playing truant, a stolen moment.

They had been navigating for less than half an hour when Marnie pointed ahead.

'That's the place, isn't it? That gap between the trees on the opposite side to the towpath.'

Ralph craned his neck to scan the area. 'You don't think it might be too shallow there?'

'I think we've tied up there before. Shall we risk it?'

'Let's go for it,' Ralph said, easing back on the accelerator.

****

There was a relaxed atmosphere in the saloon on *Sally Ann* that lunchtime. To Marnie it felt like she'd turned a corner. Her work as executrix to Iris Winterburn's estate was completed, and the sad saga of Sylvia Harris was now out of her hands. True, there were a few loose ends to Iris's will to tie up, but they only involved a few signatures. Also, she'd had a discussion with Ralph and had made a major decision.

Ralph was pouring Marnie a second glass of wine when her mobile warbled. The caller was Roger Broadbent. Her first instinct was to let it go to voicemail, wanting nothing to disturb the congenial ambience of the picnic lunch. But Roger's calls were never trivial, and he'd never fobbed her off in the past. Marnie excused herself and hopped up to the stern deck, pressing the green button on the way.

'Convenient time?' Roger asked.

'Sure, Roger. What can I do for you?'

265

'It's about Sylvia ... inevitably.'

'Okay.'

'I've just had a meeting with Max Frobisher. He's an old friend, a very experienced barrister. Marnie, we're going with diminished responsibility. We both agreed the temporary insanity line probably wouldn't stick.'

'So she had a spur-of-the-moment aberration?' Marnie said.

'We don't think there's any better option.'

'What about the fact that she saw him, planned it and bought a hammer?'

'It was for self-preservation. She was sleeping rough and had already been groped and manhandled by various unstable individuals in the night. Buying a hammer is not unusual for women in that position, desperate to defend themselves.'

'Would she be up to handling cross-examination in the dock? Couldn't she be accused of premeditation?'

'Max thinks it would be wise not to make her testify.'

'Wouldn't that count against her?'

'Not necessarily. In court he'd argue that she was too disturbed to be able to cope. That would be consistent with a plea of guilty of manslaughter with diminished responsibility.'

After ending the call, Marnie reported back to the others. Ralph thought Roger's strategy made sense. Donovan offered no opinion. Anne asked a question.

'Does Roger think she'll go to prison?'

Marnie picked up her glass and examined the dark red wine. She swirled it gently before replying.

'I think that's anybody's guess. Roger hasn't said that in so many words, but I suspect he's looking at damage limitation. Let's face it, Sylvia did kill that man. There's no way around that.'

Ralph said, 'Court cases are notoriously unpredictable. Sylvia will be in the hands of her barrister, the jury and the judge on the day. Who knows how it will turn out? I doubt if Roger would want to make a prediction at this stage.'

Anne sighed. 'It's tragic for Sylvia. I know that hateful man didn't deserve to die, but he shattered her life. I can't imagine what it would be like to find yourself suddenly losing your home and ending up out on the street.'

Marnie looked pointedly at Ralph before turning back to face Anne. 'You'll never have to,' she said.

'I'd hope not.'

'No. I meant that literally.'

'What d'you mean?' Anne asked.

Marnie and Ralph exchanged glances again. Ralph nodded and Marnie spoke.

'I've come to a decision, Anne. I've talked it over with Ralph and –'

'Not that it's strictly speaking any of my business,' Ralph interjected.

'Well, I think it is, given that we're getting married.'

Ralph shrugged. 'Fair enough, but you know I'm in agreement.'

Anne looked puzzled. 'Agreement to what? I don't get it.'

'You will, Anne,' said Marnie, 'in more ways than one.'

Anne said, 'Is it National Talking in Riddles Day or something?'

Marnie grinned. 'I've decided to give you April Cottage, Anne.'

Anne was speechless. She was stunned; her jaw dropped.

Donovan smiled at her. 'You're going to catch flies like that, you know.'

Anne's mouth snapped shut. 'You're ... I mean ... You mean ...'

'I mean with any luck,' Marnie said, 'you might manage to finish a sentence.'

Anne spluttered. 'April Cottage?'

Marnie nodded. 'In the village of Little Haddon in the County of Hertfordshire. I've just asked Roger to make the necessary arrangements.'

'Blimey!' said Anne.

'He didn't say that,' said Marnie.

'Good decision,' said Ralph.

Marnie smiled. 'He did say that.'

****

Nobody felt like working that afternoon. Glebe Farm had an end-of-term feeling. After bringing *Sally Ann* home to base, Marnie suggested relaxing by the water. She set up the large parasol while Ralph and Donovan tied the boat's mooring ropes and put out sun loungers on the grassy bank. Anne did nothing; she was floating in the air with no hope of her feet touching the ground or coming remotely into contact with planet Earth for the rest of the day. She hovered at the edge of the canal, staring ahead, silent, until Donovan guided her to a recliner and sat her down.

Marnie disappeared for several minutes and returned through the spinney carrying a tray holding a large glass pitcher covered with beads of condensation, plus four glasses. There was also a cluster of hors d'oeuvres dishes: pistachios, cashews, olives and peanuts. She set them down on a picnic table and invited everyone to help themselves to homemade lemonade and nibbles.

Donovan served Anne whose mind was still orbiting in the stratosphere. As he was placing a small selection of nuts and olives in the palm of her hand, she looked up at him and spoke quietly.

'Donovan, answer me this. Did Marnie *really* say she was giving me the cottage or did I imagine it?'

'You heard correctly.' Donovan leaned down and kissed her on the forehead. 'Now sit back, try not to choke on the peanuts, and enjoy the moment.'

Anne still bore a confused expression. 'I will,' she said, 'when I regain consciousness.'

The group sat in the sunshine and sipped the chilled lemonade, munching on the occasional nut or olive. It was an afternoon of pure self-indulgent pleasure, and they wallowed in it. Minutes slipped by while no one broke the silence. Eventually Marnie stirred herself, picked up the jug and did the rounds, topping up the glasses.

'This is wonderful,' Ralph said. 'A perfect choice ... unforgettable.'

Anne joined in. 'It's a day I'll certainly never forget.'

Marnie stooped and kissed her lightly. 'You won't?'

'No. It's not every day that people queue up to kiss me on the forehead.'

Marnie chuckled. 'Idiot!'

Anne became serious.' Thanks, Marnie. If you want to change your mind about the cottage, that's fine by –'

'I'm not changing my mind about anything.' She smiled. 'It will be one less thing to worry about. I've had enough to occupy me for one year.' As she regained her seat, she said to Ralph, 'Were you right that I'd completed my tasks as executrix? Is that a fact?'

'Well, you'll have to pay the solicitor's fees out of the estate, but once you've done that, there can't be much else. All the bank accounts are closed. You'll just have to transfer the shares to your name and transfer the ownership of the cottage to Anne.'

'There's Mrs Allen and Mr Edwards,' said Anne. 'Got to think of them.'

'And decide what you want to do about letting the cottage,' Marnie added. 'We can talk to a local agent, then Roger can draw up the papers.'

Ralph said, 'I think Iris deliberately made everything as simple as she could in the will, knowing that you'd have all that business with Franz to handle.'

Marnie nodded thoughtfully. 'I suppose that's all behind us now, too.'

Donovan said, 'There's nothing more can be done to trace his family in Germany. It seems that like Franz the rest of them have died out. They may never have known what became of him. The dog-tag proves that.'

'He may have been an assassin, a Nazi and an SS officer,' Marnie said, 'but he was undeniably brave, dropping behind enemy lines like that.'

'And fanatical,' said Donovan. 'Something has just occurred to me. Franz probably wrote a letter to his family to be delivered in the event that he didn't return from his mission.

It was common practice in the military at that time. So his family may have got that message.'

'He must've known he stood little chance of getting out alive,' said Marnie.

'That's certainly true,' said Ralph. 'And he made an impression on the life of Iris Winterburn from which she probably never recovered.'

'I'm sure she never did,' Marnie said.

When Marnie's mobile trilled she looked at the screen and announced, 'It's Roger again.' As soon as she heard his voice she knew something was wrong.

'I've just had a call from the police station, Marnie. Sylvia has ... hanged herself in her cell.'

Marnie leaned back in her chair. 'Oh my God ... Is she ...?'

'I'm afraid so.'

'But how could this happen? Don't they do things to prevent ... I mean, did they just leave her without ...? Oh Roger, I don't know what I'm saying.'

Roger said quietly, 'I understand she used her tights.'

'Bloody hell ... Look, Roger, I'm going to have to ring you back. My head's in a spin.'

Even before Marnie disconnected, the others had guessed the reason for Roger's call. They all sat back in their chairs, desolate and despairing. Silent tears were rolling down Anne's cheeks. She had been brought down to earth with a bump. Marnie gave them the details that they hadn't heard. Without speaking, Anne got up and walked off slowly through the spinney. Donovan exchanged looks with Marnie before setting off to follow.

'What a strange year,' Ralph said quietly. 'Two women whose lives were deeply impacted by circumstances outside their control, both of them suicides; two men who no doubt thought they were acting for the best and lost their lives as a result; two wills with far-reaching consequences.'

Marnie turned her head to face Ralph. 'A deadly symmetry,' she said. 'It sounds like the title of a crime novel. What a tragic mess.'

'Now's probably not the time to reach a balanced judgment, Marnie, but perhaps in some ways it's not all tragic. Iris Winterburn's story was certainly heart-rending, but she trusted you to put things right, and I'm sure she'd think you've done her proud. We can ask Angela to arrange for Franz's remains to be buried in the churchyard here, where he spent his final days, if you think that's appropriate.'

'Yes, or perhaps even arrange a green burial in a plot alongside Iris, so that they can be together, all conflicts behind them.'

'You choose, Marnie, whatever you think would be for the best. Iris would trust you to do the right thing, and she'd be happy with your decision.'

'You think?'

'There can't be any doubt about it,' Ralph said emphatically.

'And what about Sylvia?' Marnie asked.

'You didn't fail Sylvia. What happened to her can't be laid at your door. You did your very best to help her in her hour of need. She made some tough choices ... right to the end, but they were her choices.'

'I hope you're right, Ralph.' Marnie shivered. 'Is it my imagination, or is it getting chilly?'

'Time to go in, I think,' said Ralph.

Chapter 27

On that previous Tuesday evening nothing more had been said on the subjects of Iris Winterburn, Franz von Weidlingen or Sylvia Harris. It was as if everyone wanted to put those episodes behind them or perhaps needed time to absorb and process what had happened in their lives.

Anne came back into the office on Wednesday after serving coffee to the gardeners and began preparations for the morning break in the office. Ralph arrived a few minutes after ten and Donovan descended the wall-ladder from Anne's attic room, where he'd been working on his dissertation.

When everyone was present and supplied with mugs of coffee Anne said, 'Marnie, I didn't really thank you properly for your generosity yesterday. I think I was too knocked out to be able to make sense of what you'd said. So thank you ... very much.' She grimaced. 'Boy, doesn't that sound inadequate!'

'You're very welcome, Anne. We both thought, Ralph and I, that it would set you up for the future. I just need to check with our accountant, whether a straight gift is the best way to handle this, but effectively that's what it will be. Once that's resolved, we can get Roger to draw up a contract – or whatever – and then it will be yours.'

Anne shook her head. 'I'm still speechless.' She looked down at her coffee mug and added, 'It somehow makes it all the more vivid to me to think what Sylvia lost.'

'And what drastic steps she took to exact her revenge,' Marnie said.

They fell silent, focusing on their coffee, lost in their private thoughts. Marnie returned to her desk and picked up the phone to dial a familiar number.

'Roger, I think I'm *compos mentis* again. Sorry I had to break off before.'

'It was a shock to all of us, Marnie.'

'Can I ask you ... what will happen to Sylvia now?'

'That depends. Do you know if she had any family?'

'I don't think she did, but I expect the police will check. Will there be a post-mortem?'

'Probably. Sudden death in custody ...'

'I'd just like to say that once the situation is clarified, if there's no one else involved, I'm prepared to take on the funeral arrangements and costs.'

'That's an expensive commitment, Marnie.'

'I don't care. I want to do the right thing ... for once.'

'You have nothing to reproach yourself for.'

'Even so.'

'Actually, there's something I wanted to say to you. You and Ralph will both need new wills once you're married. Marriage automatically renders any previous wills invalid. I think you knew that.'

'Vaguely. Let me think about it. Right now, I've had enough of wills to last me a while. Let's talk again about this when Ralph and I get back from Venice after the wedding.'

Roger was glad to have changed the subject and did his best to lighten it further. 'Let's hope you avoid a murder on the Orient-Express!'

Marnie groaned. 'Don't even think about it!'

Anne was collecting the used mugs on a tray when there was a flash of movement across the plate glass window. It was followed by a hasty knock on the door, and Sammy, one of the gardeners, looked in.

'Marnie ... got a minute? We've found something. You ought to see it.'

They all trooped out and followed Sammy to the furthest part of the walled garden, close to Franz's shallow grave. Ray, the other gardener, was kneeling in the corner, scraping soil with a trowel. It reminded Marnie of the archaeologists who had worked at Glebe Farm in the past.

'What have you found?' Marnie asked.

'I haven't touched it,' Ray said. 'Look. There it is.'

They craned forward, peering into the dirt. Lying in the soil was a small lump of metal not much more than a centimetre in length, as thick as a child's finger. It was a dull brown colour, pointed at one end. Donovan stepped forward and picked it up. He held it out in the palm of his hand for the others to see.

'You know what it is, don't you?' said Marnie.

Donovan nodded. 'It's a nine millimetre bullet, the kind fired by a Luger pistol.'

'You're sure of that.' It wasn't a question.

'Oh, yes. No doubt about it. I've seen a lot of these. This one's in really good condition, considering how long it's been in the ground and how it got there.'

Marnie and Ralph and Anne stared down at the small piece of metal that had had such a drastic effect on the lives of Iris and Franz. In their minds they heard the gunshot, imagined the bullet ripping through uniform, bone and flesh before exiting the body. They realised they were standing on the very ground where Franz had fallen.

Marnie reached forward. 'May I?' she said.

Donovan tipped the bullet into her outstretched hand. For a few moments she gazed down at it.

Sammy the gardener said, 'What d'you want to do with it?'

Marnie glanced at him in silence before turning to the others. Without a word she tossed the bullet lightly back into the trench.

'Let this be its grave,' she said. 'Just bury it here. This is where it belongs.'

Chapter 28

Marnie had set aside the first stint in the office on Saturday morning to tie up the remaining loose ends concerning the last will and testament of Iris Winterburn. She signed the final letters and documents relating to the transfer of shares and savings and made a substantial payment into a savings account in the name of Anne Price. Anne knew nothing of this arrangement or of the account itself. Marnie had set it up when they first began working together three years earlier. The aim was to give Anne a firm foundation for her future.

Marnie's last act as executrix was to sign a cheque for the fees of Seymour Lang. This time she was sure that this would be the final contact between them. And then there was one last matter.

She looked at the small pile of letters on her desk. They were on cream vellum notepaper of good quality, in Iris's distinctive handwriting, resting on top of her notebook with its faded green cover, her 'notes in time of war'. The collection had dominated Marnie's life for the past few weeks and brought back to life an episode that had taken place in the very barn in which Marnie was now sitting. What tragedy that place had known over the centuries!

Marnie picked up the letters and slotted them together into a new light green folder, together with the notebook. On its label she wrote simply: Iris. It fitted perfectly into the box file in which all the other papers and documents pertaining to Iris's affairs were stored. Marnie stood and placed the box file on the shelf with all the other project files.

For some moments she stood silently reflecting on a chapter in her life that had struck when she least expected it. Two women whose lives had been scarred by tragedy; two men whose actions had brought about their own deaths; two wills at the heart of everything. Ralph's summary had been correct. The sequence of events and repercussions had led to a tragic ending.

A deadly symmetry.

About the author

When not writing novels, he is a linguist and lexicographer. As director of The European Language Initiative he compiled and edited twelve dictionaries in fifteen languages, including English, since the first one was published by Cassell in 1993.

They include the official dictionaries of the National Assembly for Wales (English and Welsh), the Scottish Parliament (English and Gaelic) and a joint project for the Irish Parliament and the Northern Ireland Assembly (English and Irish).

For the record, the others are specialist dictionaries in Basque, Catalan, Danish, Dutch, French, German, Greek, Irish, Italian, Portuguese, Russian, Scottish Gaelic, Spanish and Welsh.

Since 2015 he has devoted his time entirely to writing fiction.

He lives with his wife, cookery writer Cassandra McNeir, and their delinquent cat, Marmalade, in a three hundred year-old cottage in a Northamptonshire village. Delightful as it is, it bears no resemblance to Knightly St John.

Books by Leo McNeir

Book 1 - Getaway with Murder

Book 2 - Death in Little Venice

Book 3 - Kiss and Tell

Book 4 - Sally Ann's Summer

Book 5 - Devil in the Detail

Book 6 - No Secrets

Book 7 - Smoke and Mirrors

Book 8 - Gifthorse

Book 9 - Stick in the Mud

Book 10 - Smoke without Fire

Book 11 - Witching Hour

Book 12 - To Have and to Hold

Book 13 - Beyond the Grave

Author's website **www.leomcneir.com**

Printed in Great Britain
by Amazon